MICHAEL TENNANT

DEATH

IN THE

VIEUX CARRÉ

Also available
by
MICHAEL TENNANT

**CAN YOU
SLEEP
ON A
STORMY NIGHT**

ISBN: [979-8-9912069-9-0]

Printed in [United States of America]

First Edition: [March 14, 2025]

Library of Congress

Control Number:

michaeltennant@mail.com

PART ONE

PROLOGUE

NEW ORLEANS NIGHTS had a way of promising possibilities that the mornings never delivered. Charles knew this better than most as he climbed out of the weather-beaten 2003 Ford pickup, the humid air immediately clung to his freshly pressed suit.

"Last chance," the big man said, sitting behind the wheel and leaning out of the open window. The engine's rumble drifted through the New Orleans air like distant thunder. "Real music at the Striped Cat tonight—my quartet's playing our best set in months."

Charles adjusted his collar, glancing up at the glowing sign of Le Bayou Jardin. "I'll have to take a rain check. And maybe I can bring Sarah next time —she loves jazz."

A deep, genuine laugh rolled out from the truck. "What would the folks at the courthouse say?"

"They'd probably say I finally found someone in that building with real talent." Charles smiled, the lines around his eyes deepening. "I'll talk to Sarah, and maybe we can make plans for next Friday."

"Can you promise me that? I'll save you a seat by the stage."

"I can promise you I'll certainly try."

"I'm gonna hold you to that, judge," the driver tapped his fingers against the steering wheel in a rhythmic pattern. "You sure you don't want me to wait? You know that flat tire of yours ain't gonna—"

"No, I'll catch a cab. This dinner meeting shouldn't take that long."

"Alright then. Have a good night," the driver said cheerfully, shifting the truck into gear.

"Have a good set. See you Monday," Charles replied as he headed into the restaurant.

"Monday, it is," the driver repeated before pulling away from the curb. "See you then."

As the pickup's taillights disappeared into the night, Charles turned toward Le Bayou Jardin. The maître d' nodded in recognition as he approached.

"The gentleman is already waiting, sir. Your usual table."

The corner table, partially shielded by decorative palms, offered a clear view of the entrance while still remaining discreet. Perfect for a man who preferred privacy but always wanted to know who was coming and going.

Robert rose when he spotted Charles approaching, noting his easy, confident smile. The tailored suit revealed that Charles had clearly climbed the ranks since their acquaintance years ago.

"Charles," Robert extended his hand warmly, "great to see you. It's been too long."

"Hello, Robert." Charles shook his hand, nodding with approval. "You're looking well. Success seems to agree with you."

Robert laughed. "Business has been good. Very good." He gestured to the wine already breathing beside two crystal glasses. "I took the liberty. The '82 Bordeaux I remembered from last time."

Charles settled into his chair, looking pleased. "You remembered. I'm impressed."

"Some things are worth remembering," Robert replied as he poured the wine. "To old friends?"

"To old friends," Charles agreed, raising his glass. Their glasses met with a gentle ring before they tasted the aged Bordeaux.

Their conversation flowed naturally, punctuated by occasional laughter and shared memories. The piano player shifted to a soft rendition of "Moonlight in Vermont" As they continued their conversation.

Halfway through their main course, the maître d' approached the table. "Excuse me, sir. There's a phone call for you. They say it's urgent court business."

Charles nodded, "I should take this. Won't be long."

"Take your time," Robert said, pushing his chair back. "Nature calls, as they say."

Charles followed the maître d' to the host stand where the telephone was waiting. From there, he could see their table as he lifted the receiver to his ear.

At the back of the restaurant, Robert approached the restroom. A man in a dark suit was leaning against the wall. As Robert drew near, he murmured, "Now," his lips barely moving.

The man gestured with his head, then walked toward the dining area.

"Hello? Hello?" Charles waited, hearing nothing. "Hello, this is Charles Taylor."

While Charles remained on the phone and Robert disappeared into the restroom, the dark-suited man approached Charles's table. And in seconds, he was gone, melting back into the crowd of diners.

Charles set the receiver down, "Line's dead," he told the maître d'. "If it's important, they'll call back."

He returned to the table, which stood momentarily empty.

A minute later, Robert returned from the restroom, sliding back into his chair. "Everything alright with your call?"

"No one was there," Charles replied with a slight shrug. "Line was dead."

Robert nodded, reaching for his own wine glass. "Well, where were we? Ah yes…"

The easy conversation about the project continued. Charles swirled the rich Bordeaux in his glass, enjoying the taste as Robert launched into a discussion of his latest business venture.

The wine tasted expensive. Complex. And somewhere beneath the notes of cherry and oak, something else. Something Charles couldn't identify.

As the waiter glided over with dessert menus in hand, Charles became aware of a subtle shift in his perception. The room's elegant lighting began to blur, walls and ceiling tilting at increasingly odd angles. He blinked hard several times, struggling to bring Robert's face into focus across the table. The candlelight between them seemed to stretch and dance unnaturally. When he attempted to decline dessert, Charles discovered his tongue felt strangely weighted, his words refusing to form properly in his mouth.

"What did you... Something's wrong..."

"You're just tired, Charles," Robert said, his voice floating as if from a distance despite his seemingly genuine concern. "Let me call you a cab."

The next moments melted into one another as Robert's arm steadied Charles through the restaurant. The maître d' held the door open while the cool night air washed over them, doing nothing to clear Charles's fog. A taxi materialized at the curb, and he vaguely registered Robert's voice providing an address he couldn't comprehend.

"6464 Prytania Street," Robert was saying to the driver. "His daughter will be waiting. Poor guy had a few too many."

The taxi pulled away from the curb, carrying Charles into darkness as Robert's figure grew smaller behind them. Through the fog in his mind, Charles fought to stay conscious, to understand what was happening. But the drug was too strong, the darkness too inviting.

Later, when the taxi stopped at an unfamiliar address, strange hands helped him from the vehicle. A woman's voice cut through his haze: "Dad, not again." He vaguely registered a man tipping the driver. Together, the couple guided him across an unfamiliar lawn to a porch, where they gently settled him into a wicker chair, the night air doing little to clear his clouded thoughts.

As the taxi's taillights disappeared around the corner, Charles heard the crunch of tires on gravel—a black SUV. New hands—rougher, purposeful—lifted him from the chair. The woman leaned over him inside the vehicle, her face professionally blank as she applied something to his torso. Two small patches, their effect immediate.

The last thing Charles felt was the vehicle moving through the night, carrying him far from the city he'd spent his life trying to protect.

CHAPTER 1

THE MORNING HEAT PRESSED down on New Orleans like a damp wool blanket, the kind of suffocating humidity that made even breathing feel like work. Detective Renee Dubois knew these streets better than most. With her dark hair swept back from her face and green eyes fixed ahead, she navigated the narrow cobblestone alleys that honeycomb the French Quarter with the confidence of a local who had walked them a thousand times before.

Her tan skin told the story of years working under the Louisiana sun, with the weathered look of someone who belonged to these streets rather than just visiting them. She moved through the Quarter like a local, knowing which shortcuts to take, which shopkeepers to nod to, and which corners to approach with caution. New Orleans wasn't just where she worked; it was home, with all its beauty and flaws.

Morning light changed the Quarter, washing away the night's mystique. Wrought-iron balconies hung over buildings in faded colors that had weathered decades of their share of hurricanes. Shopkeepers sprayed down their sidewalks, washing away the remnants of last night's parties—beads, plastic cups, and other souvenirs of celebration. The neighborhood was shifting from one life to another, as it did every day.

At twilight, the Quarter's duality was most evident: a place where jazz could be heard from the open doors on Frenchmen Street to the clanging of the streetcars on Canal Street. Neon lights flickered invitingly from bars that never seemed to close while street performers set up their acts on corners worn smooth by two centuries of foot traffic. It was a realm where shadows were thick enough to hide in, and whispered deals in back rooms could instantly turn deadly.

Next to her, Detective Kelsey Griffith sat, his sandy hair still damp from an early shower, a contrast to Renee's more practical approach to the morning. His blue eyes were always alert, watching the morning crowds as if trying to determine who belonged there and who didn't. His pressed shirt and neatly knotted tie revealed an attention to detail that sometimes seemed at odds with their line of work.

He knew the city's elegant charm could win over the not-so-streetwise tourist, but he was also keenly aware of its darker undercurrents. The same streets that drew visitors with promises of jazz and beignets also hosted transactions involving narcotics, flesh, and influence—an economy as old as the city itself.

"You can almost hear the music in the air, can't you?" Kelsey said as he strolled beside Renee through a square where pigeons pecked hopefully at remnants of yesterday's food, gesturing toward a group of street musicians setting up for the day. The sound of a trumpet was already weaving through the air as the city began to shake off its slumber; the brassy notes bounced off the ancient buildings, just as they had for generations.

"Yeah, I hear the music, and everything else that goes with it," Renee said under her breath, her eyes fixed on a man slipping into a side street, moving with the careful deliberation of someone who didn't want to be noticed. It was way too early for a tourist; it seemed more like someone who would be familiar with the darker rhythms of the city—the comings and goings that happened when most visitors were still sleeping off their Bourbon Street indulgences.

The French Quarter was an attraction for millions, a place where the old-world charm of New Orleans collided with the realities of modern excess. Beneath the grandeur of Jackson Square and the elegance of old Creole courtyards lay a seedier undercurrent. Drugs moved through hidden passageways, carried by couriers who blended seamlessly with the tourists. Shady deals were struck in the dim back rooms of dive bars—places that never seemed to close, their stained bar tops and creaking floors worn down by decades of unspoken transgressions.

And then there were the people who vanished into the night, never to be seen again. The missing persons reports that piled up on desks at the precinct, most eventually filed away unsolved. In a city where people came to reinvent themselves, to disappear into the crowd, it was too easy to slip from one life into another—or out of life altogether.

For Renee and Kelsey, this wasn't just another morning patrol. They weren't here for the tourists, the jazz, or the coffee stands selling chicory-laced brew strong enough to wake the dead in St. Louis Cemetery. Their presence had a purpose; their eyes scanned the morning bustle for something specific.

The corruption they were investigating ran deep, like the veins of the old oak trees that lined the city streets. It crept into the businesses, the politics, and the culture of New Orleans, rooting itself in the Quarter's very foundations. Like the termites that silently devoured historic buildings from within, this corruption ate away at the city's institutions, leaving facades that looked intact while the structures behind them rotted.

"You think this is bigger than we know?" Kelsey asked, folding a case briefing and slipping it into his inner jacket pocket. His eyes followed a patrol car as it rolled slowly down the narrow street.

Renee sighed, her breath visible in the morning air despite the growing heat. "It gets bigger every day and more dangerous. Like trying to drain the bayou with a teacup."

They'd been the lead investigators on a narcotics case that initially seemed straightforward—a mid-level dealer, a predictable network, and the usual patterns of distribution. But as they'd pulled on threads, the fabric of the case had unraveled to reveal something far more complex. It quickly became clear that this was no ordinary drug case; it was like a tangled web of power and money that stretched from the streets to the highest offices in the city.

Whispers floated through the streets of men who wore suits by day and masks by night, smiling in the public eye while holding the city's soul in their pockets. Names mentioned in hushed tones in back rooms, powerful figures whose influence reached into every corner of New Orleans life.

With each new piece of evidence they uncovered, the stakes grew higher. Witnesses became reluctant to talk, evidence disappeared from lockup, and court dates were mysteriously postponed. The pattern was too consistent to be coincidence, too pervasive to be the work of a few corrupt individuals.

As they turned onto Royal Street, passing antique shops with windows displaying Civil War artifacts and century-old Mardi Gras masks, a text message alert chimed on Renee's phone. She glanced at the screen and fell silent, her jaw setting into a firm line as she slid the phone back into her pocket.

"Another case thrown out," she said, showing Kelsey the screen. "Judge Harrison found a 'procedural error' in the warrant application. Three months of work down the drain."

Kelsey just shook his head, frustration showing in the tightening of his jaw. "That's the fourth one this month. And always the same judges, the same excuses."

"The same results," Renee added, pocketing her phone. "Dealers back on the street within hours, evidence returned, charges dismissed."

They walked in silence for a moment, headed for Courtroom Three, the weight of their investigation settling around them like the morning mist that sometimes rolled in from the river, obscuring the familiar, making the city feel alien and unpredictable.

The Orleans Parish Criminal District Court squatted on Tulane Ave like an old, weathered building, its limestone face darkened by years of New Orleans rain and grime. It had seen generations pass through its doors, a silent witness to both justice served and justice denied, its hallways echoing with the steps of those seeking a fresh start and those trying to escape what they deserved.

Sunlight sliced through the high windows of Courtroom Three, stretching shadows across the worn wooden benches as Assistant District Attorney Rachel Sullivan made her opening move. The room smelled of aged wood, paper, and the lingering cologne of attorneys who had passed through earlier that morning.

"Your Honor," Sullivan began, her voice steady despite the tension visible in her shoulders, "the State has clear evidence that Antoine Domingo was in possession of over two kilos of heroin with intent to distribute." She approached the bench, moving as if this case were already won, her confident stride masking the uncertainty she felt. "Furthermore, we will prove this was not an isolated incident but part of a systematic drug operation that has claimed countless lives in our city."

From her seat in the gallery, Detective Renee Dubois watched Judge Maurice Leblanc's face. Six months of surveillance, wiretaps, and careful police work had led to this moment. The Domingo organization had seemed untouchable until now, their tendrils reaching into every corner of New Orleans' drug trade. But something in the judge's expression— a slight tightening around the eyes, an almost imperceptible shift in his posture—made her stomach knot with apprehension.

Next to her, Detective Kelsey Griffith leaned forward, his knee bouncing with nervous energy, the wooden bench creaking slightly beneath him. They'd worked this case together, spending countless nights in unmarked cars, following leads, building evidence piece by piece. The Domingo organization had been operating with impunity for years, their product finding its way into every neighborhood from the Garden District to the Ninth Ward.

Stepping into the courtroom, you couldn't help but notice the faded grandeur. The high ceilings, decorated with intricate moldings, drew your gaze upward, while the judge's bench, worn smooth by countless hands, commanded the room. Behind the judge, American and Louisiana flags stood in their holders, a slight layer of dust covering them. The jury box was empty today, as this was just a preliminary hearing, but it would decide whether the case would go to trial.

Defense Attorney Steven Beaumont rose slowly from his chair, his bespoke suit rustling softly as he straightened to his full height. Everything about him spoke of old money—from his gold cufflinks to the slight aristocratic drawl in his voice, honed at expensive schools and polished in exclusive clubs.

"Your Honor, before Ms. Sullivan continues, the defense moves to suppress all evidence obtained through electronic surveillance."

Renee felt Kelsey stiffen beside her. They'd done everything by the book, double-checking every warrant and procedure. The magnitude of the case required a strict protocol. The Domingo organization wasn't just another drug ring; it was an institution in New Orleans, as much a part of the city's underground as the crypts in the city of the dead.

"Your Honor, all surveillance was conducted with proper judicial authorization," Sullivan countered, maintaining her professional composure despite the sudden challenge. "We have signed warrants for every phase of the investigation."

"Signed by Judge Langley." Beaumont interrupted, producing a thick folder from his briefcase. "Who, as this court is no doubt aware, is currently under investigation by the judicial review board."

The gallery erupted in whispers, the sound like dry leaves rustling across a courtyard. Renee watched Antoine Domingo sitting at the defense table in an expertly tailored suit that probably cost more than her monthly salary. The track marks on his arms were carefully hidden beneath Italian cotton, but she'd seen them clearly the night of his arrest. Now, he sat there, the hint of a smirk playing at the corners of his mouth, his confidence seemingly unshaken by the proceedings.

LeBlanc peered over his reading glasses at Sullivan, his expression carefully neutral. "Counselor, were you aware of this investigation when you submitted these warrants?"

"No, Your Honor," Sullivan replied, her voice steady despite the blindside. "And I would argue that any investigation of Judge Langley has no bearing on the validity of these specific warrants. The evidence they yielded is solid—"

"The foundation rests on potentially compromised judicial oversight," Beaumont cut in, his voice carrying the perfect mixture of concern and righteous indignation. "Your Honor, I have here a motion to suppress all evidence obtained through these questionable warrants and any evidence derived from them."

Renee felt the case slipping away like sand through her fingers. She glanced at the back of the courtroom where Jean-Paul Domingo, Antoine's father and the true power behind the organization, sat watching the proceedings. His expression reminded her of a man observing a play he'd already seen—and paid to produce.

At the prosecution table, Sullivan fought back with the desperate determination of someone who could see victory transforming into defeat before her eyes. "Your Honor, even without the surveillance evidence, we have physical evidence recovered during the arrest, testimony from multiple confidential informants."

"Which was executed based on information obtained through the suppressed surveillance," Beaumont countered, closing the trap he'd carefully laid. "Your Honor, without this illegally obtained evidence, the State has no case. I move for dismissal."

The gallery erupted in murmurs again, voices rising and falling like waves against the seawall. Renee watched a young couple in the back row clutch each other's hands tightly. She recognized them—the parents of Amy Lester, an honor student at Warren Easton High, found dead in the school bathroom from heroin traced back to Domingo's operation. They had come seeking justice for their daughter, clinging to the hope that the system would work for them despite everything they'd already lost.

"Order," LeBlanc called, though his gavel tap was oddly gentle, almost apologetic. "Given the circumstances, this court has no choice but to grant the defense's motion. Case dismissed."

The sound of the gavel's final fall echoed through the courtroom like a gunshot. Six months of work, countless hours of surveillance, all the evidence pointing to Domingo's guilt—gone in twenty minutes of legal maneuvering.

Antoine Domingo stood, accepting handshakes and back slaps from his legal team with the casual grace of someone accustomed to winning. His father made his way forward from the gallery, every inch the proud patriarch despite his son's obvious track marks and lengthy arrest record. The Domingo organization had been operating in New Orleans since the old French Quarter days, their narcotics empire passing from father to son like some twisted family legacy.

Beaumont paused by the prosecution table where Sullivan sat, still shuffling papers with trembling hands. "Better luck next time, Rachel," his voice carried just far enough for Renee and Kelsey to hear, laden with smug satisfaction. "Though you might want to be more selective about your cases. Some families in this city have operated here since before there were courts to argue in."

He turned, catching Renee's eye as he passed their bench, his confidence unshaken. "Detectives. Perhaps you should focus on simpler matters. Leave the Domingo territory to those who understand its... complexities."

Kelsey started to rise, his face flushed with anger, but Renee's hand on his arm held him back. "Not here," she muttered, aware of the eyes on them. The department's reputation was always hanging by a thread.

They watched the Domingo entourage file out, followed by Judge LeBlanc, who didn't spare them a glance. The Lesters were the last to leave, their quiet grief a stark contrast to the celebratory mood of the defense team. Mrs. Lester's shoulders shook silently as her husband guided her toward the door, his own face a mask of resigned despair.

Finally, only Sullivan remained, still at her table, staring at her carefully prepared arguments that would never be heard, the papers spread before her like the remnants of a battle lost before it began.

"Rachel," Renee said softly, approaching the prosecution table. "You did everything you could."

Sullivan looked up, her eyes reflecting the defeat they all felt. "Did I? Or did I just play my part in their show?" She began roughly shoving files into her briefcase, her movements betraying her frustration. "You know what the worst part is? I heard LeBlanc was at the Domingo family compound last weekend. Some charity fundraiser for their youth foundation. The same foundation that somehow always has teenagers selling their product near schools."

"The judge is dirty," Kelsey said flatly, his voice low enough that only the three of them could hear.

"The judge is connected," Sullivan corrected, closing her briefcase with a decisive snap. "In this city, that's better than clean." She paused, shaking her head. "James Callahan warned me about this case. Said some families are untouchable, no matter how guilty they are." A bitter smile crossed her face. "I should have listened to him."

The trio stood in silence for a moment, the empty courtroom seeming to mock their efforts, the scales of justice invisibly weighted in favor of those with enough money and influence to tip them.

Through the tall windows, New Orleans continued its daily rhythm, oblivious to the corruption that had just been enacted in the name of justice. Outside, streetcars rattled along their tracks, tourists wandered the nearby district with cameras and expectations, and somewhere in the city, the Domingo organization prepared their next shipment, secure in the knowledge that the system would continue to protect them.

Renee felt the familiar burning in her chest—the mix of anger and determination that had driven her since her first days on the force. The Domingo organization might have won today, but the war was far from over. There were other avenues, other approaches. And somewhere in this city, there was a thread they could pull that would unravel the entire corrupt tapestry.

The question was whether they could find it before more bodies piled up, before more families like the Chens were left with nothing but grief and the hollow promise of a justice system that served only those who could afford to corrupt it.

CHAPTER 2

"YOU READY?" RENEE ASKED, starting the car.

Kelsey leaned back in his seat, his smirk fading as the weight of what was coming settled on them.

"No, but let's do it anyway."

The afternoon traffic thinned as they left downtown. The streets had given way to the sprawling outskirts of the city, where the trees grew taller, and the skyline faded into a mess of high-rise buildings. Kelsey had been quiet for a while but finally glanced over at Renee. "Hey, I was—"

"Unit 12, return to headquarters. Repeat, return to headquarters immediately for briefing. Captain's orders."

"That's never a good sign," Kelsey said, watching Renee's hand tighten on the steering wheel.

"Well, looks like our day just got a hell of a lot more interesting," she said, yanking away from the curb. The tires squealed as she spun the wheel hard, throwing the car into a tight U-turn that earned a couple of dirty looks from folks clutching coffee cups on the sidewalk.

They turned out of the Quarter, heading back to HQ, both wondering what kind of case could have them called in so abruptly.

When they pulled into the lot, Kelsey stepped out of the car and took in the sight of the building. The place was a testament to the city's no-frills attitude—a concrete block that might have been painted once upon a time but had long since been worn down by the elements. Kelsey looked up at it as if seeing it for the first time, even though he had walked through those doors a thousand times before.

"Every time I look at this place, I wonder why they even bother."

Halfway to the entrance, Renee threw him a glance over her shoulder. "It's not about looks, Kelz. It's about the institution itself."

Inside, they were hit by the cool blast of an air conditioning unit that had seen its better days. Officers moved through the bullpen, phones rang, and the shuffle of paperwork echoed through the halls. But the mood was tenser than usual, and Renee could feel it.

Captain Roy Simmons was waiting near his office, his expression as hard as usual. He motioned them over, not wasting time with pleasantries.

"Briefing room. Now," he said, already leading the way down the hall.

Renee and Kelsey followed without a word, looking at each other as they moved through the narrow corridor. The paint on the walls was peeling due to its age and lack of care, and mold was growing on the ceiling tiles from the leaky roof.

Simmons wasted no time. He closed the door as soon as everyone entered the room and launched straight into it.

"We've got a body," he said. "Found early this morning in the swamps near Barataria. A few Swampers spotted it half in the water and half caught on a cypress knee. By the time the state boys arrived, the gators had already done what gators do."

Kelsey grimaced. "Nice."

"Here's the thing," Simmons continued. "The body's in rough shape—no ID yet, and we can't even confirm the age because, well, because of the gators. But the state boys found something that got their attention. A Loyola Law School ring was found on his finger."

"A Loyola law grad floating in the bayou?" Renee looked puzzled. "That's not exactly a place you'd expect to find a college guy."

"Exactly," Simmons said. "There's no telling who this guy is yet, but we need to get on it. State police are holding the scene but want us to lead the investigation. So remember, first things first—we need to get that body over to forensics and see what they can pull from the remains."

Renee shifted in her seat. "Cap," she began, "I don't understand. Why are narcotics being assigned to a floater in the swamp?"

"Look, you both know how short-staffed we are right now. We've got to pitch in wherever we can. Homicide's swamped, and you two are some of our best. I need you on this. And besides, you both were in homicide before you moved over to narcotics, so you know the ropes."

"So, we're just supposed to drop our ongoing cases?"

"No," Simmons replied, shaking his head. "Consider this a temporary reassignment. Your narcotics cases are still yours, but I need you to prioritize this floater. Something about it doesn't sit right with me, and I want you two on it."

Renee sighed, realizing there was no point in arguing further. "Alright, Captain. We'll head out to the swamp. But if this interferes with our ongoing investigations..."

"I know, I know," Simmons cut her off. "Just do what you can. That's all I'm asking. So please, I need you two to get out to the scene, take over from the state boys, and work with forensics to extract whatever you can from the body."

Kelsey, letting out a groan, said. "Not the kind of case I was expecting to be given today."

"Me either," Simmons said bluntly. "But it is what it is."

Renee stood up and began walking to the door.

Kelsey pushed his chair back. "Guess I'm skipping lunch."

CHAPTER 3

THE SILENCE BETWEEN RENEE and Kelsey lingered for most of the ride. As the city disappeared from view, the wilds of the swamp closed in, the landscape growing more remote and untamed with every passing mile.

They left the precinct and drove toward Barataria, the city gradually giving way to open marshland and the suffocating heat of the bayou. The closer they got, the more the air thickened, and the road narrowed until they were surrounded by swamps on either side. They could smell the wet earth from the marsh as they drove deeper into the winding roads.

Kelsey glanced sideways at Renee. "You grew up around here, didn't you?"

Renee kept her eyes on the road as memories began to fill her mind. "Yeah, I did. I lived in the swamps 'til I was fourteen."

"I didn't know you were out here that long. What was it like?"

Renee inhaled and then let out a breath. "It was… different. You had to know the land, every inch of it. My folks were old swamp people. Dad fished, trapped, and did whatever he could to make ends meet. Mom helped out where she could. We lived in a small house on stilts, where you could hear the water underneath when it got quiet. No neighbors for miles."

She paused, her fingers grabbing the wheel a little tighter as the road narrowed. "It wasn't easy, but it was home. Out here, you don't get much help from the outside. You learn to survive and rely on yourself. But the swamp has a way of getting under your skin. It's peaceful in some ways, but it's also unforgiving. You have to respect it, or it'll eat you alive."

Kelsey nodded. "Sounds like a different world."

Renee glanced at him. "Seriously, though, it's not at all like a city person would think. Living out there, you understood things in a different way. Life and death felt a lot closer.

You saw it in the animals, in the people. Neighbors you'd known for years would just... disappear."

Kelsey grinned. "Sounds like the city."

Renee caught his eye with a brief, wry smile. "I guess in that respect, it does. My parents did the best they could, but they didn't want me stuck out here. They thought the city could offer me better opportunities. So when I turned fourteen, they sent me to live with my aunt. She had married out early—left the bayou and never looked back."

Kelsey looked out the window at the thick trees and winding waterways, trying to imagine a young Renee growing up in such a place. "Must've been a hell of a change, going from this to the Big Easy."

"It was." Renee's voice softened. "City life was loud, chaotic. I didn't fit in at first. The streets were confusing, and I missed the quiet. But I got used to it. My aunt showed me the ropes and made sure I stayed in school. And after a while, the city started feeling like home, too. But this place…the swamp, it stays with you. No matter how far you go from it."

Kelsey stared out the window, watching the swamp pass by outside. "I can't imagine what it's like growing up where the only thing around is the water and trees. You ever miss it?"

Renee considered the question, the distant call of a heron echoing through the marsh. "Sometimes. There's a simplicity out here, a way things make sense. You know what you're up against. In the city, it's different. The dangers are harder to see."

Kelsey chuckled. "Yeah, but out here, the gators are literal."

Renee smiled, though her eyes remained focused on the road. "Yeah, at least you know where you stand with a gator."

As they turned, the swamp opened into a vast stretch of water. Renee's smile faded as reality settled back in.

"This was my home," she said quietly, "but it's not the same when you come back for something like this."

"I can understand that," Kelsey remarked.

The car slowed to a stop near the blinking lights that marked the scene's perimeter. The swamp they had just spoken of was now the backdrop for a grisly investigation.

"Loyola law grad out here..." Kelsey said, opening the door. "I wonder what connection he had with the swamp."

Renee shook her head. "No way of telling."

* * *

Across town, in a sterile laboratory hidden within an innocuous warehouse in the industrial district, Antoine Domingo slammed the door behind him, making the glass beakers on the shelves tremble. Dr. Lucia Vasquez didn't look up from her microscope, accustomed to his dramatic entrances.

"The purity is off again," Antoine said, tossing a small package onto her workstation. "The Rivera cartel is flooding the Quarter with product that's ninety-four percent pure. Ours tested at eighty-eight."

"Your father approved the current formula," Dr. Dr. Vasquez replied calmly, finally looking up. "The higher the purity, the higher the overdose risk. Jean-Paul was explicit about keeping it below ninety percent."

Antoine paced the sterile white laboratory, his designer shoes squeaking against the polished floor. "My father's caution is becoming a liability. The market is changing, and we're falling behind."

Dr. Vasquez watched him carefully. In the many years she'd worked for the Domingo organization, she'd observed the growing tension between father and son. Jean-Paul built his empire on calculated risks and strategic patience. Antoine wanted expansion, dominance, and immediate results.

"I can adjust the formula," she offered. "But your father will notice the change in the financial reports. The process costs more."

"Let me worry about my father," Antoine replied. He checked his Rolex, the gleaming timepiece a calculated display of his success. "Just make it happen."

As he turned to leave, his phone rang. He checked the caller ID and answered immediately, his tone shifting from command to guarded apprehension.

"Yes, Judge Harrison... Of course... The Rodriguez case, yes." He listened intently, nodding though the judge couldn't see him. "I understand completely. I'll have Mendoza handle it personally." His expression tightened as he calculated the cost. "Yes, sir. The usual arrangement. I'll make sure it's delivered tomorrow."

After ending the call, Antoine's expression darkened. "That was Harrison. He wants another fifty thousand for the Rodriguez dismissal. Says the prosecutor is being difficult."

"Your father handles the judicial arrangements," Dr. Lucia reminded him.

"My father isn't here," Antoine snapped. "He's meeting with investors in Houston, playing his respectable businessman role." He tapped his fingers rapidly against the lab table. "Harrison also mentioned something interesting. Judge Taylor's been asking questions about case dismissal patterns. Specifically, our cases."

Dr. Vasquez's hands stilled over her work. "That sounds concerning."

"It's being handled," Antoine said, his voice dropping to a dangerous whisper. "I've got someone reaching out to Taylor. An old connection." A cold smile spread across his face. "Did you know my father once offered Taylor a million dollars to play ball with us? He turned it down."

"Your father told you this?"

"My father doesn't tell me anything important," Antoine replied bitterly. "But I have my own sources in his inner circle. People who recognize which Domingo will be running things soon."

Dr. Vasquez watched him through the glass walls as he left the laboratory, speaking intensely on his phone. Antoine had always lived in his father's shadow, fighting for recognition, for respect. In her experience, men with that particular hunger often made deadly miscalculations.

She returned to her microscope, adjusting the formula as requested, wondering which Domingo would still be standing when the inevitable collision between father and son finally came.

* * *

When they arrived at the scene, state police had already taped off the area, their vehicles parked haphazardly on the dirt road leading to the water. A few officers stood by while the occasional gator bellow echoed faintly from the distance.

"Welcome to paradise," Kelsey muttered, stepping out of the car and taking in the stagnant, swampy air. "Damn, this place stinks."

They were greeted by a state police sergeant. "You're NOPD, right?"

Renee nodded. "What do we have?"

The sergeant gestured toward the murky canal that led deeper into the swamp. "We got ourselves a floater. Found him about fifteen minutes in, where the canal widens out past the cypress grove. No telling how long he's been in the water. Gators got to him. Not much there to look at. Forensics is going to have their hands full with this one."

Kelsey glanced toward the water. "Do you have an idea about his age?"

The sergeant shook his head. "Not really. It could be anywhere from twenties to forties, maybe older. Between the water and the gators, it's hard to say at this point. The only thing that stood out was the ring—Loyola Law School. That's what got us to call you guys."

Renee scanned the scene. "Were you able to get him out of the water yet?"

"Was waiting for you," the sergeant replied. "We've kept the scene as intact as possible, thought you might want to look before we move him."

Renee nodded. "Okay, we'll get some pictures first. We need to get as many details as we can."

Kelsey stuffed his hands in his pockets, taking in the dense marshland around them. "Not much out here but water and gators. How does a lawyer end up out here anyway?"

"That's what we're gonna try and find out," Renee said, looking at the place she once called home.

Kelsey slapped at a mosquito on his neck. "Got any bug spray? These things are eating me alive."

Renee managed a smile, but being back here stirred up memories she'd tried to forget. Old ghosts that had nothing to do with the body they'd come to investigate.

"Right there," she pointed to where a dirt road disappeared into the cypress grove. "Half a mile down, up on stilts. Daddy built it himself." The wood and tin structure was long gone now, claimed by Hurricane Katrina like so many other pieces of her past.

She could still see her father standing on their small dock, showing her how to read the water. "The swamp don't lie, baby," he'd say, his calloused hands gesturing at the ripples. "Everything leaves a trace—

gators, fish, boats. You just gotta learn to read the signs."

Now, looking at the body, those lessons echoed in her mind. The swamp was still teaching her to read signs, only now they might be carved in human corruption instead of nature's honest brutality.

"Over there," she pointed to a weathered cypress, its trunk wider than a car. "That's where Daddy would meet the hunting parties. Judges, politicians, businessmen—all wanting to bag themselves a trophy gator." She paused, remembering the night that changed everything. "He'd guide them through the bayou, cook up his famous jambalaya, listen to them talk..."

"Must've heard some interesting conversations," Kelsey observed carefully, noting the tension in his partner's voice.

"Yeah." Renee's hand unconsciously moved to the badge on her belt. "One night, he heard something he shouldn't have. Next week, there was a 'hunting accident.'" The last words came out bitter as marsh water.

She walked to the water's edge, her boots sinking slightly into the soft earth. A bull gator glided past, barely causing a ripple—a reminder that the deadliest things often moved in silence.

"I was thirteen when they brought his body back. Mama couldn't handle it. That's when she sent me to live with my aunt." She turned to Kelsey, a tear in her eyes. "You know what the official report said? 'Accidental discharge of hunting rifle.' No investigation, no questions asked."

Renee picked up a piece of driftwood, tossing it into the water. A nearby egret took flight, startled by the splash. "You know what Daddy used to say about the swamp? 'Out here, there's no hiding what you are. The swamp strips away all pretense.' Funny how the same people who come out here to play at being hunters are the ones hiding behind their benches and badges back in the city.

"When I became a cop, I thought I was choosing a different path than my father. Turns out I'm still reading signs, still tracking predators. Only difference is, the ones I'm hunting now wear suits instead of scales."

Kelsey watched his partner, seeing her in a new light. The tough detective facade had cracked just enough to reveal the swamp girl underneath—the one who learned about justice not from law books but from the unforgiving laws of the bayou.

The noise of the wild sounded in the distance, and the cypress trees creaked in the rising wind. Kelsey noticed Renee's posture had changed—straighter, more focused. The bayou had reminded her not just of who she was but also of why she wore the badge.

"The swamp doesn't lie," she said, echoing her father's words. "And neither do I."

As they moved closer to the water, they knew the Louisiana swamp was something to contend with. The gators had done their work, but still, they had to find something—some piece of the puzzle that hadn't yet come into focus.

"We need to get forensics everything they can use," Renee said quietly, scanning the area. "And then maybe they can figure out who this guy is—and why he ended up here."

Kelsey sighed, his usual humor replaced by the grim sight of the corpse floating before him. "I've seen some horrible things in this job, but… this? I didn't need to see."

* * *

Captain Roy Simmons sat behind his cluttered desk, waiting for the coffee maker in the corner to finish brewing. The office was dimly lit, the blinds half-closed, letting in only slivers of light. He liked his coffee with a splash of French vanilla and two sugars—just enough sweetness to cut through the day's bitterness. As the rich aroma filled the room, Simmons saw Renee and Kelsey through the section of glass that looked out onto the precinct floor.

Opening the door with a file in hand, Simmons said, "Hey, you two, come sit." His eyes never left the paper he was reading.

"What's up, Captain?" Renee and Kelsey responded in unison, their voices so in sync it was as if they shared the same thoughts.

Simmons leaned back in his chair, rubbing his tired eyes. "Judge Charles Taylor didn't show up to work today or yesterday."

"Whoa," Kelsey grunted. "Did he graduate from Loyola?"

"Bingo," Simmons said without looking up.

Kelsey gave a slow nod. "The body we found. The ring. Judge Taylor being MIA."

Renee walked over to the coffee pot in Simmons's office and helped herself to a cup. Simmons watched her as she poured the cream and two spoons of sugar.

"Help yourself to some coffee, why don't you?" Simmons said.

"Thanks, Cap, already did."

Simmons shook his head and laughed.

She took a sip of coffee before speaking. "What's the connection? Why dig this up now when our caseload is already through the roof? I don't see why we're getting pulled into this."

Simmons picked up the file and slid it across the desk toward them. "Judge Taylor was assigned a high-profile drug case—big money, influential names. He was supposed to start hearing motions this week, but he's been off the radar."

Renee glanced at Kelsey. "And now there's a body in the bayou with a Loyola Law School ring."

"Are you implying that the body is Taylor?" Simmons asked.

"No," Replied Renee.

"Well, I might be," said Simmons.

"So, the judge's disappearance might not be just about him not showing up for work." Kelsey implied, "If that body is Taylor, we've got a big mess on our hands."

"Let's not get ahead of ourselves," Simmons said. "First things first: we need to identify who this guy is. If it turns out to be Taylor, we need to manage the situation before it blows up in our faces. The news media already knows he would be handling a high-profile case, and we don't want them tipping anyone off—not just yet."

Swirling the spoon in her coffee cup, Renee looked up at Simmons, "Alright. We'll head back to forensics and see what they've got on the body. If it's Taylor, we'll have to dig into his connections—find out who would want him dead."

Simmons nodded. "Keep me updated on anything you find."

As they stood to leave, Kelsey glanced at Renee. "Looks like the swamp's not done with us yet."

Stepping out of the police complex, the heavy door swinging shut behind them, Renee's phone buzzed in her pocket. Glancing at the unknown number on the screen.

"Hold up," she muttered to Kelsey, answering the call, "Dubois."

A voice came through, low and distorted, as if run through a voice modulator. "Going to forensics is a waste of time."

Renee shot Kelsey a quick look. "Who is this?"

The voice kept going like it hadn't heard Renee's question at all. "The body belongs to Taylor. You'll confirm it eventually, but I'm telling you now—it's him. Do your due diligence. I know you have to. But it's Taylor."

Kelsey moved closer, trying to catch what was being said.

"Who are you?" Renee pressed.

The voice went quiet, then after a pause, said, "You're being watched. Be careful."

Renee's grip tightened on the phone. "Who the hell is this?"

But there was nothin' but silence—the line had gone dead.

Renee lowered the phone slowly as she looked at Kelsey. "Well, that was subtle."

"What was," Kelsey said, "what did they say?" Renee slid the phone into her pocket. "That the body's Taylor and that we're being watched."

Kelsey glanced around, scanning the street. "Great. Just what we needed—ghost callers and stalkers. You believe him?"

Renee shrugged as she looked out over the Quarter. "Don't know. But we're gonna find out."

"Can we trace the call?"

Renee shook her head. "Probably not. You can bet it's a burner."

"Why would someone go through the trouble of feeding us that information? Is he an insider? Is he trying to help us?"

Renee leaned against the car. "Maybe. Or he's playing us. If he is an insider, assuming it's a he—it could mean he's playing with our minds, trying to lead us into a dark alley."

"This is strange. Why reach out now? What's the angle?"

Kelsey's eyes narrowed in thought. "I mean, think about it. This mystery caller drops this bomb on us out of the blue. What's he playing at?"

"Maybe he was in on something and now thinks killing a judge probably crossed the line."

"Or," Kelsey paused momentarily, "maybe he's the killer."

"Well," Renee said, "whatever the reason, we've been assigned the case."

"Yes, but Renee, that just happened. How did he know so fast?" His mind worked through the thought. "What are we supposed to take from that? Is he involved? If he's trying to help, I guess we'll hear from him again?"

Renee took a moment to consider the question. "You know, if this guy is trying to help us, he's doing it in a weird sort of way. It makes me think he's either scared or..."

"Or he's yanking our chain," Kelsey blurted out. "For all we know, he could be behind all this, just leading us around in circles."

"Yeah, he could be," Renee said. "We need to look at it from both angles. Let's say he's trying to keep his hands clean and maintain a low profile. But then again, if he's pulling all the strings..."

Kelsey finished Renee's thought: "And we fall for it, thinking he's trying to help; we could be setting ourselves up for trouble. Either way, we need to watch our step with this one."

"Ya think?" Renee said sarcastically. "But let's not get ahead of ourselves. First things first—we need to make sure the body belongs to Judge Taylor, and if our shadowy friend isn't yanking our chain. Then it probably means he's holding back more than he's letting on."

"And if he's lying...?" Kelsey asked.

"Then we're being played." Renee shrugged. "Guess we'll find out soon enough."

"True," Kelsey remarked. "Let's see what the lab rats have to say. If the caller is right, we know at least he's connected somehow."

CHAPTER 4

THE FLUORESCENT LIGHTS of the forensics lab buzzed overhead as Renee and Kelsey made their way down the hallway. The antiseptic smell hung in the air—harsh but still preferable to Bourbon Street on any given night.

Upon entering, they saw Dr. Lefort, the Medical Examiner, hunched over a microscope. He looked up, his gray hair disheveled and dark circles under his eyes indicating another long night.

"Detectives," he greeted them as he straightened up. "I was wondering when you'd show up. I heard you two had the case."

Renee nodded at a face she knew all too well. "Hi, Doc."

They'd been there before, in this room of last resorts, piecing together the final chapters of lives cut short.

"Welcome, my friends. We have to stop meeting like this," Lefort said. "Come to check on gator boy?"

His attempt at levity fell flat in the somber atmosphere, but the detectives appreciated the effort. In their line of work, gallows humor was sometimes the only thing keeping the darkness at bay.

"Sure thing, Doc," Kelsey said, rubbing the sweat from his forehead. "You think you can ID him?"

"Possibly. There may be enough here, but it'll take some time. The ring's a good start, but I wish we had more to go on."

LeForte sounded frustrated. The ravages of nature hampered his skilled hands, which were capable of unraveling the mysteries of death.

"Maybe we'll have a stroke of luck," Renee said. Thinking of the anonymous call and the missing judge, but neither wanted to jump to conclusions.

Lefort let out a humorless chuckle. "Luck? In this job? You're funny, Dubois." He gestured to the sheet-covered body. "This poor soul's been gator food. Identifying him will be about as easy as finding an honest politician in this crazy town."

Kelsey chuckled, "Come on, Doc. Not our politicians."

"Of course not," Lefort remarked. "I wouldn't dare insinuate that. Besides, you never know who's listening."

"Walk us through it, Doc," Kelsey said. "What are we looking at here?"

"Well, normally, we'd start with photos, you know? But that's out unless we had more of our friend here to take pictures of."

"What about fingerprints?" Renee pressed.

"Nope. See, detective, when a body's been marinating in the bayou this long, fingerprints tend to go the way of the dodo. We could try rehydrating the fingertips, but it's a long shot. And even if we get prints, they're useless if our Vic isn't in the system."

"DNA, then?" she pressed.

Lefort scratched his head, thinking. "Well, we can use bone, hair, whatever's left. But DNA's slow, and we need something to match it to. This ain't CSI, where you get results before the commercial break."

Renee exchanged a loaded glance with Kelsey, then dropped her bombshell. "What if I told you we got a strange call from someone who didn't identify himself—said the body was Judge Taylor. And when we got back to the precinct, we found out Judge Taylor didn't show up for court yesterday or today. Plus, he's a Loyola alum."

The change in Lefort was instant. His eyes sharpened, fatigue momentarily forgotten. "Well, well. Now that's interesting. A missing judge? Suddenly, our boy here got a whole lot more important."

The casual atmosphere evaporated.

"So, doc, how quickly can we get a positive ID?" Kelsey asked.

Lefort circled the body. "Well, now that we've got a name to work with, dental records are our best shot. We're lucky the gator left us half a head to work with. It's quicker than DNA, that's for sure."

He paused. "Look, it's not foolproof—teeth aren't like fingerprints. They're not one of a kind. But throw in the other evidence, the general description...what we have left of this poor soul, and we might just be able to nail this down."

Lefort's eyes lit up. "Tell you what? If you can snag Taylor's dental and medical records, I might be able to give you an answer sooner rather than later. It's not perfect, but much better than shooting in the dark."

"Okay, so you think maybe in a week?" Renee asked.

Lefort considered his response.

"Possibly in a day or two," Lefort said. "Give me a minute, and I'll write you a provisional order to seize the records. I'll leave it up to you to find out who his physician and dentist are." He leaned in and lowered his voice to a whisper, though only the detectives were present. "But listen—from all my years of doing this, when someone important is murdered, and what you said about an anonymous caller saying it was Judge Taylor... you can bet multiple people with connections are involved. This could be a high-profile and dangerous case."

"We know," Renee said.

"Our friend here," Lefort said, looking at the corpse. "I want to see if I can find any sign of a struggle."

"If you're thinking foul play," Kelsey said, "we're way ahead of you."

Lefort spread his hands. "I'm not thinking anything yet. But if this turns out to be your missing judge, well... let's say you might be opening one hell of a can of worms."

"We'll get you the dental records, Doc," Renee said, "and whatever else you need."

As they turned to leave, Lefort called after them. "Oh, and detectives? One more thing. Teeth can tell us where he's from, you know. The minerals in drinking water leave distinctive signatures in dental enamel over time. If he spent most of his life here, our local water would have left its mark." Lefort shrugged. "It might help confirm whether he's truly a local or from somewhere else entirely."

"Thanks, Doc," Renee nodded.

"And, detectives. If this is who you think it is, watch your back. In this town, dead judges tend to bring out all kinds of nasty creatures. And I'm not just talking about gators."

CHAPTER 5

YANKING HIS TIE LOOSE, sweat darkened his collar despite the early hour. The Mississippi rolled past them, thick as oil and twice as dirty.

Renee squinted against the glare bouncing off the water. "Dental records won't hunt themselves down. Though something tells me identifying the judge will be the easy part."

"Ain't that the truth." Kelsey paused at their Crown Vic, hand resting on the sunbaked metal. "Remember when we thought this was just another floater?"

"Yeah." Renee rummaged through her pockets, finally fishing out her keys after an awkward search. "Now we may have a dead judge and gator tracks leading nowhere."

The street stretched before them, heat waves dancing off the hot concrete. Kelsey glanced over the car's roof at his partner. "One thing's for sure: you never know what this city will vomit up for you next."

Renee shook her head. "Where do you come up with this stuff?"

Kelsey smiled and folded himself into the passenger seat, his holster snagging on the upholstery that had seen too many stakeouts and not enough care. The door slammed shut with the kind of finality usually reserved for courthouse moments—the same kind Judge Taylor used to deliver back when he was slamming down his gavel.

* * *

The Orleans Parish Courthouse stood before them, its weathered stone facade reminding them of the countless dramas that had unfolded within its walls. As Renee and Kelsey climbed the many steps, the heat quickly took its toll. And it wasn't long before they were both breaking a sweat. Halfway up, Kelsey paused to wipe his face, saying, "It's like walking through a sauna."

They entered the corridors, finally arriving at a door marked "Judge Charles Taylor." Outside, a middle-aged woman sat at a desk, her fingers flying over the keyboard.

"Excuse me," Renee said, flashing her badge. "I'm Detective Dubois, and this is Detective Griffith. Could you help us get some information on Judge Taylor?"

The secretary looked up. "Is everything OK? I mean, is everything alright with the judge? He hasn't been seen for a few days, and I'm a bit concerned."

Trying to be as sympathetic as possible, Kelsey replied, "That's why we're here; we're trying to locate Judge Taylor. When was the last time you heard from him?"

"It was Friday afternoon, I believe. By the way, I'm Margaret Landry—I've been his secretary for more years than I want to count." Margaret smiled and then said, "He mentioned a dinner date and said he'd see me on Monday. But he never showed up, and I haven't been able to reach him on his cell."

Renee nodded, jotting notes. "Has he ever done this before? Missed court without notice?"

"Never," Margaret said firmly. "The Judge is very dedicated. This isn't like him at all."

"We understand," Renee said. "Ms. Landry, we might need to check with the Judge's medical providers. Sometimes, people leave alternate contact information with them. Do you happen to have those details?"

Margaret's expression changed, a hint of a smile crossing her face. "Oh yes, I have all that information. The Judge often asked me to make appointments for him. He was always so busy, you see. Said it was easier to have me handle those things."

"Wonderful, that will be of great help. How often would you make these appointments for him?"

"Oh, quite regularly," Margaret replied. "Just last week, I made an appointment for him with Dr. Johnson for his six-month cleaning."

"And his doctor?"

"That would be Dr. Randall at Tulane Medical Center," Margaret said, consulting her planner. "Though he hasn't needed an appointment there in a while."

"Can you give me their contact information?"

"Yes, I'll write it down for you."

Renee nodded, setting down her notebook. "Thank you, Ms. Landry. You've been more help than you know." She paused, choosing her next words carefully. "One more thing—did Judge Taylor ever mention taking trips to Barataria? Maybe for hunting or swamp tours?"

Margaret let out a small laugh, though there was no humor in it. "Oh no. Judge Taylor wouldn't go near a swamp. He was strictly a country club man—golf and tennis. Said the mosquitoes in his own backyard were more wilderness than he could handle."

Renee smiled. "Thank you again, Ms. Landry. Here—let me give you my card. Please let us know immediately if you hear anything from the judge."

"Sure thing, detectives."

* * *

"You think the Judge was mixed up in something?" Kelsey asked as he started the car.

"I think we're about to find out. And something tells me we might not like what we discover."

* * *

The bell chimed as Renee and Kelsey pushed open the door to Esplanade Dental. The waiting room was empty, except for a young receptionist behind a sleek desk. She looked up, her smile faltering slightly at the sight of Kelsey's badge attached to his belt.

"Good afternoon," Renee said as she approached the desk. "I'm Detective Dubois, and this is Detective Griffith. We'd like to speak with Doctor Johnson."

The receptionist's eyes widened slightly. "Oh, um, certainly. May I ask what this is regarding?"

Kelsey stepped forward, speaking a little above a whisper, "It's a police matter. We prefer to discuss it directly with the Doctor."

"Of course," the receptionist nodded. She picked up the phone and spoke quietly for a moment. Setting it down, she turned back to the detectives. "Dr. Johnson will be out in just a moment. Please, have a seat if you'd like."

Renee and Kelsey remained standing, their eyes scanning the room out of habit. The waiting area was tastefully decorated, with soft jazz playing in the background—a quintessential New Orleans touch.

A few minutes later, a door opened, and a man in his late fifties emerged. He wore a crisp white coat, and his salt-and-pepper hair was neatly combed. "Detectives? I'm Dr. Johnson. How can I help you?"

Renee stepped forward. "Dr. Johnson, do you mind if we speak privately for a moment?"

"Not at all. Follow me, please."

Dr. Johnson led them down a short hallway to his office. Once inside, he closed the door and gestured to two chairs across from his desk. "What can I do for you?"

Renee handed him the document. "We have a request from the medical examiner's office for Judge Charles Taylor's dental records."

Dr. Johnson's eyebrows rose slightly, but he maintained his professional demeanor. "I see. May I?" He held his hand out for the document. "Everything seems to be in order. I'll have my assistant retrieve the files."

"Dr. Johnson, would you mind getting them yourself?" Renee said. "The fewer people who know, the better."

They followed the dentist to a small, well-appointed office. "Here you go. Is there anything else you need from me?"

Kelsey shook his head. "Not at this time, Doctor. Thank you."

Renee nodded. "Thanks, Doc. If we need anything else, we'll be in touch."

As they stood to leave, Dr. Johnson asked. "Detectives, without violating confidentiality, may I ask if Judge Taylor is... all right?"

Kelsey answered calmly, "We're not at liberty to discuss any details, Doctor. But we appreciate your concern."

Dr. Johnson nodded, understanding the professional boundaries. "Of course. If there's anything else I can do to assist, please don't hesitate to contact me."

Making their way back to their car, Kelsey said, "That went well."

Renee nodded, already leafing through the file. "Yeah, but now comes the real work. Let's get these to the M.E. and see if we can finally put a name to our John Doe."

As they pulled away from Esplanade Street Dental, both detectives could feel the weight of the judge's possible death pressing down on them. They thought they were getting one step closer to unraveling the mystery. But in a city like New Orleans, they knew that answers often led to more dangerous questions.

CHAPTER 6

"GOT SOME TIME TO KILL," Kelsey said.

"Poor choice of words, considering." Renee squinted up at the sun-bleached sky. "Can't think on empty. Café Du Monde?"

"Works for me. My liver's already filing a protest."

"So, show some restraint for once."

Kelsey snorted. "If I knew how to do that, I'd be selling the secret instead of chasing dead judges."

The French Quarter wrapped around them like a worn leather glove—familiar, comfortable, hiding old stains. A saxophone wept through "Blueberry Hill," the notes drifting between buildings that had seen three centuries of times gone by. Tourist season was in full swing, the sidewalks crowded with folks learning the hard way that New Orleans didn't give up her secrets cheap.

Café Du Monde's ancient fans pushed around air that smelled of sugar and chicory, tempered with river mud and yesterday's rain. They found a table beneath the striped awning, where generations of cops had nursed hunches.

Their waiter appeared, crisp whites defying the humidity. "Sorry for the wait. Been slammed since sunrise." His accent placed him uptown, probably working his way through Tulane.

"Two orders of beignets," Kelsey said, then caught Renee's look. "Make that one. And café au lait."

"What happened to that liver protest?"

"Filing an appeal tomorrow." He grinned. "Maybe."

Renee ordered her usual and settled back as Jackson Square came alive with fortune tellers and featured artists, each selling their version of truth.

"When forensics comes back..." She let the words hang in the humid air. "If it's the Judge, we'll have answers. The question is—will we want them?" As she watched powdered sugar drift like evidence across their table.

Kelsey tapped on the table with his fingers as he watched tourists dodge pigeons in Jackson Square. "We've got pieces that don't fit yet, a half-eaten body in the bayou, a missing judge, and an anonymous caller who knows too much." He leaned closer, lowering his voice. "And we still don't know if any of it is connected. What's your take on the caller?"

"I don't know, but if the body turns out to be Taylor, then the caller knows something either way."

"Alright, so we've got two possibilities here. The caller is genuinely trying to help us but doesn't want to get involved or tip his hand. Maybe he's scared, or he's got something to lose."

Renee nodded. "Or the caller is involved and is trying to scare us off. And that means he knows something, and that bothers me."

"Exactly," Kelsey said. "And here's the kicker: if the caller knows about our investigation, others probably do too. If the criminal element is involved, then they must be aware of us poking around."

Their order arrived in the waiter's practiced two-step—the kind of graceful dodge perfected by years of navigating tourists, cops, and confidential informants, sometimes sharing the same powdered sugar. Steam rose from the café au lait, warm and steady, briefly fogging the edge of the glasses before fading into the air.

Renee eyed her black pantsuit, then the snow-white mountain of beignets. "Fifteen years on the force, you'd think I'd learn." She brushed at the visible sugar, already claiming territory on her lapel. "Like wearing a ball gown to a crawfish boil," she said, shaking her head.

The first bite melted on her tongue. She took a sip of her coffee, then set the cup down, her brow already furrowed. "This caller bothers me. Who finds out about a dead judge before the labs even do?"

They sat in silence, their table a quiet island in the afternoon noise. Nearby, tourists laughed and snapped photos, unaware of the weight pressing down across from them. Somewhere in the distance, music played— a low, steady rhythm that didn't lift the tension but only gave it a pulse.

"Bottom line," Renee said, brushing powdered sugar from her lap, "we can't take any chances. If a judge is involved in something shady, you can bet some police might be too. We don't know the caller's motives, and we don't know who else might be aware of our investigation."

"OK, then. We need to operate as if we're being watched at all times. Trust no one outside us two, and even then, we must be careful about what we say and where we say it."

"Agreed," Renee said. "We keep digging, but we do it quietly. No discussing the case at the precinct, no leaving notes or files where others might see them. We treat everyone as a potential leak until we know otherwise."

Kelsey raised his coffee cup. "Just us, then."

Renee tapped her cup against his. "Just us." She took a sip, wondering if someone was watching, reporting their every move to whoever was pulling the strings.

* * *

"Well, is that quick enough for you?" Dr. Lefort said as the detectives walked through the door.

"I was wondering what was taking you so long," Renee laughed. "Just kidding, Doc. Seriously, though, I didn't expect to hear from you so soon."

We're the McDonald's of forensics. You know, fast food, fast service... oh, never mind." His eyes twinkled, as if to have amused himself.

"Good one, doc," Kelsey smiled. "I also thought it would take longer."

"Normally, it would. But there were some interesting developments that moved things along quickly for me. Come take a look at this." His eyes moved from the detectives to the body and back again. "The dental records are a match, that's for certain. But there's more." He pulled back the sheet, revealing a long, thin scar on the left side of the torso. "See this? It's a surgical scar, consistent with a splenectomy."

"A spleen removal? Why?" Renee asked. "That's not exactly common, is it?"

"No, it's not," Lefort said. "Which is why I followed up with Dr. Randall at Tulane Medical Center; you listed him as his physician. It turns out Judge Taylor had a condition called idiopathic thrombocytopenic purpura. ITP for short. It's an autoimmune disorder that causes low platelet counts."

Kelsey raised an eyebrow. "And that's related to the spleen, how?"

"In severe cases, when ITP doesn't respond to other treatments, doctors sometimes resort to a splenectomy."

"And Taylor had this procedure?" Renee asked.

"According to Dr. Randall, yes. About five years ago. So, between the dental records and his rather unique medical history, I can say with near certainty that this is indeed Judge Charles Taylor."

Renee's jaw clenched. "Damn," she muttered, echoing Kelsey's earlier sentiment. "So, our mystery caller was right on the money."

"That's not all. While examining the body, I noticed something odd. Look here, at the fingertips."

The detectives leaned in. The skin on the fingertips was rough, almost synthetic in appearance.

"What are we looking at?" Kelsey asked.

"Someone tried to alter the fingerprints, probably with some acid. It's crude but effective. If it weren't for the scar and dental records, identifying the body through normal means would have been nearly impossible."

They left the ring, Renee said. How do you miss a ring when you're tampering with somebody's fingerprints?"

"Exactly," Lefort nodded. "Whoever did this thought they were thorough, but not thorough enough. I guess they were counting on the gators and the water to do their work for them."

"They were probably trying to get out of there," Kelsey said. "The swamp isn't the kind of place you want to be hanging around, especially with gators staring at you."

Dr. Lefort pulled the sheet back over the body, "I'll have the full report for you by morning, but I wouldn't wait to inform your captain. This isn't the kind of news that keeps well."

"It looks like we're not dealing with professionals, or the would-be professionals hired amateurs to do their dirty work." She turned to Dr. Lefort. "Is there anything else we should know, Doc?"

"No, not right now. If I find anything else out, you'll be the first to know."

"And detectives, I've said this before, but be careful out there. These individuals are ruthless. Whatever this is, Taylor must have been a threat to them. Keep your eyes open and watch your backs."

* * *

Renee rubbed the sweat from her forehead with the back of her hand. "I've lived here all my life," she muttered, "and I still don't think I'll ever get used to this heat." She squinted into the sunlight, her thoughts still tangled in what Lefort had just confirmed.

"We need to call Simmons," Kelsey said, "let him know we've got a positive ID."

"Remember, let's not say too much. We don't know who might be involved."

Looking around, Renee noticed a sleek black sedan idling across the street, its windows tinted so as to hide the riders from view,

She nudged Kelsey, nodding her head towards the sedan. "Don't look now, but we may have company."

Kelsey casually glanced in the direction Renee was alluding to. "How do you know they're following us? It's just a car parked across the street."

"Because I saw that same car parked by the Café Du Monde."

"Well then," he murmured. "Let's find out."

"Get in, Kelz. I'm driving." As she pulled out of the parking lot, the black sedan smoothly merged into traffic behind them.

"Well, that confirms it," Kelsey said, "we're being followed."

Renee's eyes were glued to the rearview mirror. The sedan was two cars back, matching their every turn.

Renee hung a sharp right onto Rampart Street, then another quick left. The sedan followed, closing the gap.

"Definitely not nothing," Kelsey murmured, twisting in his seat to keep an eye on the tail.

Renee's palms slid on the steering wheel. "Hang on," she said before abruptly cutting across two lanes of traffic and diving down a narrow side street.

Horns blared behind them as they made their maneuver. Kelsey looked over his shoulder for any sign of pursuit. After a moment of tense silence, "I don't see them." He said, "Where did they go?"

Renee's eyes darted between the road and her mirrors. "They were too close. We couldn't have lost them that easily, and they were definitely following us."

Kelsey leaned back in his seat. "Another scare tactic, maybe? Like the mysterious phone call. Just trying to let us know that we're being watched."

With the sedan no longer in sight, Renee loosened her grip on the steering wheel. "Could be," she admitted. "Could be."

They drove in silence for a few blocks, wondering if this was another intimidation tactic they were dealing with.

"You know what this means, don't you?" Renee asked.

"Yeah. Whoever we were up against, they wanted us to see them. They're sending a message."

As they merged back onto the main street, both detectives scanned their surroundings. The black sedan had vanished, but its menacing presence still weighed on their minds.

"So, our next move would be, what?" Kelsey asked.

"We keep digging," Renee replied.

They were silenced by the ring of Renee's phone. Answering it on speaker, "Dubois."

"Can you two come back here?" Lefort said. "I noticed something after you left. You're going to want to see this."

"On our way, Doc," Renee responded, changing course back to forensics.

Kelsey glanced at his watch—9:45 PM. "Late calls from the morgue were never good news."

As they entered, Dr. Lefort led them to the examination table and pulled back the sheet. "Look here," he said, pointing to several marks on the skin. "See these?"

Renee leaned in closer. "What are we looking at, Doc?"

"Street fentanyl. High concentration." Lefort's voice was grim. "Found it in his blood work. But here's what's interesting—it was administered twice. The first dose was in his drink; these patch marks on his skin were applied later. Whoever did this wanted to make damn sure he didn't walk away."

Raising his hands to rub his forehead, Kelsey said, "You're saying someone slipped it to him and then went back for seconds?"

"Exactly." Lefort moved to his desk, picking up a lab report, "The first dose was in his system through ingestion—found traces of wine in his stomach. The fentanyl was mixed in."

"Someone wanted this guy dead," Renee added to the conversation, her eyes fixed on the patch marks. She'd seen enough murder scenes to know the difference between opportunity and intent. "This wasn't some random hit. The way it was set up, the wine, the patches—they planned every detail." She looked at what was left of the body on the examination table, her voice dropping to match the morgue's hollow quiet. "But they got sloppy. And in my experience, when killers get sloppy, it's usually because they're working under someone else's orders."

"Could be." Lefort gestured back to the body. "After the wine did its job, the patches finished him off. They wanted to make sure this guy wouldn't wake up." He shook his head. "But you're right, Renee, they got sloppy with the details."

Renee remained silent for a moment, taking in all in. "So, our killer has ties to street dealers."

"High-level ones," Lefort confirmed. "This wasn't corner boy stuff. The fentanyl was nearly pure—that comes from someone near the top of the supply chain. So, whoever applied the patches knew exactly what they were doing."

"Well," Kelsey said, "We know he didn't do it to himself."

Lefort snorted. "Not a chance. The wine would've knocked him flat. Someone else put those patches on him. They weren't taking any chances; they wanted him out of the picture."

"This is cartel-level purity but applied by someone trying to imitate medical precision. Amateur hour meets professional product." He looked up from the report. "And here's another thing, the wine. Who puts two grand worth of wine in a judge's glass just to spike it with street drugs?"

Kelsey looked up from the body. "So, they poisoned him, then dumped him in the swamp?"

"Looks that way," Lefort replied. "Killer probably hoped the swamp would take care of the rest."

"Smart move, Kelsey said. "No body, no crime. Just a missing person case."

Lefort nodded in agreement. "Yes, and it almost worked. If those swamp boys hadn't found him when they did, there might not have been anything left to find."

"Time frame?" Kelsey asked. "You have a time frame?"

"Based on decomp and gator activity, I'd say he was in the water about 48 hours before he was found.

"That lines up with when he went missing," Lefort asked. "Over the weekend, right?"

"Yeah," Kelsey responded. "He was last seen Friday evening and reported missing Monday morning when he didn't show up for court."

"Given how fast fentanyl works," Lefort added, "I'd say our killer didn't waste any time."

Renee frowned. "So, we have to find out how it got into his wine. He was probably dining out. But with whom?"

"Someone must have slipped it into his drink," Lefort said.

"So," Kelsey added, "The judge must have trusted whoever he was with and maybe left the table for a moment. What do you say, doc? Does that sound about right?"

"I would say so." Lefort replied, "Maybe he had dinner with someone he trusted."

Looking bothered by the thought, Kelsey remarked, "Someone close enough that the judge wouldn't think twice about turning his back on or leaving his plate or glass unattended."

"So, if what you say is correct," Renee commented. "We're looking at friends, colleagues, maybe family."

Lefort shook his head. "Damn, That's cold. Sharing a meal with someone and then watching him die."

"Must have been really planned out," Kelsey added. "Poison him Friday night, get him in the vehicle before the drug had time to work, and…"

Renee interrupted, "That means Taylor must have been riding with someone. The perp certainly wouldn't want him driving under the influence, especially if he were going to dispose of the body. The perp needed to be in complete control."

"Yep," Kelsey continued, "then drive out to the swamp and dump him before anyone notices."

The wheels in Lefort's mind were turning rapidly. "They probably put the patches on him while in the vehicle."

Renee, picturing the scene, said. "Alright. We need to trace the judge's movements on Friday—every person he saw, every place he went. Focus on meals, drinks, and any social gatherings."

"Thanks, Doc, for calling us back," Renee said. "This opened up a whole new avenue for us."

As they turned to leave, Renee stopped in her tracks for a moment. "They must have really thought they were clever. But they just gave us a whole lot to work with. We know now he was targeted."

"Yes, and now we just have to put these pieces together and find out who the judge trusted enough to let his guard down."

CHAPTER 7

SIMMONS WAVED THEM into his office. "Get in here, you two. Tell me you got something."

The door closed, shutting out the precinct's usual buzz, phones ringing, papers shuffling, voices overlapping.

"It's Taylor, Cap," Renee said, sinking into a chair. "Forensics confirmed it. And it wasn't any accident. Someone wanted him dead."

Simmons sank back in his chair. "That's the last thing I wanted to hear."

"There's more," Kelsey added. "Before forensics even confirmed him, we got a strange call. Someone told us it was Taylor."

Simmons leaned forward. "Like a tip-off?"

"Maybe. Or someone's playing us. Hard to say."

"Hell," Simmons said, tapping his pencil on the desk. "What exactly did they say?"

"Not much. Just that it was Taylor, then they hung up."

Simmons' face fell as the full implications hit him. "This isn't just a random act of violence. We're talking about the assassination of a judge."

Kelsey's jaw tightened. "Homicide should have had jurisdiction from the beginning," he said, his voice edged with frustration.

Simmons gave him a warning look but didn't press. "Keep me posted. Every lead, every gut feeling. And watch your backs. Around here, the gators aren't just in the swamps."

Outside, Kelsey nudged Renee. "You buying his 'concerned boss' act?"

Renee shook her head. "Right now, I'm not buying anything from anyone. This case is as murky as the Mississippi. And probably just as dangerous."

* * *

Kelsey pulled into his driveway that night, though the usual sense of relief didn't hit. Not tonight.

As he reached the front door, he heard it—the low rumble of an engine starting up. He turned, catching a glimpse of a black sedan with tinted windows pulling away from the curb.

Inside, Kelsey tried to sound casual. "Hey, hun, that car across the street? Did you happen to notice how long it's been there?"

"For a while, I noticed it when I got back from the store a few hours ago."

"Did you happen to see anyone inside?"

"No... I didn't, wasn't really paying that much attention." Her eyes searched his face. "Why? What's going on?"

Kelsey sat at the table. This case, that call, the tail—it was all adding up to something dark. And now this. Trouble wasn't just at the station; it was sitting outside his house.

He studied Laura's face, caught between full disclosure and protective silence. "This case—it's complicated. Potentially dangerous."

"Dangerous? Kelsey, what aren't you telling me?"

"We might be dealing with people who don't appreciate questions." His eyes darted to the front door, his voice dropping barely above a whisper. "That car out there... could be a coincidence."

But the tightness in his chest told him otherwise. His fingers trembled slightly as he retrieved his phone. "I need to reach Renee."

Keeping his back to the wall, Kelsey edged toward the window, careful to stay hidden behind the frame as he peered through the narrow gap in the blinds. The street appeared normal—too normal. He held his breath as the call connected, each ring stretching into eternity until finally, Renee's voice cut through.

"Dubois."

"Renee," Kelsey said, "that black sedan that we saw earlier—it was sitting across from my house when I got home."

"Damn," Renee said, "is it still there?"

"No, it drove off as soon as I got home. I think they just wanted me to see them. They definitely want us to know they're watching."

"Agreed."

"And Renee? Watch your back. If they're watching me, they're probably watching you too."

After hanging up, Kelsey turned back to Laura, who had listened to his side of the conversation. He took her hand. "Laura, I need you to do something for me. I want you to stay with your sister for the next few days. Take the kids, too."

"Kelsey, no. I'm not leaving you here alone." Laura shook her head. "Besides, Nicole is in Nevada. That's a thousand miles away."

"You're scaring me now." Laura's voice tightened. "What aren't you telling me?"

Kelsey squeezed her hand. "It's just a precaution. I'll sleep better knowing you're all somewhere else until this blows over."

"The kids have school, and I have work. We can't just disappear because you have a hunch."

"Laura, please. I wouldn't ask if it wasn't important."

Laura saw the resolve in her husband's eyes and knew there was no point in arguing. She nodded reluctantly. "Okay, but promise me you'll be careful."

Kelsey pulled her into a tight embrace. "I love you, Laura, and yes, I promise."

As Laura went upstairs to call her sister, Kelsey sat back at the kitchen table. The case had just become personal, and the danger was no longer an abstract concept but a genuine threat to his family.

He thought about Judge Taylor's position, the cases he might have presided over, the influential people he might have angered or threatened. What had the judge stumbled upon that was worth killing for? And more importantly, who else might be involved or in danger?

As Kelsey pondered the past few days, thoughts began swirling. What if this was more than just the death of a judge? What if Taylor's murder was merely the tip of the iceberg?

* * *

Renee walked into the precinct the following day and noticed Kelsey leaning back in his chair, staring straight at the wall.

"You know, Renee, if we're going to investigate Judge Taylor's death, we need to know more about him. What kind of man was he? Was he corrupt? Was he honest? We can't just assume we know who he was based on his position. We need to go deeper. Does he have a relative or someone who knows him well?"

"We can't go to just anyone," Renee said. "We already discussed how the person who poisoned him might be someone close to him, someone he trusted. We need to find a close relative like a brother or sister, or a confidante he might have opened up to."

* * *

Renee and Kelsey sat in Charles Taylor's sister's living room that afternoon. The room was filled with family photos, many featuring a younger Charles in various stages of his career.

Vanessa, a woman in her early sixties with the same piercing blue eyes as the judge, settled into an armchair across from the detectives. "I'm not sure how much I can tell you that will help," she began, "but I'll do my best. Charles... he was always a good man. Stubborn as a mule sometimes, but good to his core."

She reached for a framed photo on the side table, extending her arm as she passed it to Renee. It showed a young Charles Taylor in a police uniform. "Before he became a judge, Charles worked as a detective for the NOPD. That's where it all started, I think. He saw things... things that troubled him deeply."

Vanessa's eyes grew distant. "He went to law school after leaving the force. He said he wanted to fight corruption from the inside. After he graduated, he became a legal advisor to several high-profile political figures in New Orleans. That's when things really started to change."

"In what way?" Renee asked.

"He had access to the corridors of power, you understand. He saw things." Vanessa paused, collecting her thoughts. "There was this land development deal the city council approved—the Riverside Project. The day after the vote, Charles came home completely different."

Kelsey and Renee exchanged glances, letting her continue at her own pace.

"He came to me that night," Vanessa's voice softened. "He was shaken, more scared than I'd ever seen him. Said he'd uncovered something big, something that could bring down half the city if it ever came to light."

"Did he tell you what it was?" Kelsey asked.

"Evidence of corruption. Widespread, deep. Local politicians, prominent business leaders, even members of the judiciary." Vanessa's hands trembled slightly. "He said it had spread like poison through every level of city government."

"And he confided all this in you?" Kelsey's tone was gentle but probing.

"Oh, yes, but he wouldn't tell me who they were. He didn't want me getting involved." Vanessa glanced back and forth between them. "He kept really detailed records, though. He said they were his insurance policy."

Kelsey glanced at Renee and saw the same realization in her eyes. The magnitude of what they were hearing was staggering.

Vanessa, quite the storyteller, seemed to relish sharing her brother's story. "The cover-up lasted for years," she continued. "Charles and a handful of other honest officials mounted a quiet resistance. However, as the corrupt elements tightened their grip on the city, resources began to disappear. Honest cops found themselves reassigned or forced out. Whistleblowers were silenced. With no support from above and no way to bring their evidence to light, Charles and his allies were forced to operate in the shadows."

Kelsey, shaking his head in disbelief, said, "And the public had no idea."

"Exactly," Vanessa replied, her hands clasped tightly in her lap. "The decent people fighting against this corruption had no choice but to keep their efforts hidden. They were outnumbered, outmaneuvered, and simply running out of options." Her voice remained composed, although her eyes revealed the depth of her feelings about her brother's struggle.

She stood up and walked to the window, thinking about the city she'd watched change over decades. "After a while, it just became another one of those things in New Orleans that everybody knew about but nobody talked about. Just swept under the rug like so many other scandals happening here."

Her voice grew softer, tinged with old memories. "Charles was different, though. Sure, he moved on— had to, really. Said becoming a judge wasn't about giving up the fight—it was about getting a better vantage point."

"Like climbing to higher ground?" Renee asked.

Vanessa nodded, a sad smile crossing her face. "Exactly. From the bench, he could see patterns more clearly. Connections between cases, names that kept popping up. He'd act all proper in his robes, but underneath? He was still that same detective, putting pieces together."

She sank back into her chair, suddenly looking tired. "He might've changed positions, but never changed who he was. Still, that same stubborn cop who couldn't let go of a case, even after all these years."

'*And now he's dead,*' Kelsey thought, making sure not to utter the words. The room fell silent as the sadness of his thought sank in.

The implications were clear as Renee and Kelsey left the sister's house. Judge Taylor's murder wasn't just about silencing one man; it was an attempt to put an end to a man who couldn't be bought.

* * *

The New Orleans rush hour traffic crawled along at a snail's pace, the usual chaos amplified by the torrential downpour that had engulfed the city. This wasn't just rain; it was as if the Mississippi itself had decided to fall from the sky. Sheets of water cascaded down, turning streets into shallow rivers and overwhelming storm drains that gurgled helplessly against the deluge.

Through the fog of rain on their windshield, Renee and Kelsey could barely make out the brake lights of the car in front of them, a blurry red smear in a world gone gray. The wipers fought a losing battle against the onslaught, creating a hypnotic rhythm that only added to the surreal atmosphere.

In New Orleans, rain wasn't just weather; it was a force of nature that reshaped the city. The air, already thick with humidity on a typical day, now felt almost soupy. The scent of wet asphalt mingled with the ever-present notes of bourbon and beignets, creating a cocktail of smells unique to the Big Easy.

Water pooled in the dips and hollows of the old streets, hiding potholes that could swallow a tire whole. Locals knew to navigate these temporal lakes with the caution of seasoned sailors while hapless tourists and newcomers risked flooding their engines with one wrong move.

A few hardy souls braved the elements on the sidewalks, huddled under umbrellas that seemed comically inadequate against the biblical downpour. Steam rose from storm grates, adding an ethereal quality to the scene as if the underworld was exhaling into the storm.

The blare of horns punctuated the constant drumming of pavement. It was a symphony of frustration, a chorus of drivers who knew that this commute, usually a test of patience, had become an endurance event.

Inside their unmarked sedan, Renee and Kelsey were cocooned in a bubble of relative calm, the outside world muffled by sheets of rain against the windows.

Despite the chaos outside, or perhaps because of it, the detectives were deep in conversation as they reviewed their visit with Judge Taylor's sister. The rain had created a strange sense of isolation, as if they were the only two people in a city drowning in secrets as surely as it was drowning in the rain.

Renee's eyes darted constantly between the road ahead and the rearview mirror, a habit born of years on the force and intensified by the high stakes of their current case.

As they inched forward in the heavy traffic, both detectives knew that this rain, this traffic, was more than just an inconvenience in a city like New Orleans, where danger could lurk around any corner, where corruption ran as deep as the roots of the old oak trees, even a rainstorm could be used as cover for those who operated in the shadows.

And so, they talked, piecing together the puzzle of Judge Taylor's life and death, all too aware that somewhere in this rain-soaked city, answers were waiting to be found—answers that some would kill to keep hidden.

* * *

"So, if what the sister told us is true," Kelsey said, "Taylor's been fighting corruption since his beat cop days. That's a lot of years to make enemies."

Renee nodded, her eyes fixed on what she could see of the sea of brake lights ahead. "Yeah, and any of them could have decided Taylor had finally crossed a line. But which one? And why now?"

The shrill ring of Renee's phone cut through their speculation. She fished it out of her pocket, frowning at the unfamiliar number on the screen. "Dubois."

The voice was distorted, clearly disguised, and hauntingly familiar. It was the same as before.

"Captain Simmons," the voice said, "trust no one but Simmons." Each word was clear and deliberate. "He's a good man and trustworthy. But trust no one else."

Before Renee could respond, the line went dead. She stared at the phone momentarily, then slammed it down on the seat. "Damn it!"

"Who was that? "Kelsey asked.

"Our mysterious caller. He said to trust no one but Simmons, that Simmons is the only one we can trust."

Kelsey rolled his eyes. "Simmons? Why him specifically?"

"I don't know," Renee shook her head, "but whoever this guy is, he seems to know a lot about what's happening. And if he's right..."

"If he's right, then we're surrounded by people we can't trust," Kelsey finished as if anticipating her very words. "Cops, lawyers, maybe even other detectives. Hell, for all we know, the chief could be involved."

Renee nodded slowly, trying to think it through. "This case is getting more complicated day by day. If we can only trust Simmons, how are we supposed to conduct this investigation? We can't do everything ourselves."

"So, what's the verdict?" Kelsey asked. "Do we trust Simmons?"

"I don't know, Kelz. Simmons is complicated. He's not afraid to bend the rules, maybe even break them. But he does appear to want to do what's right."

"Even if his methods are questionable?" Kelsey added.

"Especially then," Renee replied. "Maybe that's exactly what we need."

"But here's the thing, Renee. We're not just deciding whether to trust Simmons. We're also taking the word of some caller who wants us to trust him. And we sure as hell not gonna do that until he proves himself."

"For all we know, this could be an elaborate setup," Renee said, "The caller, Simmons, and who knows who else."

"Exactly. Someone could be trying to manipulate us into trusting the wrong person."

"Or trying to make us distrust everyone, leaving us isolated and vulnerable.

"Before we can trust Cap, we need to do our due diligence."

* * *

The soft glow of computer screens illuminated Renee and Kelsey's faces as they huddled in a quiet corner of the precinct's records room well after hours. The rest of the building was dark and silent, but here, the air hummed with tension and the quiet tapping of keyboards.

"I can't believe we're doing this," Kelsey muttered, not taking his eyes off the screen. "Investigating our captain."

"We need to trust someone, Kelz. Right now, Simmons is our best bet. But first, we need to know who we're dealing with."

They had started with Simmons's official record, but now they were digging deeper, searching for the man behind the accolades and commendations.

"You know," Renee said, "Simmons was in the military. Maybe we can check some military records and get a better sense of his background."

Kelsey looked up from his screen. "That's not a bad idea. That will give us something else to go on."

"Only one problem, Kelz. How do we get that information? It's not exactly public."

The thought hit him right between the eyes. Getting his father-in-law involved just didn't sit right with him. After reasoning it out for a moment, he finally said, "I... I might have a way."

Renee noticed the apprehension in his voice. "Kelz, what is it? You look like you're unsure."

"My wife's father is in the military—a high-ranking officer. Maybe he can help us."

"Sounds good, but you don't seem thrilled about it. What's the catch?"

Kelsey leaned forward. "It's complicated. The Colonel—what we call him—never approved of me. He didn't want Laura to marry a cop. He said it was too dangerous. He favored her marrying a military man, go figure. And now, with everything that's happening... I'm afraid he'll be proven right if something goes wrong. Laura will be in danger because of me, and I'll be the one to blame."

"Oh, Kelz..."

"But here's the thing," Kelsey continued, "I also know that the only way I can protect my family and still do my job is to get any information we can, especially on Simmons. We need to know if he's a man we can trust."

He looked up at Renee, determination mixed with fear in his eyes. "If Simmons is dirty or involved in this mess somehow, my family could be in even more danger. I need to know, Renee. I must know who I can rely on to have my back, our backs."

Renee nodded. "So, you're willing to risk proving your father-in-law right to keep your family safe? I certainly can't find fault with that."

"Remember that suspicious vehicle I spotted outside my house?"

Renee nodded,

"Well, it got me thinking. Whether we like it or not, our families might already be at risk. That's why I asked Laura to stay with her sister for a while."

Kelsey took a deep breath. "It's about Laura, the kids, and everyone I care about, including you, that could be affected if we don't get to the bottom of this.

"If involving the Colonel can help us figure out whether Simmons is trustworthy, then it's a risk I have to take. Even if it means swallowing my pride and facing my father-in-law's judgment."

Renee reached out and squeezed Kelsey's shoulder. "So, how do you want to approach this?"

"I'll call Laura first. She's at her sister's now, which makes this conversation a bit easier. She might be able to smooth things over with her father before I talk to him. It's a long shot, but it's the best chance we've got."

As Kelsey reached for his phone, he knew he was about to cross a line, blurring the boundaries between professional and personal in a way that could have far-reaching consequences. But with the safety of everyone concerned and their investigation hanging in the balance, they knew they had no choice. They knew they had to tell if Simmons could be trusted.

Kelsey's fingers hovered over his phone for a moment before he finally dialed Laura's number. As he waited for her to pick up, he silently hoped that this decision wouldn't come back to haunt him—that he wouldn't be proving his father-in-law right after all. Each ring seemed to last an eternity, his heart pounding. Finally, he heard Laura's voice.

"Kelsey? Is everything okay? It's late."

He could hear the concern in her voice, making what he had to say even harder. "Hey, honey," Kelsey said, trying to keep his voice steady. "I need your help."

"You need my help?" Laura asked.

"Yes, I need to talk to you about something important."

There was a pause on the other end of the line. "What's going on, Kelsey? You're making me nervous."

Kelsey took a deep breath. "Laura, remember that case I've been working on? The one I couldn't tell you much about?" He glanced at Renee, who nodded.

"Well, it's bigger than we thought. And potentially more dangerous."

"Dangerous?" Laura's voice rose slightly. "Kelsey, what have you gotten yourself into?"

Kelsey grimaced. "I can't go into all the details, but I need your help. It's about Captain Simmons."

"Your captain? What about him?"

Kelsey closed his eyes, bracing himself for what he had to say next. "We need to know more about his background, especially his military service. And... I need to ask your dad for help."

The silence on the other end of the line was deafening. "You want to involve my father? Kelsey, you know how he feels about your job. About us."

"I know, I know," Kelsey said quickly. "Believe me, I wouldn't ask if it wasn't absolutely necessary." He heard Laura's sharp intake of breath.

"I knew something was wrong when you asked me to stay at my sister's. Are we already in danger?"

Kelsey hesitated, not wanting to frighten her more, but knowing he needed to be honest. "There's been... some suspicious activity. Nothing concrete, but I want you and the kids safe, just in case."

"Oh, God," Laura whispered.

"Listen," Kelsey continued, "I know your dad has never approved of me being a cop. He's probably going to see this as proof that he was right all along. But

Laura, I need his help to keep you safe, to keep our family safe. And to do my job."

There was a long pause, and Kelsey feared she might refuse. Then, Laura's voice returned, "Okay. I'll talk to Dad. But Kelsey, promise me you'll be careful. And when this is over, I want the whole story."

Relief washed over Kelsey. "I promise. Thank you, Laura. I love you."

"I love you too," Laura replied, her voice a little softer. "I'll call Dad first thing in the morning. It's too late to bother him now."

Kelsey nodded to Renee. "You're right. The first thing tomorrow is fine. Thanks again, honey."

As he hung up, Kelsey felt a mix of gratitude and guilt. He was dragging his family into this mess, potentially proving his father-in-law's worst fears correct. But he knew it was necessary. He just hoped that whatever information the Colonel could provide would be worth the risk.

Kelsey looked up at Renee, who had been waiting patiently. "Laura's going to talk to her father in the morning," he said. "Now we wait and hope he's willing to help."

Renee nodded, understanding the weight of what Kelsey had just done. "You're taking a big risk, Kelz. I hope it pays off."

"Yeah," Kelsey said, hoping the same thing, "me too. Because if it doesn't, I've just put my family in the crosshairs."

As they settled in to wait for the morning, both detectives felt the stakes of their investigation rising. They were no longer just risking their careers—now, Kelsey's family was on the line. Whatever they discovered about Simmons had better be worth the price they might have to pay.

* * *

The afternoon sun slanted through the blinds in Kelsey's office when his phone rang. An unfamiliar number flashed on the screen.

"Hello, Detective Griffith."

"Kelsey." The voice was crisp, no-nonsense—exactly what you'd expect from a Colonel. Straight to the point, no small talk.

Kelsey straightened instinctively. Old habits from when dealing with his father-in-law kicked in. "Colonel."

"Laura called me." There was a hint of disapproval in the Colonel's tone, but also something else. Maybe a bit of concern. "She said you needed information on Roy Simmons."

Kelsey waited. He knew better than to interrupt. The Colonel always worked at his own pace and followed his own rules.

"I'll see what I can find out," the Colonel said after a pause, already sounding like he was forming a plan. "I'll get you the information as soon as I have it."

A longer pause followed, then the Colonel's voice softened slightly. "Oh, and Kelsey…"

"Yes, sir?"

"Keep my family safe." It wasn't quite an order, but it wasn't a request either—a rare moment of vulnerability from a man who usually kept his emotions locked down.

Kelsey gripped the phone a bit tighter. "I will, sir." He put everything he had into those three words, wanting his father-in-law to hear his commitment.

The line went dead—classic Colonel style. No goodbye, no extra words, just the mission, the order, and then silence.

Kelsey lowered the phone slowly, staring at it. For the first time since marrying Laura, he felt like he and the Colonel might finally understand each other. Nothing brought people together quite like worrying about family.

* * *

The harsh, unforgiving landscape of Afghanistan's Korengal Valley, nicknamed "The Valley of Death" by U.S. troops, was where Captain Roy Simmons's legend was born. In 2009, then-Staff Sergeant Simmons led a small team of Army Rangers on a high-risk reconnaissance mission deep in Taliban territory.

What should have been a 48-hour operation turned into a nightmare when a large group of insurgents ambushed Simmons's team. Outgunned and outnumbered, Simmons made the gut-wrenching decision to split the team, drawing enemy fire to allow the wounded to escape. In the chaos of the firefight, Simmons was separated from his unit.

For weeks, the Army scoured the region but found no trace of Simmons. As days turned into weeks, hope dwindled. After two months, Simmons was officially declared 'Missing in Action' and presumed dead. The news hit his family and fellow soldiers like a thunderbolt, leaving a void that seemed impossible to fill.

But Simmons wasn't dead. Severely wounded and stranded in enemy territory, he had been taken in by a local Pashtun family, adherents to the ancient code of Pashtunwali that demands protection for guests.

Despite the risk to their lives, they nursed Simmons back to health in a hidden cave system.

As Simmons recovered, he learned the local dialect and customs. He discovered that his hosts were part of a network of villages resistant to Taliban control. Over the next year, Simmons became a ghost in the mountains, working with local fighters to disrupt Taliban operations. His intimate knowledge of U.S. military tactics and the locals' understanding of the terrain made their small resistance cell formidable.

Their actions were like pebbles creating ripples in a pond. Supply routes were mysteriously disrupted, Taliban commanders disappeared, and crucial intelligence found its way to U.S. forces through unnamed sources. The Taliban put a price on the head of the "American ghost," but Simmons remained elusive.

It wasn't until a joint U.S.-Afghan operation in the region that Simmons's true fate was discovered. As U.S. forces approached a suspected Taliban stronghold, they were stunned to be greeted by Simmons, now sporting a long beard and traditional Afghan clothing, leading a group of local fighters.

Simmons's return was nothing short of miraculous. His actions during his time "missing" earned him the Silver Star, the Bronze Star, and a Purple Heart. But more than the medals, the experience changed Simmons fundamentally. He returned to the U.S. with a nuanced view of the conflict and a deep respect for the Afghan people who had saved his life.

Captain Simmons was an enigma to the officers under his command—an authoritarian, no-nonsense leader with an unexpected wellspring of empathy. He demanded excellence but understood the gray areas of life and law enforcement. His time in Afghanistan had taught him that the world rarely offered simple solutions to complex problems.

In the end, the rugged mountains of Afghanistan had forged Roy Simmons into more than just a war hero or a police captain. They had shaped him into a unique leader who could navigate the complex, often morally ambiguous law enforcement landscape in a city as intricate and troubled as New Orleans.

* * *

"Okay," Renee said. "So, everything we can see about Simmons seems to say he's a stand-up guy. But to be sure, I have one more idea I'd like to try. It's a bit risky, but I think it's necessary. We need to test Simmons directly without him knowing."

"I'm listening," Kelsey said, sitting up straighter.

"Here's what I'm thinking..."

* * *

Renee's knuckles rapped against Simmons's office door. Cap, we've got a lead on Judge Taylor's death. We're supposed to meet the CI tonight under the Elysian Fields overpass at 11 o'clock."

Simmons looked up from the stack of paperwork that seemed to multiply on his desk like weeds. "Do you trust this guy?"

"He's been reliable so far," Kelsey said, "Claims he has information about corruption connected to Taylor's murder."

The captain's pen tapped once against the desk. "Okay, check it out. Let me know what you find."

"Will do, Cap," Kelsey said. "Maybe this is the lead we need."

"Hope so." Simmons was already reaching for another file. "Be careful out there."

* * *

Renee and Kelsey positioned themselves in the shadows of an abandoned warehouse at 10:00 PM. Far enough from the overpass to avoid detection, close enough to watch every approach through binoculars. The distant hum of late-night traffic echoed against the walls of the empty warehouse as they settled in to wait.

Hours crawled by. Occasional headlights swept across the overpass like searchlights, illuminating nothing but concrete and darkness.

At midnight, Renee lowered her binoculars with a sigh of relief. "Not a soul in sight. No surveillance, no one trying to identify our CI. I guess we have our answer," she said.

Kelsey scanned the area one final time, the silence speaking louder than any surveillance team could have. "If Simmons were dirty, he would've sent someone to identify who our informant was. Someone claims to have information about Taylor's murder, and he doesn't even ask for a name?"

Renee looked back at the empty overpass, its shadows holding nothing but their own doubts. "He's clean—between this and his military record. He's gotta be, at least let's hope so… Time to bring Simmons in. Fully."

"If we're wrong, we'll find out the hard way."

"Then let's hope our mystery caller was right about him."

CHAPTER 8

WHEN THE STORY BROKE, the early morning smell of beignets began to waft through Decatur Street. The rhythmic churn of newspaper presses gave way to an urgent buzz as editors scrambled to update the morning edition. By 6 AM, news vans from every local station had descended upon the courthouse, their satellite dishes facing toward the sky.

Renee Dubois stood in the precinct's break room, her eyes fixed on the small TV in the corner. The ticker at the bottom of the screen screamed in bold red letters: **"BREAKING NEWS: MISSING JUDGE FOUND DEAD IN BARATARIA."**

The anchorwoman appeared flawless, but it was her grave expression that stole the spotlight. "In a shocking development, sources close to the investigation have confirmed that a body discovered in a swampy area of Barataria last week has been positively identified as that of Judge Charles Taylor. Judge Taylor had been missing for several days, failing to appear for court..."

Kelsey appeared at Renee's side. "It was only a matter of time," he said, holding up his phone to show the news alerts. Times-Picayune, The Advocate, and even national outlets were picking it up.

The TV flickered to a live shot outside the courthouse, where a crowd of reporters fought for position. The courthouse steps, typically quiet and dignified, had become a chaotic scene of flashing cameras, with everyone poised to hurl their questions.

All that could be heard was the steady, snapping rhythm of cameras capturing every second. Reporters eagerly waited for information regarding Judge Taylor's death. Lieutenant Gabriel Smith stepped up to the makeshift podium, followed by several City Council members who didn't bother hiding their desire to be in full view of the cameras. "Good morning," he began, "as you know, the body of Judge Charles Taylor was found in Barataria."

The crowd of reporters moved ever closer as they waited for Lieutenant Smith to finish his opening statements.

"The New Orleans Police Department can confirm that the body of Charles Taylor was found in a swampy area in Barataria.

"Let me be clear—this is still an ongoing investigation, and we don't have all the facts just yet," Smith continued. "Our department is fully committed to this investigation, and I know people are concerned, especially given the high profile of the case. But we're doing everything we can to ensure we handle this correctly."

He glanced at the group of reporters; he could tell they were waiting for a slip or some hint of a scandal. "We're working around the clock to get answers, and as soon as we know more, we'll share what we can. It is essential that we do not compromise or jeopardize our investigation."

As soon as he finished, the reporters burst into a flurry of questions, talking over each other and not showing any courtesy to their fellow reporters.

"Lieutenant, was Judge Taylor murdered?"

"Do you have any suspects yet?"

"Could this be tied to any of Judge Taylor's cases?"

Smith held up his hands, trying to gain some control. "I understand you all have many questions. At this time, we cannot provide any further details. We ask for your patience and cooperation as we continue our investigation. Thank you."

He stepped away from the podium, ignoring the continuing barrage of questions.

* * *

Antoine Domingo stood at the floor-to-ceiling windows of his penthouse apartment, overlooking the French Quarter as the late afternoon sun cast its glow on historic buildings. The morning news reports about Judge Taylor's body being identified played on three different screens behind him. In his hand, he swirled an expensive bourbon in a crystal tumbler.

The apartment was minimalist and modern, deliberately different from his father's antique-filled mansion. On his desk sat a framed photograph, the only personal item visible in the otherwise austere space. It showed a much younger Antoine standing beside Jean-Paul, both in hunting gear, Antoine proudly displaying a duck while his father's hand rested on his shoulder. The glass over the photo was cracked—had been for years—but Antoine had never replaced it.

His phone buzzed. Another message from his father, requesting his presence at the estate to discuss the "recent developments." Antoine ignored it, just as he'd ignored the previous two.

"You'll need to answer him eventually," said the woman lounging on his leather sofa—Lucia Vasquez—his confidante, occasional lover, and the organization's medical specialist.

"He can wait," Antoine replied, downing the bourbon in one swallow. "He's made me wait my entire life."

Lucia glanced at the news footage showing police at the courthouse. "The judge is becoming a problem even in death."

"A problem I handled," Antoine said, "Father would still be negotiating, trying to buy him off. Some people can't be bought."

"Your father built an empire from nothing," Lucia said, rising to pour herself a drink. "That deserves respect."

Antoine laughed bitterly. "An empire he won't let me run. Twenty years I've worked for him, and he still treats me like I'm eighteen and reckless."

"Aren't you?" she challenged with a slight smile.

Antoine moved to a sleek cabinet and retrieved a small vial. The white powder inside was nearly pure fentanyl—the same product used on Taylor. He studied it, rolling it between his fingers.

"You know what the difference is between my father and me?" He didn't wait for Lucia to answer. "He still pretends. All the charitable donations, the respectable businessman's act, the careful political connections. He needs people to think he's legitimate."

"And you don't?"

"I see what we are," Antoine said, his voice hardening. "We're businessmen. We sell what people want, and we eliminate threats. No pretense necessary."

He returned to the window, watching darkness settle over the city. "My father built his empire playing by old rules. But he doesn't see how the game has changed."

"Is that why you went after Judge Taylor without consulting him?"

Antoine's jaw tightened. "Taylor was collecting evidence and investigating the organization. My father would have dragged his feet, tried to negotiate, and trusted the wrong people. I saw the danger and took care of it."

"And if Jean-Paul discovers what you did?"

Antoine's reflection in the window showed a cold smile. "By the time he fully understands, I'll have secured the organization's future. My way."

He turned to face Lucia. "The judge was just the first step. Once I handle these detectives investigating his death, Father will see my approach works better than his caution."

Lucia studied him for a long moment. "You've never forgiven him, have you?"

"For what?"

"For loving the organization more than he loved you."

Antoine's hand tightened around his empty glass. The truth of her words hung in the air between them, unacknowledged but undeniable. The cracked photograph on his desk seemed to watch him accusingly.

"These detectives," he said finally, ignoring her question. "They'll lead us to the evidence Taylor gathered. Then they'll meet the same fate."

Lucia set down her glass. "You're playing a dangerous game, Antoine."

"It's the only game that matters." He refilled his bourbon, eyes drawn back to the news footage of the courthouse. "My father built his empire on whispers and handshakes. I'm building mine on fear and absolute control."

His phone buzzed again. Jean-Paul, for the fourth time.

"You should answer," Lucia said softly. "He's not a man who likes to be ignored."

"Neither am I," Antoine replied, but picked up the phone nonetheless. It was time to play the dutiful son again—at least until his plans fully matured.

* * *

Back at the precinct, Renee and Kelsey watched the monitors, where reporters lingered outside headquarters like they were waiting for the start of a Mardi Gras parade. Just then, Captain Simmons appeared in the doorway. His somewhat weathered face took on a more hardened look. His shirt sleeves were rolled, revealing forearms marked with faint scars—badges of survival that told stories he rarely shared.

"Hey, you two," he said. In that moment brought on by the newscast, something changed in him. The battle-hardened commander replaced the easy-going captain who shuffled papers and drank coffee in his office daily. His shoulders straightened, and his eyes took on a look they hadn't seen before. Renee and Kelsey's careful vetting of Simmons hadn't been wasted. He seemed to be transforming from their superior officer to something more: a battle-tested ally who would stand with them in the trenches. As he moved, they could feel the weight of command settling around him like an old, familiar coat. At that moment, they knew their instincts about trusting him had been right.

"I need to see you in my office. Now." His jaw tightened slightly as if something was brewing. He glanced quickly down the hallway, checking for any unwanted ears.

His tone left little room for questions—the kind of voice that had once commanded troops through the mountains of Korengal Valley. The set of his shoulders and the slight forward lean of his posture made it clear that whatever he had to say wasn't going to wait. This wasn't a routine briefing or a casual check-in. This was something that needed to be discussed behind closed doors, away from walls that might have ears and where loyalties could shift like the Mississippi's currents.

They followed him through the bustling precinct, where phones rang incessantly with calls about the breaking news. Inside his office, Simmons closed the blinds and locked the door.

"This is about to become a three-ring circus," he said, settling into his chair. "And I need to know everything you two have. No holding back."

Renee and Kelsey exchanged glances. After their careful vetting of Simmons, this was the moment of truth.

"Cap," Renee began, "what we're about to tell you... it goes deeper than just Taylor's murder. According to his sister, the judge had been investigating corruption at every level of city government."

"How high up?" Simmons asked.

"We don't know, it could be anyone. City council, judges, maybe even higher," Kelsey replied. "And there's more. The anonymous caller who knew about Taylor? He specifically told us to trust only you."

Simmons was taken aback by that statement. "Me? Why?"

"That's what we've been trying to figure out," Renee said, watching Simmons carefully. "We did some digging into your background, Cap. Your military service, your time in Afghanistan..."

"You investigated me?" Simmons leaned back in his chair, a hint of a smile playing at the corners of his mouth. The words carried no anger, only a touch of approval. After all, he'd known about their investigation—it was exactly what he would have done in their position.

He took a moment to study them both before speaking. "Most cops would've been hesitant to question their captain, worried it would hurt their careers." Now there was a hint of pride in his voice. "But you two... You didn't let rank get in the way of doing what needed to be done—I admire that."

"Had to be sure," Kelsey said, not backing down. "In this case, we have to be careful who we trust."

"Even with your own captain," Simmons nodded, a hint of respect shining through in his voice. "That's exactly what Charles would've done. He saw so much more. He never took anyone's word at face value either." He drummed his fingers on his desk, a familiar gesture whenever his curiosity sparked. "So, what did you discover in my background that made you feel you could trust me?"

The two detectives looked at each other, waiting to see who would answer first. After what felt like an eternity, Renee spoke up. "A man who spent a year fighting alongside local villagers in Afghanistan after being presumed dead... who chose to protect those people instead of just trying to get home... that's someone who understands loyalty isn't about following orders. It's about doing what's right, no matter the cost."

Simmons seemed to be at a loss for words, memories of those mountain valleys playing behind his eyes. "Sometimes," he said finally, "the only way to fight corruption is to risk everything. Charles understood that, and I'm glad to see that in you two." Simmons nodded. "Smart. Damn smart, that's what I would have done." He stood and walked to his window, peering through a gap in the blinds at the city beyond. "Taylor and I... we served together."

"In the military?" Renee asked.

No, not in the military, here, in New Orleans. He was a beat cop when I first joined the force."

"You knew him?" Renee asked.

"Knew him? Hell, he was my first ride-along. That was before he went to law school and then became a judge. Taylor was one of the good ones. He saw the corruption eating away at this city and decided to fight it from the inside."

"Why didn't you tell us this before?" Kelsey asked.

"You vetted me," Simmons replied, "I figured one good turn deserves another."

It finally dawned on Renee. "That's why you assigned us to homicide–to see how we'd react."

"It was," Simmons acknowledged.

Renee's mind raced, pieces falling into place. "Did you know it was Judge Taylor in the swamp from the beginning?"

Simmons shook his head. "I wasn't sure, but I had my suspicions. Taylor had been investigating a drug ring in the city. His wife called me Sunday night, frantic because he hadn't come home all weekend and wasn't answering his phone." His words stalled, and a shadow crept into his expression. "Then I heard about a body in the swamp wearing a Loyola Law School ring. Charles always wore his. I figured right then this was more than just routine."

"So, you teamed us up with homicide to see if we could be trusted," Kelsey said, the puzzle pieces finally clicking into place.

"The case needed the right detectives," Simmons replied. "People who wouldn't back down, wouldn't be bought off, and wouldn't miss the deeper implications."

"When did you figure out we could be trusted?" Renee asked.

Simmons shook his head and gave a slight smile. "Actually, pretty much right away. I wanted to see your reaction when I put you on homicide. If you'd leaped at the chance, I would've figured you saw it as a way to conceal the case details." He leaned back in his chair, his eyes shifting between the two detectives. "But when you pushed back against it, that's when I started thinking you were okay."

He continued. "That's when I knew for sure. You weren't taking anything at face value—not even your captain. That's exactly the kind of detectives I need." Simmons paused, letting his remarks sink in. "Taylor contacted me a month ago. He said he had evidence that could bring down half the fentanyl trade in New Orleans. I don't know exactly what he had, but it must have been some type of document, picture, or something worth killing a judge for."

"What can you tell us about Judge Taylor himself?" Renee asked. "His ways, his thought patterns, where he might have gone with the information he had. Understanding the man better could give us leads on his contacts and movements. At this point, anything could help."

Simmons walked over to the coffee maker in his office and poured himself a cup. "Charles... he was methodical, always had been. Even back when we were patrol officers, he'd keep these little notebooks. Wrote down everything—names, dates, patterns he noticed. Used to drive me crazy sometimes, but those notes of his solved more cases than I can count."

"I don't get it," Kelsey interrupted, shaking his head. "Why would a judge go through all this trouble? Aren't they supposed to just sit on the bench and hear cases?"

A faint grin tugged at Simmons's mouth. "That's what most people would think. But not Charles; ever since his days in the NOPD, he couldn't let go of investigations. When he went into law and finally became a judge, it became something like a hobby— but I think it was more than that." He paused, taking another sip of coffee. "I think he'd lost faith that anyone else in law enforcement really wanted justice. So, in his spare time, he'd dig. Man burned the candle at both ends but was careful about it. Had to be—if anyone caught wind of what he was doing, it could've jeopardized cases he was sitting on."

"Did he ever handle cases he investigated?" Renee asked.

"No, never," Simmons replied firmly. "He was too smart for that. But what he did do was study patterns. If a similar case came before him, he had this deeper understanding. Could see connections others might miss."

He settled back against his desk, coffee cup warming his hands. "One thing about Charles—he never trusted electronics for the important stuff. Said computers could be hacked, phones tapped, but good old-fashioned paper was reliable. It wouldn't surprise me if whatever evidence he had is written down somewhere. And knowing Charles, he'd have used a personal code—initials instead of full names, references only he would understand. His way of keeping secrets even on paper."

"Any idea where he might've kept something like that?" Kelsey asked.

"That's the thing about Charles—he was smart about it. He never kept anything sensitive at home, or anywhere people would think to look; he was paranoid that way. He had a fascination with historical places. Used to say New Orleans was full of perfect hiding spots. Places people walk past every day without a second glance."

Simmons leaned back, like always when memories started flooding back. "You know, Charles wasn't always the strait-laced judge everyone saw in court. Back when we were beat cops, he had this way of making even the worst shifts bearable. Used to bring these awful gas station sandwiches and tell the worst jokes."

He shook his head, smiling slightly. "But man, when it came to the job, he was like a dog with a bone. Never let go once he caught wind of something fishy. Remember that time we were working on a routine burglary case? Everyone else wrote it off as just another break-in, but Charles... he kept digging. It turned out it was connected to this huge insurance fraud scheme. That was Charles—always looking deeper."

Renee, with a puzzled look on her face, said, "So, why do you think he wanted to become a judge?"

"I think it was around '95 or '96. Some well-connected kid got busted with enough cocaine to lock him up for years. But then, like magic, the charges disappeared, evidence vanished, and it was as if the whole thing never even happened."

Pacing around the room, Simmons stopped at the window, peering out over the city. "Charles was livid. Said the system was a game for those who could pay. That's when he started talking about law school—he thought maybe he could do something from the inside. First, he considered DA, but why he aimed for judge instead, I never figured out."

"Bet that didn't win him many friends," Kelsey said.

"Hell no, it didn't," Simmons laughed, but there wasn't much humor in it. "Charles made enemies like some people collect baseball cards. In every case, when he threw the book at some rich kid or politician's friend, he'd get another target on his back. But he didn't care. He used to say, 'Roy, the day everybody likes you is the day you've stopped doing your job.'"

"What about his family?" Renee asked. "Must've been hard on them."

"Yeah..." Simmons' voice softened. "His wife, Sarah, stuck by him through everything. Even when they started getting threats, even when they had to move twice because someone kept vandalizing their house, they lived with security systems and looked over their shoulders. But Charles... he wouldn't back down. He kept saying he needed to stand up for what's right."

He ran a hand through his hair, looking suddenly tired. "You know what kills me? Just last month, he told me he was thinking about retiring. He said he wanted to spend more time with Sarah and maybe do some teaching. But he had this one last thing he needed to finish first."

Kelsey caught Renee's eye. "The drug ring investigation?"

"Yeah," Simmons nodded slowly. "He said it was bigger than anything we'd seen before. That it went all the way to the top. I told him to be careful, but..." He trailed off, then slammed his hand on the desk. "Damn it, I should've known they wouldn't let him get that close. Should've put protection on him or something."

"Cap, you couldn't have known," Renee said quietly.

"Maybe not," Simmons sighed. "Charles knew the risks. He used to say there are two types of corruption in this city—the kind everybody sees and pretends not to notice, and the kind that kills you if you notice it at all. Guess we know which one he stumbled into."

The office fell quiet, only the distant sound of phones ringing in the bullpen breaking the silence.

Each of them sat with their thoughts, wondering what Judge Taylor had discovered that was worth dying for.

"Where's this evidence now?" Renee asked.

"I don't know," Simmons replied. "Taylor was supposed to hand it over to me the weekend he disappeared. He never showed."

The office fell silent as the implications sank in. "Somewhere in New Orleans, I'm sure," Simmons said. "That cache held secrets that powerful people would kill to keep hidden."

"So now what?" Kelsey asked. "If what you're saying is true, we're not just looking for a murderer. We're looking for whatever Taylor discovered."

Simmons nodded grimly. "That's why they're watching you. They know you're working the case. They're probably hoping you'll lead them to whatever Taylor had."

"The black sedan," Kelsey said, "the one following us, parked outside my house..."

"I don't believe they're trying to scare you off," Simmons said. "I believe they're waiting to see if you'll lead them to what they want."

"If I was trying to do that," Renee said, "I certainly wouldn't let anybody see me."

"They're probably trying to scare you into speeding up the investigation. They wanted you to see them. They know they're racing against time."

"Okay, so how can we use that to our advantage?"

"It's risky," Simmons warned. "These people—they've killed a judge. They won't hesitate to kill two detectives."

"We don't have a choice," Kelsey said. "If we don't find that evidence, Taylor died for nothing."

Simmons studied them both for a long moment. "Alright. But from now on, we play this smart. No paper trails, no electronic communications. Everything stays between us three."

"We were already on board with the first two."

"Thinking ahead, I like that," replied Simmons.

"What about the anonymous caller?" Renee asked.

"That puzzles me," Simmons said, "Either he's in on it, or he's on our side working this from another angle. I guess we'll find out eventually, so do your due diligence with this guy, and be careful what you say to him.

"If he makes contact again," he said, wiping sweat from his forehead, "push for a meeting. These types down here like to watch first. See if we're Uptown stupid or French Quarter smart." His watch caught the glow of the dying sun through the window blinds—the kind of sunset that turned the Mississippi into liquid gold and made the dim-lit alleyways darker.

"Taylor had something on somebody. Something that files and recordings may lead us to. Something worth turning a judge into gator bait." He looked up, his eyes were strained with the weight of too many similar cases. "Whatever it was, I want it found."

A streetcar bell rang out as it traveled down St. Charles Avenue. Simmons pushed his chair back from his desk, creating a deeper dent in the already worn wooden floor. "Get out of here, you two. Go home. We'll address this with clearer eyes in the morning."

As they prepared to turn the day over to the night shift, they knew their colleagues would arrive wondering what the night might bring—drunken brawls, maybe a shooting or two, all the usual chaos that kept them running. None of it would compare with a darker truth: that somewhere between the mansions and the bayou, a judge's killer was sleeping soundly, untouched by the city's nightly madness.

CHAPTER 9

ROOSTERS SEEMED TO CROW early for the NOPD, and Simmons's face looked pale in the white fluorescent light of his office. "Come in, you two." A phrase that was becoming all too familiar. "The ME's report showed he was poisoned with street fentanyl in wine? Like some kind of twisted cocktail?"

"That's what came down from forensic," Renee said, looking over at Cap's old worn coffee pot, wondering why it wasn't percolating.

Simmons rubbed his temples. "You two going back to the courthouse?"

"That's the plan," Kelsey said. "We need to know what Taylor did that Friday night—who he trusted, where he went. Any info we can muster up."

* * *

"Something's not right," Renee said, stepping into the hallway. "No coffee. First time in ten years that ancient percolator hasn't been burning yesterday's grounds in there."

Kelsey caught her look. "That's your way of saying you need a fix?"

"What do you think? It's too early to go to the courthouse?"

"Alright. Beignets and that 'olé' stuff," Kelsey drawled, already heading for the stairs.

"*Au Lait*. Café au lait, not olé." Renee shook her head. "How many years have you been in New Orleans, and you're still butchering French like a tourist from New York?"

Kelsey looked at Renee as if to say, 'KIDDING.' "Born in Memphis, raised in Birmingham. What did you expect?" Already pulling his keys out, knowing they'd end up at Café Du Monde like always. Some habits in the Big Easy had their own kind of ritual.

* * *

The sun hadn't yet burned through the morning haze as Renee and Kelsey sat at Café Du Monde, watching the Quarter come alive. Suddenly, the whimsical notes of a calliope drifted across from the river, its steam-powered melody floating over the rooftops.

Kelsey tilted his head. "Listen," he said, "Natchez must be heading downriver. Sounds like an old Fats Domino tune today.

"Sometimes I just don't appreciate this place like I should," looking at the city's uniqueness. "The balconies overlook the nostalgia of the city and the smiling faces of the people passing by. The way the vines creep up those old brick walls. Each one's got two centuries of stories built right into the mortar."

"Every morning, same time," Renee said, watching a gallery owner unlock her doors, revealing glimpses of oil paintings—jazz musicians bent over their instruments, quiet courtyards shaded by banana trees, and the cracked stone paths of old cemeteries.

"The city wakes up like this—art, music, history, all mixed together."

Through the iron fence of Jackson Square, they could see artists arranging their work—watercolors of streetcars gliding past Garden District mansions, charcoal sketches of street performers, vibrant acrylics of second-line parades. A trumpeter had taken up his spot near the corner, his mournful notes weaving between the calliope's cheerful tones.

"You see those tourists?" Kelsey nodded toward a group clutching maps and cameras. "They come for the parties and tours but miss the real magic. Like that lady up there-" he pointed to a second-floor balcony where an elderly woman in a faded house dress was carefully tending to her morning glories. "Been here longer than both of us combined. Probably knows more secrets than all our case files put together."

"That's what makes this place different," Renee agreed, watching the morning light shine on old Andy Jackson sitting atop his trusty horse in the middle of Jackson Square. "It's not just a tourist attraction. It's still a neighborhood. Still has its own heartbeat."

The calliope's song changed to "New Orleans Ladies" as they sat in comfortable silence, letting the city's morning rhythms wash over them. Somewhere in this beautiful, troubled place, a killer walked free. But for now, they could take a moment to remember why they fought so hard to protect it.

"You know what gets me?" Renee said, pushing her empty coffee cup aside. "How this neighborhood refuses to die. In other cities, their historic districts become museum pieces. Here? People still live above these shops. Grab groceries at the corner store and argue with their neighbors over food prices."

From somewhere down the street came the distant clang of a streetcar, its brass bell cutting through the mix of voices, music, and cooking smells that made up the Quarter's morning symphony.

"Hard to believe," Kelsey said quietly, "all this history, and underneath..." He let the thought trail off, both of them knowing what lay beneath the postcard-perfect surface they were sworn to protect.

Renee stood, brushing the inevitable powdered sugar from her clothes. "That's exactly why we do what we do, Kelz. Some things in this city are worth fighting for."

They left their table, stepping back into the flow of Decatur Street, where the past and present seemed to meet, and even the darkest mysteries couldn't completely shadow the magic that drew people here from around the world.

* * *

The courthouse was quieter now. Margaret Landry was at her desk as always. From appearances, you would think Judge Taylor was in chambers, and business was as usual. She looked up as they approached, her eyes tired but alert.

"Detectives," she said softly.

Renee pulled up a chair. "Ms. Landry, we need to know everything about Judge Taylor from last Friday. Anything you can remember? No matter how small it might seem. How did it start, who he trusted, where he might have gone."

"Well, his day was always the same. Always came to the courthouse in his jogging clothes, took a shower, and then reviewed his cases for the day."

"So, he jogged every morning?" Kelsey asked.

"More like a fast walk. But yes, every day."

Margaret's hands trembled slightly as she opened her desk drawer. "I... I've been thinking about that night, though. I remembered something." She pulled out a small leather-bound notebook. "The judge kept his personal appointments in here. He..." She swallowed hard as if she was having trouble completing it. "He left it on my desk that Friday afternoon. Said he might need me to reference it later."

Kelsey leaned forward. "What kind of appointments?"

"Mostly dinners, social events. The judge had certain places he liked, certain people he met regularly." She opened the notebook carefully. "That Friday... he had dinner plans at Le Bayou Jardin. Eight o'clock reservation."

"Who was he meeting?" Renee asked.

"He didn't say. Just wrote 'dinner—important' in his usual handwriting. But..." Margaret hesitated. "He was nervous. I could tell. Kept checking his phone all afternoon."

"Did he tell anyone else about these plans?"

"I don't know. He was being very careful that day. But there's something else." She flipped through the notebook. "He had a name in the back—then there was this lone word written by it, 'TRUST.'

That's all it said, 'TRUST.' James Callahan from the DA's office were on it."

"This James Callahan," Kelsey said carefully. "Did the judge meet with him often?"

"Sometimes, usually at Vivien's Corner for lunch." Margaret's voice dropped. "The last time they met was about a week ago. The judge came back upset. Started pulling case files right after."

"Ms. Landry," Renee leaned forward, "did the judge ever mention being worried about someone close to him? Someone he thought might have betrayed his trust?"

Margaret's hands stilled on the notebook. "The week before he died, he said something strange. We were closing up for the day, and he looked... tired. He said something like, 'The people closest to the light cast the longest shadows.'" She looked up. Her eyes seemed a little wet. "I didn't quite understand what he meant."

"The dinner reservation," Kelsey cut in. "Would he have driven himself?"

"No. In fact, that Friday night, he had Boggles drop him off at Le Bayou Jardin."

"And who is Boggles?" Renee asked.

"Oh, he's the janitor. Everybody here calls him *Boggles*. I don't know why. I asked him one time, and he said it was a nickname his father gave him."

"Do you have Boggles' phone number?

"Yes, everybody has Boggle's phone number. He's the janitor; we need him from time to time, you know, to take out the trash and stuff. Here, I'll write it down for you."

"Thank you," Renee said. "We'll also need that notebook, Ms. Landry."

"Of course." Margaret handed it over, then added, "Detectives? The judge... he was a good man. But in the last few weeks, he seemed different, as if he was carrying something heavy on his mind. Seemed like... whatever it was, it was making him uncomfortable."

As they walked back to their car, Kelsey flipped through the notebook. "Le Bayou Jardin. Fancy place. Real fancy."

"Yeah," Renee said, starting the engine. "The kind of place where you might serve expensive wine to a judge you're about to murder."

"Whoever killed Taylor was at that dinner." Renee pulled out into traffic. "And they were probably on his list of trusted people."

"Which means," Kelsey said grimly, "we're not just looking for a killer. We're looking for a traitor."

The New Orleans night leaned heavily against the car windows. Somewhere out there, someone had sat across from Judge Taylor—watched him lift a glass of poisoned wine, maybe even toasted him—then smiled as he drank to his death.

"You know what bothers me most?" Renee said, "Taylor knew something was wrong. He left breadcrumbs, the notebook, the names, the files. He just didn't know which of his friends was really his enemy."

"Well," Kelsey replied, "that's what we're going to find out."

CHAPTER 10

BOGGLES LIVED IN A SMALL shotgun house in the lower nine, its weathered blue paint peeling in the afternoon heat. Wind chimes made from old brass keys tinkled softly on the front porch, where an ancient rocking chair swayed gently in the breeze.

"You sure this is it?" Kelsey asked, double-checking the address Margaret had given them.

"That's what his personnel file says," Renee replied, climbing the creaking steps.

Before they could knock, a deep voice called from inside. "Doors open. Come on in, detectives."

They found Boggles in his kitchen, a big man with gentle hands brewing coffee in an old-fashioned percolator. His courthouse janitor's uniform was draped neatly over a chair.

"Been expectin' you," he said, not turning around. "Figgered you'd show up once you talked to Miss Margaret." He pulled three cups from a cabinet. "Real shame what happened to Judge Taylor. He was a good man, and I called him a friend."

"Did you know the judge well?" Renee asked, accepting a cup of coffee that smelled far better than anything their Cap. ever brewed.

"Fifteen years cleanin' them halls, you get to know everybody. But Judge Taylor?" Boggles shook his head slowly. "He was diff'rent, though. Treated me like I was somebody, not jus' the man with the mop. Would stay late sometimes, talkin' 'bout the city, 'bout justice. 'Bout things that weren't right."

"And that Friday before…?" Kelsey prompted. "Margaret said you gave him a ride."

Boggles settled his large frame into a kitchen chair that creaked under his weight. "Yeah, I'd sure did. Axed me to drop him off at some fancy eatin' place. Said he was meetin' somebody for dinner."

"Did he usually ask you to give him a ride?" Kelsey asked.

"Naw, that was the first time ever. He tol' me he went down to the garage for his car and seen he had him a flat tire. Didn't wanna be late, said he'd catch hisself a ride home and get that tire fixed come mornin'."

Boggles went quiet for a moment, remembering. "He'd did say one thing, though. When he'd was gettin' out, he'd turned to me and said, 'Boggles, sometimes the best way to hide somethin' is to put it where everybodies could see it.' Dunno why he'd said it. He'd jus' said it."

Renee caught Kelsey's eye, and the meaning passed without a word. Taylor's words had that familiar coded quality—another breadcrumb deliberately left for someone to follow.

"That was the last time I'd seen him alive," Boggles said quietly. "Twenty years, I'd been cleanin' that man's chambers. Watched him workin' late into the night, tryna do right by folks. And somebody just..." He trailed off, his big hands clenchin' into fists.

"We're going to find who did this, Boggles," Renee assured him.

"Boggles paused, his voice catching slightly as he wiped his face with the back of his hand. "Judge Taylor was a good man. The kinda man makes you wanna be better yourself. Whatever happened to him—it jus' ain't right."

CHAPTER 11

LE BAYOU JARDIN looked different in the harsh light of day. The crystal chandeliers that had cast such a warm glow over Judge Taylor's last dinner now seemed cold and lifeless. Renee and Kelsey stood in the empty dining room with Marcel, the maître d', who'd been working that night.

"This was their table," Marcel said, gesturing to a corner spot partially hidden by a decorative palm. "Judge Taylor and his guest. Judge Taylor always requested this specific location whenever he ate here."

Renee studied the table's position. "Good vantage point. You can see the entrance, but it's tucked away enough for a private conversation."

"The security cameras," Kelsey said, looking up at the discreet black domes in the ceiling. "How many angles cover this area?"

Marcel pointed them out. "Two. One by the entrance, one over the bar."

"We'll need the footage," Renee said.

They huddled around a monitor in the restaurant's small office while Marcel queued up the footage. The time stamp showed 8:05 PM.

"There," Kelsey pointed as Taylor appeared on screen, being led to his table where another man was already waiting.

"Do you know who the other man is?" asked Renee.

"The judge has different people he meets with from time to time. I don't know who that man was."

They watched the silent drama unfold: a wine bottle sitting on the table, casual conversation, everything looking normal until they saw Marcel approach the table.

"That's when I told him about the phone call," Marcel said. "A man had called, very insistent. Said it was urgent court business."

On the security footage, Taylor stands and walks to the phone at the host podium, keeping his back to the entrance but facing toward his table. His dining companion then leaves the table, heading toward the restrooms.

The camera captured two men pausing near Taylor's table, standing together with drinks in their hands. While they stood there, a third person in a dark coat approached the table from the rear. After approximately four seconds, he moved away from the table. The two men who had been standing there then walked in separate directions.

Taylor returned to the table after the men had departed. His dining companion returned shortly after.

"Can you zoom in?" Renee asked.

Marcel adjusted the image, but the figure remained frustratingly unclear.

By 9:30, the footage showed Taylor becoming visibly unsteady. His companion called for the check.

The final images showed Taylor being guided out of the restaurant, barely able to walk.

"That's when I helped his dinner guest get the judge out to the front of the restaurant," the Maître d' told the detectives. "We waited together for the taxicab."

"Who called for the taxi?" Renee asked.

"His friend did, Crescent City cab," the Maître d' replied.

* * *

Outside Le Bayou Jardin, Renee pulled out her phone while Kelsey started the car.

"Crescent City Cab, dispatch," a woman's voice answered.

"This is Detective Dubois, NOPD. I need information about a pickup from Le Bayou Jardin on Friday night, around 9:45 PM."

"Hold, please." The sound of typing filtered through the line. "Got it. Pick up at 9:42 PM, Le Bayou Jardin. The driver was William Baptiste. The destination was 6464 Prytania St."

"Is he working today?"

"Lucky for you, he just started his shift. Want me to radio him?"

"Yes, please have him come to Le Bayou Jardin."

Forty minutes later, they sat across from the cab driver in a corner booth. Baptiste was a thin man with greying temples and eyes that had seen too much of the city's darker side.

"Mr. Baptiste. We're investigating the death of Judge Charles Taylor. Do you remember picking up a man outside of Le Bayou Jardin two Fridays ago?"

"Yeah, I remember that fare. Guy could barely walk. A man helped him into the cab, paid cash up front—more than the fare would've been."

"This friend," Renee said. "What can you tell us?"

"Not much, he gave me an address in the Garden District, I think. Mentioned something about the guy's daughter... Oh yeah, said she'd be waiting." Baptiste frowned. "When I pulled up, there was a couple already waiting outside on the front porch steps."

Kelsey leaned in a little closer and said, "What happened next?"

"They came right down to the cab, real concerned-like. The woman said something about him tying one on again, like this was a regular thing. They helped him out of the cab and got him up to the porch."

"Could you identify them?" Renee asked.

Baptiste shook his head. "It was dark, and they stayed mostly in the shadows. I just stood out of the way until they removed him from the cab."

"The house," Kelsey said. "Your dispatch said he was taken to 6464 Prytania St."

"That sounds about right." He took a sip of his coffee. "I saw the news about the judge. Never thought it had anything to do with my fare."

Renee looked over at Kelsey as if she were reading his mind. Another piece of the puzzle—the careful handoff, the waiting couple.

"Mr. Baptiste," Renee said carefully, "would you be willing to take us to that house and go through all the details on the premises?"

"Sure thing. I just need to inform dispatch."

* * *

Streetlights cast pools of yellow light along Prytania Street as they pulled up to 6464. Only the porch light was on, just as it had been that night. Baptiste leaned forward from the back seat.

"This is the place," he said. "Looks exactly the same as it did the other night." He squinted through the darkness at the lawn. "I don't remember that for sale sign being there."

"Walk us through what happened," Renee said.

Baptiste stepped out of the car, moving to the spot where he'd stopped his taxi. "Well, it was pretty simple, really. I pulled up right here. A man and woman came down the steps when I arrived."

"You said you didn't get a good look at them, right?" Kelsey asked.

Baptiste shook his head. "Not really. It was dark like this, and I was mostly focused on making sure the passenger got out of my cab okay. The man reached for his wallet and handed me some cash. I told him that it was already paid for, but he said this is for my trouble and gave me extra."

He gestured toward the porch. "They helped him up the steps, got him settled in one of those wicker chairs. Said they'd take it from there."

"Did anything seem unusual to you?" Renee asked.

"No, not really. Just looked like folks helping someone who'd had too much to drink. Happens all the time in this city, especially on weekends." Baptiste shrugged. "They said they had him, so I left."

"Did you notice any lights on in the house?" Kelsey asked.

"No, just the porch light. Didn't pay much attention to the house itself."

* * *

After dropping Baptiste back at his cab, Renee and Kelsey drove back to 6464 Prytania Street. The house loomed before them in the darkness, its empty windows like black holes in the brick facade.

"The cab driver noticed two things," Renee said, parking across the street. "The porch light was on that night, but he doesn't remember seeing that for-sale sign."

Renee pulled out her phone and dialed the realtor's number. It rang twice before a woman answered.

"Sharon Miller."

"Ms. Miller, this is Detective Dubois with NOPD. I'm calling about 6464 Prytania Street."

"Oh, that property! Is everything alright?"

"Yes, ma'am. Can you tell me how long it's been for sale?"

"That house hasn't been lived in for several months now."

"And the for-sale sign has been up for how long?"

"Same amount of time. Several months."

Renee caught Kelsey's eye as she ended the call. The house has been empty for months. No rentals, no occupants."

"So, our couple with their perfectly timed arrival, their careful show of helping the judge..." Kelsey let the thought hang. "They picked this house because they knew it would be empty."

Renee finished, "And the for-sale sign? They must have moved it and then put it back before leaving."

CHAPTER 12

RENEE WAS HALFWAY through her third report of the morning when Kelsey's familiar weight settled on the corner of her desk. "Just got a call from Jenkins," he said. "He's at some club in the warehouse district. EMTs are working multiple overdoses, some fatal. They're requesting patrol and narcotics on the scene." Renee straightened in her chair. "How many we talking about?"

"Four so far. Two DOA, two critical." Kelsey stood, already moving. "Whatever they took, hit hard and fast. EMTs say the reaction pattern isn't typical."

"Bad batch, maybe?" Renee grabbed her jacket from the back of her chair.

"Could be. Or something new on the street." He waited as she checked her weapon. "Clubs called 'The NOLA Night.'"

"Real imaginative." Renee rolled her eyes. "One of those converted warehouses?"

"Yeah, the newest hot spot in the district. Guess their opening night isn't going as planned."

Something nagged at Renee as they headed toward the warehouse district. The morning sun slanted through the windshield as she turned to Kelsey. "Why didn't we get this call directly? Narcotics should have been first on the dispatcher's list."

"Jenkins and I go way back," Kelsey said, navigating around a delivery truck. "Known him since I was walking a beat in the Quarter. I was a rookie then, and he taught me a lot. He knows I'm in narcotics, so he probably just called my cell to cut through the red tape."

Renee frowned, looking a little puzzled. "Let's check this scene out; then, we need to find out why this call bypassed us." She paused, a new thought occurring to her. "Come to think of it, we haven't been getting any calls lately."

When Kelsey pulled up to The Warehouse, emergency lights from patrol cars streaked across the weathered brick, none of the frantic activity that you would typically see at a scene with multiple overdose victims.

"Isn't that James Callahan? The ADA standing over there by the club entrance," Renee asked, nodding toward the man. Despite the early hour, he was dressed in a crisp charcoal suit, looking more like he was headed to court than a crime scene.

Renee and Kelsey shared a quick glance. A name from Taylor's 'TRUST' list had suddenly appeared at a scene they'd been called to through irregular channels—that was the kind of coincidence that made good detectives nervous.

"Since when does the DA's office respond to overdose calls?" Kelsey muttered as they got out of the car.

"Since never," Renee replied under her breath, already studying Callahan's body language as they approached. The ADA seemed unusually relaxed for someone at a scene with multiple fatalities.

Kelsey walked up to Jenkins, who stood slightly apart from the others. After their usual greeting of brief nods—a holdover from years of working together—Kelsey asked, "Why did you call me about this? What happened to dispatch?"

Jenkins shifted his weight, glancing briefly toward Callahan before answering. "It was the ADA that wanted me to call you." He lowered his voice, adding, "Said something about keeping this contained until we know what we're dealing with."

The explanation did nothing to settle the unease growing in Kelsey's gut. If anything, it added weight to his suspicions. He'd known Jenkins long enough to read between the lines—the older officer seemed to be confused by it, too.

Renee had made her way over to them, her sharp eyes taking in every detail of the scene. The usual organized chaos of a major incident was notably absent. No crime scene techs. No photographers. Even the EMTs seemed to be moving with an unusual lack of urgency.

"Jenkins," she said quietly, "where are the victims?"

"Two DOA inside, two transported critical about twenty minutes ago," Jenkins said quietly. "But here's the thing—EMTs said it was the fastest-acting overdose they'd ever seen. Victims went down almost simultaneously. Never seen anything like this—the way they're handling it. Callahan just waltzed in and took over, almost like…"

Jenkins fell silent as the ADA strode toward Kelsey and Renee.

"I want you two on this," Callahan murmured. "Your captain's already in the loop."

He walked to his car and got in. As he lowered the window, he said, "That's all I can say for now." Then he pulled away.

CHAPTER 13

"ANOTHER DAY, ANOTHER DOLLAR," Kelsey said. They sat at their usual table at the Café Du Monde, where the remains of their beignets were dusting the tabletop with powdered sugar. It was their morning ritual, a moment of normalcy in the chaos of their investigation.

As Renee sipped her coffee, she spotted a familiar face approaching. "Heads up," she murmured to Kelsey. "Callahan at two o'clock."

The Assistant District Attorney, James Callahan, wasn't the kind of man you could miss in a crowded café. His expensive suit starkly contrasted with the casual attire of the tourists around him. Heads turned as he passed, a mixture of recognition and wariness in their eyes.

Callahan was a man who collected whispers. His reputation preceded him; some said he was the last honest prosecutor in a city drowning in corruption. Others painted him as a shark in lawyer's clothing, circling the murky waters of New Orleans politics and taking bites out of anyone who got in his way.

One thing was sure: in the ten years since he'd joined the DA's office, Callahan had amassed a conviction rate that made career criminals lose sleep. He had a reputation for relentlessly pursuing cases where he detected wrongdoing, refusing to back down until justice was served, no matter who was involved. Even when he faced setbacks, he was known for his persistence, treating temporary defeats merely as delays on the inevitable path to victory. He had a knack for being in the right place at the right time and an uncanny ability to know which way the political winds were blowing before anyone else felt the breeze.

They'd tangled with the ADA before, sometimes as allies, sometimes as adversaries. It was never clear which version of Callahan you'd get on any given day, adding an element of uncertainty to their interactions.

"Well, if it isn't New Orleans' finest," Callahan said, his voice carrying just a hint of a southern drawl. Without waiting for an invitation, he pulled out a chair and sat down, his presence immediately filling their small corner of the café.

Renee watched as Callahan's sharp green eyes flicked between her and Kelsey, missing nothing. There was a reason this man had never lost a high-profile case. He had a way of looking at you that made you feel like he was reading every secret you'd ever tried to hide.

Renee looked up, shielding her eyes from the sun. "No, you didn't," she said, a hint of amusement in her voice. "Don't tell me you came here with a dark suit."

Callahan glanced down at his impeccable charcoal suit, then, one eyebrow raised back at Renee. "What's wrong with my suit, Detective? Brooks Brothers' finest."

Renee gestured to the powdered sugar dusting their table like a delicate layer of freshly fallen snow. "One bite and you'll look like you've been caught in a snowstorm," she teased, her eyes sparkling with amusement.

A ghost of a smile played on Callahan's lips. "Are you suggesting I can't eat a simple pastry without making a mess, Detective?"

"I'm suggesting that even the great Jim Callahan is no match for Café Du Monde's powdered sugar," Renee retorted, A challenge made clear in her voice. "But by all means, prove me wrong."

Kelsey leaned back in his chair, his eyes never leaving Callahan's face. "Somehow, I doubt you came all the way down here to test your beignet-eating skills, Counselor. What's on your mind?" His tone was casual, but there was an underlying tension in the air, and a silence lingered a moment between them.

"Is it okay to join you?"

"Be our guest," Kelsey replied. "We were just discussing the Saints' chances this season."

As the waiter approached a nearby table, Callahan raised his hand to get his attention. "Café au lait," he said, turning to face Renee with a smug look. "Beignets too..." Oh, and extra of that powdery sugar, please." His smug expression softened into a smile that could win over the most ardent skeptics.

It was the kind of smile that had charmed hundreds of juries, the one that made witnesses want to tell him everything they knew. But Renee had interviewed enough sociopaths to know that charm was often their deadliest weapon. The same skills that made someone a brilliant prosecutor could just as easily serve more sinister purposes. She couldn't help but feel a shiver of unease despite the warmth of his smile.

She watched a fine dusting of powdered sugar drift away from the pristine sleeve of his tailored suit as he bit into the beignet, wondering how many of his perfectly crafted suits had escaped the infamous powdered sugar of Café Du Monde. The man who'd given cryptic orders at a crime scene was now playing the role of the genial host and doing it well enough that she might have bought the performance if she hadn't seen the steel beneath it just hours before.

They engaged in small talk for the next fifteen minutes, discussing everything from local politics to the Jazz Fest. It was just three individuals catching up over coffee to any casual observer.

Finally, Callahan, speaking barely above a whisper and almost from the corner of his mouth, began, "OK, guys, listen to what I have to say. Let's keep this conversation friendly. I want you to laugh and smile like this is anything but serious."

Kelsey chuckled, then said in a faint whisper, "So you were looking for us."

"Yes, and I knew exactly where to find you."

"I feel violated," Renee said, but she couldn't help holding back a smile herself.

"I can't talk now. We might be being watched. I will write the number of my burner on my napkin and leave it on the table. I suggest you get one and get me the number. They're not perfect, but they're safer to use."

Kelsey nodded, still smiling, as if they were discussing weekend plans. "That sounds great. We should do this more often."

"No one can know about this except us three and Simmons," Callahan stressed. "Do you agree?"

Renee raised her voice and talked a little louder, ensuring anyone nearby could hear. She leaned back, letting out a convincing laugh. "Absolutely. It's been too long since we've caught up like this."

They continued their facade of casual conversation for another ten minutes, discussing everyday chit-chat. All the while, Renee and Kelsey processed the bombshell Callahan had just dropped.

Callahan dabbed at his mouth with a napkin, still maintaining his casual demeanor. "One more thing," he said quietly, his voice barely above a whisper. "I need you to pull surveillance footage from the 2100 block of St. Charles Avenue for the morning of June 12th. Focus on the time of Taylor's walk."

Kelsey kept his expression neutral as if they were still discussing nothing more important than the weather. "Any particular time frame?"

"Six to eight AM," Callahan replied. "Taylor took his morning walks like clockwork. Always the same route, same time."

Renee leaned forward slightly, appearing to reach for the sugar. "St. Charles is a busy street. The city has cameras at most intersections. We could also check the businesses—there's that coffee shop on the corner, the bank across the street. Most of them keep their security footage for at least a month."

Callahan nodded slightly, a small gesture that spoke volumes. "Cast a wide net. The more angles, the better." With a smile, Callahan stood without a hint of powdered sugar on him. "Well," Callahan said with a bit more enthusiasm, "I should get back to the office. It's been such a pleasure catching up with you!"

As they watched him leave, Renee and Kelsey exchanged glances. Between the burner phone number hidden in the napkin and this request for surveillance footage, they had their work cut out for them. Whatever Callahan had seen—or suspected-on St. Charles Avenue that morning, he wasn't willing to say it out loud. Not there. Not now.

* * *

The day dragged on long into the night as they gathered all the footage they could of Taylor's final walk. In Simmons's office, the Venetian blinds were drawn tight, shutting out the world. The surveillance footage flickered in the dim light as Renee and Kelsey leaned in, studying the screen. The first camera angle showed only empty sidewalks and early morning traffic.

"Try the next one," Callahan said.

The second camera revealed more of the same—passing cars and a few early risers heading to work. They switched to a third angle, and there he was.

"Stop there," Callahan said. "7:26 AM."

The grainy footage showed Taylor on his morning walk and a jogger falling into step beside him.

"That's when it started," Callahan said quietly. "Taylor told me about this encounter the next day. Said he just left his house..."

As Callahan's words lingered in the air, the flickering footage continued to play, showing the judge and the jogger in what appeared to be intense conversation. In that grainy surveillance video, they were watching the beginning of events that would ultimately lead to Taylor's death.

PART TWO

CHAPTER 14

THE LIVE OAKS CAST THEIR familiar shadows across St. Charles Avenue. Judge Charles Taylor paused to let a streetcar pass, its wheels clicking against the rails. The morning air was thick with jasmine and magnolia.

A jogger in expensive Nike gear and a Tulane cap slowed beside him. "Mind if I walk a bit? Been pushing too hard, need to cool down."

"Of course," Taylor smiled, always happy for company. "Done the same thing myself. These old knees aren't what they used to be."

"Been watching you make this walk most mornings," the jogger said, breathing a bit heavy from his run. "Like clockwork. Name's Jeff."

"Charles Taylor, do you live in the neighborhood?"

"Just moved in. Garden District. Still adjusting to the humidity, but love these old homes, all this history."

"Best part of the city," Taylor said. "My wife and I used to dream about living here when we were first married. Ended up uptown instead."

"Nice area, too. Your children grow up there?"

"All three. Youngest just graduated Tulane Law."

Jeff smiled. "Must be proud."

"Very. However, I warned her about becoming a judge. Told her prosecutors have more fun."

Jeff laughed, then smoothly shifted the conversation. "Been following some of your recent decisions. Particularly interested in the upcoming Garza distribution cases."

"Ah," Taylor nodded, not yet sensing the danger. "Complex cases. Following them in the papers?"

"Let's say I represent parties with significant interests in the outcomes." Jeff kept his tone casual, friendly. "They've noticed your... strict interpretation of the law. They're hoping you might consider a more flexible approach."

"Flexible?"

"Certain cases need special handling. Technical issues with evidence and procedural questions. Nothing dramatic." Jeff's pace matched Taylor's perfectly. "Two million dollars. Cash. Same amount yearly."

Taylor felt the morning air grow cold. "You're trying to bribe a judge."

"Offering an opportunity. Others in your position understand. They see how things work here."

"I think our walk is done," Taylor said.

"Forty-eight hours, Judge." Jeff handed him a card. "Family man like you, smart man... I'm sure you'll make the right decision."

* * *

The forty-eight hours had passed. Taylor left the untouched business card in his desk drawer, his decision made by making no decision at all.

As he walked through the courthouse that evening, Taylor found Boggles finishing up his routine, humming softly while pushing his cleaning cart.

"Evening, Boggles. That sounds like 'Sweet Lorraine' you're humming."

Boggles smiled, surprised the judge knew the tune. "Sure is, Judge. My momma used to play dat one."

"Any chance of a ride to Le Bayou Jardin? The car has a flat, and I'm already late."

"Course, Judge. Lemme just put this cart away."

In Boggles' old Ford pickup, jazz played softly on the radio. Taylor noticed Boggles' fingers tapping the steering wheel in perfect time.

"You've got rhythm, Boggles. You play?"

"Piano and guitar, since I was knee-high to a crawfish." Boggles chuckled. "Momma taught piano at Xavier University. Daddy played guitar at Preservation Hall back in the day."

"But you didn't follow that path?"

"Oh, I wanted to," Boggles said, turning down Royal Street as the evening crowds parted before them. "Had a band when I was younger. Called ourselves 'Deep Fryed,' spelt with a Y. Since us New Orleans folk like's our food that way. We weren't half bad; played some of the smaller clubs on Frenchmen Street."

"What happened?"

"Life, I guess. Momma and Pops supported my dream, but they knowed how hard it was to make a livin' in music. Pops would say, 'Son, music's in our blood, but you need somethin' solid to stand on.' So, I took this job at the courthouse. Twenty-three years now."

"Do you still play?"

"Got me a regular gig every Friday at the Striped Cat. Nothin' fancy; I just sit in with some old friends. We call ourselves 'The Courthouse Kings' now." Boggles laughed. "Most of us work day jobs in the legal system, but at night, we let the music take over."

Taylor smiled. "I'd like to hear you play sometime."

"For real?" Boggles' face lit up. "Well, we playin' later tonight. Small crowd, usually just locals and a few tourists who stumble in. But the music, Judge... when it's right, it's like magic."

"Maybe next time," Taylor said. "I'll bring Sarah—my wife loves jazz."

Boggles and Taylor continued talking for a while, until they arrived at Le Bayou Jardin, the restaurant's lights gleaming in the night sky.

"You sure you wouldn't rather hear some real music tonight, Judge? Striped Cat's just a few blocks from here."

"Wish I could, Boggles. But I've got this dinner..."
"Another time, then." Boggles watched Taylor step out. "You know, Judge, my Pops used to say music was like justice—when it's true, you can feel it down in your bones."

"Wise man, your father."

"That—he was, Judge. That—he was. See you Monday."

"See you Monday, Boggles," Taylor said, stepping away from the car.

"And next Friday—don't forget," Boggles called after him.

Boggles drove away, his radio still playing softly, unaware that Saturday would come and go without Judge Taylor, or that the next time he heard 'Sweet Lorraine,' it would remind him of their last conversation.

* * *

Inside Le Bayou Jardin, a bottle of wine was waiting, already chilling.

The piano player had moved into a soft rendition of 'Moonlight in Vermont' as Taylor and his dining companion continued their friendly conversation over wine.

"The business should continue to be successful if I could only get the capital I need."

"I'm sure it will. Robert, you're a resourceful man. Besides, I've never known you to fail at anything you set your mind to. Even if sometimes it was on the shady side."

"Phone call, Judge," the maître d' said.

Taylor hesitated, glancing at his companion. "I should take this. Won't be long."

"Sure thing," Robert smiled, lifting his wine glass. "I need to go to the men's room anyway."

Taylor walked toward the restaurant's entrance, picked up the phone, and pressed it to his ear. As soon as he was out of sight, his dinner companion headed toward the restroom.

The line went dead. Taylor looked at the phone, said 'Hello' twice, then once more into the silence, and then shrugged, walking back to his table. *If it were important, they'd call back*, he thought.

The timing was perfect—he'd been away just long enough. His companion returned from the restroom a minute later, smiling as he sat down. Taylor reached for his glass.

"Everything okay?" Robert asked, looking concerned.

"Lost connection." Taylor smiled, reaching for his wine. "Now, what were you saying..."?

Thunder rolled in from the Gulf, and the first drops of rain began to fall on the French Quarter's ancient streets.

Around nine-thirty, Taylor's words began to slur slightly, his hand less steady on the wine glass.

"Charles?" Robert's concern sounded genuine. "You don't look well."

"Something's... not quite right," Taylor managed, blinking to clear his vision.

"The wine might be stronger than I thought." Robert signaled for the check. "Let me call you a cab."

Taylor tried to protest but found it difficult to focus. The restaurant's soft lights had become too bright, and the piano music was distorted. He was aware that Robert was helping him up and guiding him toward the door.

The night air hit him like a wall. Robert and the maître d' kept a steady hand on the judge as they waited on the curb. When the taxi pulled up, Taylor vaguely heard Robert giving the driver an address on Prytania Street.

"But that's not..." Taylor tried to say, but was unable to get the words out.

"It's okay, Charles." Robert then turned to the taxi driver again. "My friend here had a few too many. I don't want him driving home. Take him to 6464 Prytania Street; his daughter will be waiting for him." Robert pulled out his wallet and gave the driver more than enough money to cover the fare.

The taxi pulled away from Le Bayou Jardin, leaving Robert and the maître d' standing on the curb.

Twenty minutes later, the taxi turned onto Prytania Street and came to a stop in front of the house. There was a couple waiting on the steps of a grand old home, typical of the houses in this area of town. The porch lights cast a warm glow, making everything feel inviting.

Before the driver could shift into park, a couple hurried down the front steps.

They reached the taxi as the driver stepped out. They opened the back door without missing a beat and eased Taylor from the seat. "Oh, Greg, he must have really tied one on this time." She said in full earshot of the driver. Making it sound like this was a routine occurrence. His feet barely touched the ground as they propped him against the taxi's trunk, supporting him between them, as the man reached for his wallet.

"The fare's been taken care of," the driver said. "His friend handled it."

The man peeled off several bills anyway. "Here, a little extra for your trouble. Thanks for getting him home safely."

"We got it from here. Thanks again," he added, already turning his attention back to Taylor.

They guided the judge up to the porch, settling him into a white wicker chair where the driver could clearly see him.

The moment the taxi's taillights disappeared around the corner, a black SUV rolled silently into the driveway. Two men emerged from the vehicle. They quickly went over to the Judge and carried him to their vehicle.

In seconds, they had Taylor in the back seat. A woman leaned into the car, her gloved hands steady as she raised Taylor's shirt, placing two small patches on his torso. No words were exchanged. The car was already pulling away, slipping through the quiet streets of the Garden District, taking Judge Taylor with it as if he'd never been there at all.

CHAPTER 15

Present time

BACK IN SIMMONS' OFFICE, Renee suddenly leaned closer to the screen. "Wait. Roll that back again."

Kelsey rewound the footage to when Taylor left for the phone call. They watched in silence as the scene unfolded: Taylor walking to the host podium, his dining companion heading to the restroom, and then—

"There." Renee pointed. "Look at the timing."

Two men had stepped in front of Taylor's table, blocking the view. A third figure in a dark coat moved in from behind.

"Perfect choreography," Kelsey said. "Taylor's on the phone, but notice how he turns just enough to think he still has eyes on his table."

"But he couldn't," Callahan added, "not with those two men standing there. They weren't random patrons—they were positioned specifically to block Taylor's view."

Simmons moved closer to the screen. "The man in the dark coat—he's awfully close to Taylor's glass."

"Four seconds," Renee said, checking the time stamp. "That's all it took."

The footage continued. Taylor returned to his table, his companion coming back from the restroom. Everything appeared normal except for what had happened in those carefully orchestrated moments.

"Four people minimum involved in just the poisoning," Renee counted off. "The two blockers, the man in the dark coat. Plus, Taylor's dinner companion."

"And the footage is so bad we still can't tell who any of them are," Kelsey said.

"But now we know something else," Renee said, her eyes still on the screen. "We're not dealing with amateurs or some rushed hit job. This was planned, rehearsed. They knew Taylor's habits, knew the restaurant layout, knew exactly how to position everyone."

"Professional," Simmons finished. "Which means serious money and organization behind this."

Renee squinted at the grainy footage, focusing on the man's profile as he sat across from Taylor. "Can we clean this up at all?"

"I'll see what tech can do," Kelsey said, tapping at the keyboard. The image sharpened slightly, revealing more detail of the man's features—a slight scar near his left temple, the way his nose had been broken and healed slightly crooked.

"Those aren't the kind of scars you get from office work," Renee noted. "Run it through the database."

"It'll take time," Kelsey warned. "The angle's not perfect."

"Start with booking photos from the last fifteen years," Simmons suggested. "Focus on drug arrests in Taylor's old jurisdiction when he was still working cases."

The computer hummed as it cycled through thousands of faces. Ten minutes passed. Twenty. Thirty.

"There," Simmons said, pointing at the screen. The computer stopped on a match.

A younger version of Taylor's dinner companion stared back at them, defiant despite a swollen eye and split lip. The booking photo was from 2003.

"Robert Duran," Kelsey read. "Multiple possession charges, intent to distribute."

"I remember this case," Simmons said. "Taylor caught him selling near a school. But instead of throwing the book at him—"

"Taylor tried to help him get clean," Renee finished, pulling up the case file. "Got him into a program, helped him find legitimate work. According to this, Duran actually stayed straight for several years."

"Until now," Kelsey said grimly. "Question is— why? What made him turn on the one person who'd tried to help him?"

"Someone was paying him," Simmons said. "Buying his loyalty—or his cooperation."

"And his knowledge of Taylor's habits," Renee said. "Think about it—Duran knew Taylor from years back. Knew his routines, his favorite restaurants."

"Making him the perfect person to set up that final dinner," Kelsey concluded.

Simmons pulled out the old case file, papers yellowed with age. "Arrested in '03 for dealing near Warren Easton High. Taylor was the arresting officer."

Renee examined the original booking report. "Looking at this... Taylor had the charges reduced, then practically eliminated."

"That wasn't Taylor's usual style," Simmons noted. "He was always tough on dealers, especially ones working near schools."

Kelsey opened a sealed document from the file. "It's a CI agreement. Taylor flipped him."

"Let me see that," Renee said, taking the file. "Duran agreed to work as a confidential informant in exchange for a reduced sentence. Taylor wrote that 'Subject shows potential for rehabilitation and possesses valuable intelligence about higher-level distribution networks.'"

"Taylor told me about a CI he used to work with," Callahan said. "But that was a long time ago."

"Classic Taylor," Simmons said softly. "He was playing the long game. Using Duran to work his way up the chain."

"There's more," Renee continued reading. "Regular meeting reports, information passed. Duran was actually delivering solid intel about supply routes, key players. Taylor was building something big."

"Until it all stops," Kelsey noted, checking the dates. "The reports end in 2009. Why?"

Renee flipped through more pages. "Here— Taylor's final note: 'CI has demonstrated consistent commitment to rehabilitation. Recommend termination of CI status to allow subject to make clean break from criminal associations.'"

"So, Taylor didn't just use him," Kelsey said. "He actually helped him get out."

"Which makes that dinner even more interesting," Simmons said. "Why would Duran resurface now? After all these years?"

"And why would Taylor agree to meet him?" Renee added. "Unless..."

The implications hung in the air. "Whatever Taylor had uncovered," Callahan said, "it must have been significant enough for him to risk meeting with a former CI."

"Or Duran reached out to him," Renee suggested. "Maybe claiming he had new information."

"Either way," Kelsey said, turning to the phone records they'd obtained, "four calls from a cell phone registered to Robert Duran in the week before the dinner."

"So, Duran initiated contact," Simmons confirmed. "And Taylor took the bait."

Renee stood, pacing the small office. "Taylor was cautious, though. He chose a public restaurant, positioned himself where he could see the entrance."

"But he didn't anticipate the level of coordination," Callahan added. "The phone call, the blockers—it was too well orchestrated."

"This points to something bigger than a personal grudge," Renee said. "Someone hired Duran specifically because of his connection to Taylor."

"The Domingo organization," Simmons suggested. "Taylor was building a case against their protection network. They needed someone who could get close to him."

"And someone who had connections with him, knew his habits, his favorite spots," Kelsey added. "Duran was perfect."

Callahan checked his watch. "We need to find Duran. If he's still in the city—"

"Unlikely," Renee cut in. "After a professional hit like this, he's probably long gone."

"Still," Simmons said, "put out an APB. All airports, bus stations, train depots. If he's in the wind, maybe we can figure out where he blew."

"And we need to identify the other three men at the restaurant," Kelsey added. "The blockers and the one who drugged the wine."

"Focus on known Domingo associates," Simmons instructed. "Particularly those with specialized skills. The timing was too perfect for amateurs."

As they gathered their materials to leave, Callahan paused at the door. "One more thing—once Taylor was incapacitated, where did they take him before Barataria?"

"We know the answer to that," Renee said. "Taylor left Le Bayou Jardin around 9:45. The medical examiner puts the time of death between 11 PM and 1 AM. The cab driver already confirmed to us that he was taken to a house on Prytania Street."

"And that's where the fentanyl patches were probably placed on him," Kelsey said. "According to forensics, those were applied after he left the restaurant."

As they dispersed, the next steps of the investigation taking shape, Renee lingered a moment longer. On the screen, frozen in time, was the image of Robert Duran sitting across from Judge Taylor, raising a glass in what now appeared to be a macabre toast.

"Betrayed by his own CI," she murmured. "You never saw it coming, did you?"

The grainy image offered no response, just the ghostly tableau of Taylor's last meal, captured in the cold electronic eye of a security camera that had witnessed but could not prevent his death.

CHAPTER 16

THE CEILING FAN SPUN lazily overhead as Callahan spread his court records across Simmons' dining room table. Case files covering every available surface told a story of systemic corruption that had protected the Domingo organization for years.

"Look at this," Renee said, spreading out three more files. "Judge Harrison threw out a case against one of Domingo's lieutenants two years ago. Claimed the warrant was improperly executed."

"Same thing with the Lester case," Kelsey added, consulting his notes. "Judge LeBlanc found 'procedural irregularities' in the surveillance. Everything got suppressed."

Callahan leaned forward, his tie loosened, sleeves rolled up. "And Taylor's last case before he died—another Domingo operation. Judge Barrett was set to hear it after Taylor's recusal."

"Recusal?" Simmons looked up sharply. "Taylor never mentioned recusing himself."

"Because he didn't," Callahan said quietly. "Taylor couldn't be bought; that's what got him killed. The motion was filed the morning he disappeared. Signature looked right, all the paperwork in order, but..."

"But Taylor was already dead," Renee said, feeling a chill inside herself.

"It's not just Taylor's case," Callahan continued, pulling another file from his briefcase. "I was scheduled to prosecute a major case against Antoine Domingo himself three months ago. Big one—fentanyl distribution across five parishes. The morning of the preliminary hearing, the judge got reassigned, evidence went missing from the lockup, and suddenly, I was pulled off the case."

"Who took over?" Simmons asked.

"The DA himself," Callahan's jaw tightened. "Case dismissed within a week."

Kelsey nodded grimly. "I've seen it happen for years. Our unit arrested Domingo's people dozens of times—solid cases, good evidence. But nothing ever sticks when it gets to court, and when it does stick, it's on a low-level dealer, never Domingo himself."

"We bust our asses building cases," Renee added, "follow every procedure to the letter, and then poof—some technicality, some procedural error, and Domingo walks every time."

Kelsey spread more files across the table. "Same patterns, all of them. Three judges. Harrison, LeBlanc, and Barrett. Evidence disappeared, warrants got questioned, witnesses recanted."

"But other drug cases?" Renee was already seeing it. "Different story."

"Completely different," Kelsey confirmed. "These same judges handed down maximum sentences in non-Domingo cases. No procedural issues, no suppressed evidence, no convenient technicalities. The Vasquez cartel, the Trinh organization—they all got hammered. But Domingo? Always an escape hatch."

Simmons stood, moving to a corkboard he'd set up in the corner. "Put it up. All of it."

They worked in focused silence, pinning cases in chronological order. Red strings connected the Domingo cases, blue for others. The pattern emerged like a neon sign—three judges systematically dismantled every case against the Domingo organization while maintaining harsh sentences for everyone else.

"It's not just the judges," Callahan said, studying the board. "Look at the prosecutors assigned to the Domingo cases. Junior ADAs, most of them. No experience with major drug operations."

"Setting them up to fail." Renee nodded. "While the veteran prosecutors got the smaller cases."

"Taylor saw it," Simmons said. "He was piecing it together, tracking the pattern. That's why they killed him—he had proof."

"The question is," Kelsey stood back from the board, "how deep does it go? These cases span years. The Domingo organization has tentacles everywhere, but this level of coordination..."

"Means someone's orchestrating it from above," Callahan finished. "Someone with enough power to manipulate case assignments, influence judges, ensure the right prosecutors get the right cases."

Renee felt her stomach twist as another realization hit. "The anonymous tips that led to these busts—they all came through proper channels, right? Which means..."

"Someone in law enforcement is involved." Simmons's grim expression matched her thoughts. "They're feeding just enough information to trigger raids but not enough to make cases stick. Making it look like we're fighting the drug trade while ensuring the Domingo operation stays intact."

The room fell silent as the implications sank in. The web of corruption Taylor had discovered wasn't just about a few crooked judges or bought prosecutors. It was systematic, orchestrated, reaching into every level of New Orleans' justice system.

"We need to find out who benefits," Kelsey said. "Follow the money. Someone's getting paid to keep the Domingo organization running."

"We need those notes," Callahan said, "the evidence Taylor is hiding. The pattern is clear, but without concrete proof... Think, everyone, think. Where would Taylor have stashed them?"

Simmons thought for a moment and said, "Taylor used to say put things in plain sight and nobody will pay attention to them."

Peering through the blinds at the quiet street, Callahan said, "The courthouse. We need to check the courthouse. It will be empty at night except for security."

"But how do we get in?" Renee asked.

Kelsey straightened in his chair. "Boggles," he said suddenly. "The janitor. He's got keys to everything."

"The guy who gave Taylor his last ride?" Renee asked.

"Think about it," Kelsey continued, warming even more to the idea. "He's worked there for what, twenty years? Knows every corner of that building. And more importantly, he trusted Taylor. Taylor trusted him."

"What makes you think it's in the courthouse anyway?" Renee asked.

"It's a place to start," Simmons replied. "And besides, I know Taylor kept things close to him. He always believed in keeping important matters within arm's reach—somewhere he could monitor them. The courthouse would make sense."

"Okay, let's get back to Boggles," Kelsey said abruptly. "You saw his face when we interviewed him about Taylor. He cared about the judge. Really cared."

"And he's already involved," Callahan added. "Whether he knows it or not. Taylor chose to have Boggles drive him that night. Maybe Taylor was leaving breadcrumbs even then."

Kelsey checked his watch. "Boggles works Friday nights. He'll be at the Striped Cat now—it's his regular gig."

"He plays piano there," Renee explained. "Every Friday. Taylor knew about it—was supposed to go hear him play sometime."

They exchanged glances, the weight of those unfulfilled plans adding another layer to their determination. Taylor's life had been cut short, his simple promise to hear a friend play music now impossible to keep.

"Alright," Simmons said finally. "But we do this carefully. No pressure. If Boggles says no, we find another way."

The Striped Cat was tucked away on a side street off Frenchmen, the kind of place tourists walked past without noticing. Inside, the air was thick with cigarette smoke and the sound of well-played jazz. Boggles sat at an old upright piano in the corner, his big hands moving over the keys with surprising grace as he led the quartet through a mellow rendition of "Sweet Lorraine."

They found a table near the back and waited for the set to end. Boggles spotted them, his expression shifting from surprise to understanding when he saw their faces.

"This ain't about my music, is it?" he said as he approached their table, wiping his hands on a handkerchief.

"We need your help, Boggles," Renee said quietly.

"Judge Taylor's case?" He pulled up a chair, his large frame settling into it. "Go on, I'm listenin'"

"You know something?" Kelsey leaned forward.

"Know lots of things. Been cleanin' that courthouse longer than some of them judges been practicin' law." He paused as a waitress passed. "The judge—he seemed worried these last few weeks. Stayin' late, goin' through old papers."

Boggles lowered his voice. "Thought maybe he was writin' some kinda crime book."

The big man was quiet for a long moment, his fingers absently tapping out a rhythm on the table.

"Y'all know what you're askin'? If the wrong people find out I helped you..."

"We know," Renee said. "And we wouldn't ask if it wasn't important. Judge Taylor was killed because he found something—evidence of corruption that goes deep. We need to find what he hid before they do."

"The judge was my friend," Boggles said softly. "Twenty years, he treated me like a person. Never missed sayin' good mornin', askin' 'bout my family." His eyes grew distant. "Night he died, he said he'd come hear me play sometime. Said he'd bring his missus, make a evenin' of it."

The quartet started up again, playing a slow blues number as they waited for Boggles' decision. Finally, he reached into his pocket and pulled out a ring of keys, selecting one and sliding it across the table.

"This'll get you into the buildin'," he said, his voice barely audible above the music. "Down the hall to the right, there's a room marked 'Cleanin' Supplies.'"

His thick fingers traced an invisible map on the table. "Inside that room, there's a locker. Got my name on it." He tapped each number as he spoke them: "Combination's 8-6-4."

"You'll find an old cigar box in the locker," he continued. "Inside, there's a bunch of keys. All marked for certain areas, certain rooms." His eyes met Renee's. "They'll get you into the old service corridors."

He paused as a waitress passed their table. "From there... whole buildin' opens up, if you know where you goin'."

The unspoken warning hung between them. Renee picked up the key, feeling its cold weight against her palm.

"Boggles," Kelsey asked quietly, "did the judge know about these corridors?"

The big man's face gave nothing away as he stood to return to his piano. "Everybody got they secrets, Detective—even buildings. There's a security guard at the courthouse, makes his rounds every couple hours. First one starts right when I'm gettin' off at four. If y'all show up 'round—say—twelve-thirty tonight, you'll probably have some time to do what you gotta do 'fore he comes back 'round." He straightened his tie and said quieter, "Jus makes it count."

Still clutching the key, Renee looked up. "Are you sure about the timing?"

"Ain't no exact science, detective," he replied. "Jus find what the judge died for. Make it count."

As they watched him head back to the stage, Kelsey turned to Renee. "Tonight?"

She nodded, the key warming in her palm. "Tonight."

CHAPTER 17

THE COURTHOUSE AT 1:30 AM felt like a different world. Shadows pooled in corners where daylight never reached, and the usual bustle of justice was replaced by an eerie stillness that made every footstep sound like an accusation.

Using Boggles' key, they entered silently through the service entrance. The combination worked perfectly: 8-6-4. Inside the locker, just as promised, was the old cigar box filled with labeled keys.

"Three floors," Simmons whispered, his voice barely carrying in the marble hallway. "Kelsey, take the law library. I'll check the records room. Renee..."

"Chambers," she finished. They'd been over the plan, but saying it aloud made it real.

"Thirty minutes," Simmons checked his watch. "Then we meet at the south stairwell. If anyone sees anything suspicious, please report it by clicking twice on the radio. No voices."

They separated at the main stairs, each taking a different route to their targets. Renee watched their shadows split and fade. Then she started for her destination.

The judge's chambers sat on the third floor, at the end of a corridor that felt miles long in the darkness. Though she'd passed by this office dozens of times, she had never been inside.

The brass nameplate on Taylor's door caught a sliver of emergency lighting: HONORABLE CHARLES TAYLOR. As she entered, the chambers looked undisturbed since his death. Case files still stacked neatly on the corner desk, legal pads filled with his precise handwriting, even a half-empty coffee mug that no one had dared to move. With Taylor's words to Boggles about hiding things where everyone could see it echoing in her mind, Renee's attention fixed on the large picture behind his desk—a black and white photograph of the French Quarter from the 1920s.

Her penlight beam traced the frame's edge. Heavy oak, expertly crafted, featured a deep border that appeared slightly thicker than usual, resembling a frame within a frame. Her fingers found a nearly invisible seam where the two met, as she began to pull the frontal frame from its secondary border. A soft scrape from the hallway froze her in place.

Footsteps, trying to be quiet but given away by the old building's echo, drawing closer. Then, voices—just whispers, but in the nighttime silence, they carried loud and clear down the corridor.

"Has to be here somewhere..."

Renee killed her light, easing behind Taylor's desk. The voices were just outside now.

The door handle turned.

Renee pressed herself into the narrow space between the desk and the wall, heart thundering so loudly she was sure they'd hear it. The picture frame was inches from her face, its hidden compartment now tantalizingly out of reach.

Light spilled into the chamber as two figures entered. Their flashlight beams swept the room, catching dust motes in their glow.

"Start with the files," one voice said. "I'll check the shelves."

Renee held her breath as footsteps circled the desk. A beam of light passed inches from her, then moved on. She could see their shadows now, projected against the wall—a man rifling through Taylor's files while his companion searched through the bookshelves.

Her radio felt like a brick against her hip. Two clicks would bring help, but also guarantee her discovery. The smart play was to wait them out.

The stranger's light lingered on the photograph. "Nice shot of the Quarter," he said casually. "Looks like an original photo."

"Who cares? We're not here for the décor."

But as one of the men moved closer to the picture, Renee's hand moved to her weapon.

A dull thud echoed from somewhere below in the building. Both men froze, listening. After a moment, the first man shrugged. "Probably just building settling. These old places make noise." He moved closer to the picture, then came the unmistakable sound of shattering glass, followed by the sound of footsteps running. "That's definitely not the building," the second man said.

"Building's compromised," the first man said, stepping back from the picture. "We're out of here."

"What about—"

"Leave it. We'll come back another time."

Footsteps faded into the distance, and the door closed softly behind them. Renee sat in the darkness, counting her heartbeats to ensure they were truly gone.

She slipped out of her hiding spot moments later, her muscles screaming from being held so still. Her trembling hands grasped the frame again, fingers tracing its edge until—there was a subtle catch, barely noticeable.

The picture popped open from the backing frame like a swinging door. Behind it lay a space, only about an inch deep.

Inside sat a thin leather notebook.

Taylor's evidence. The reason he died. She couldn't believe she'd found it in the first place she looked.

Her first impulse was to grab it and run. But footsteps echoed from somewhere in the building, if someone else was still here, if she got caught with it, if it ended up in the wrong hands—too many ifs to risk it.

Instead, she carefully opened it where it lay, using her penlight to illuminate Taylor's neat, precise handwriting. The first page contained a simple heading:

"DOMINGO ORGANIZATION- PROTECTION NETWORK."

Page after page documented a complex web, including the judges who handled Domingo cases, the prosecutors assigned, and the suspicious patterns of case dismissals. Next to many entries were small notations, followed by dollar amounts. Some had dates, locations, brief descriptions of meetings.

The light from her penlight revealed something else—a small envelope tucked into a pocket at the back of the notebook. Inside were several small SD cards, each labeled with dates going back three years.

"Evidence," she whispered to herself. Taylor had been building his case methodically, gathering material to support his written notes.

Her radio crackled softly—two clicks.

Quickly, she took several photos of key pages with her phone, then carefully closed the notebook and returned it to its hiding place, making sure the frame looked undisturbed. She couldn't risk taking it—not with unknown searchers in the building or the security guard. What if she got caught? The photos would have to be enough until they could retrieve the actual evidence safely.

As she slipped out of Taylor's chambers, the faint sound of footsteps echoed from the stairwell. She pressed herself against the wall, waiting as the sounds faded. Then, moving silently, she made her way to the rendezvous point.

Kelsey and Simmons were already there.

"What was that crash?" Renee asked, speaking as softly as she could.

"I think someone threw a brick through the window," Simmons replied. "The courthouse has been vandalized several times within the last few weeks. It could be a repeat of that."

"And the footsteps," Renee asked.

"Probably the security guard," replied Simmons.

"Hope so," Renee said, "because it saved me. Those men were about to find what they were looking for."

"You found something?" Kelsey asked as they hurried toward the service exit.

"Yes," Renee replied. "Taylor kept records—I didn't have much time to look. But I did see some writings regarding Domingo."

Simmons's eyes widened slightly. "You got it?"

"No," Renee shook her head. "I left it there."

"Left it?" Kelsey's voice rose slightly. "Why?"

"Think about it," Renee whispered urgently. "I didn't know what that noise was. Who was in the building? If I'd taken it and gotten caught, it could've fallen into Domingo's hands. We don't know who's involved in this—what if the security guard had caught me? Anyone could be on their payroll."

Simmons nodded. "You did the right thing."

They slipped out through the service entrance just as patrol car lights became visible at the main doors. Moving quickly through the shadows, they made it back to Simmons's car, parked three blocks away.

Only when they were safely moving through the quiet streets did Renee finally speak again. "Someone else was looking for the same thing we were. They knew about the evidence, too."

"Which means we don't have much time," Simmons said. "If they know Taylor kept records, they'll tear that courthouse apart until they find them."

"So, how are we going to get that notebook now?" Kelsey asked. There was no mistaking the frustration in his tone.

Renee looked up, a sudden realization dawning. "Boggles."

"Boggles?" Simmons repeated.

"He cleans those rooms. Has access to everything," Renee explained. "He could get the notebook for us without raising suspicion."

"Are we really going to involve him even deeper in this?" Kelsey asked, concern replacing frustration. "He's already taken a huge risk helping us get in there tonight."

Simmons sighed heavily. "We don't have a choice. That notebook is our best evidence—those SD cards could be the key to everything."

"Besides," Renee added, pulling out her phone to show them the photos she'd taken, "he's already involved. Taylor trusted him, and so do I."

The three huddled around the phone's screen as Renee flipped through the images. Taylor's neat handwriting detailed a conspiracy that reached further than any of them had imagined. Judges, prosecutors, even high-ranking police officials—all connected to the Domingo organization through a complex web of payoffs and favors.

"Jesus," Kelsey muttered. "Look at these amounts. Hundreds of thousands of dollars."

"And these SD cards," Renee added. "Taylor must have gathered evidence somehow. Those could be our smoking gun."

"We need to contact Boggles tomorrow," Simmons said decisively. "The longer that notebook stays there, the greater the risk someone else finds it."

Renee zoomed in on one particular page that listed three locations with stars next to them. "These mean something. Taylor highlighted them specifically."

"Looks like meeting places," Kelsey suggested. "Places where the deals went down, maybe."

"Or where he gathered evidence," Simmons said. "Taylor was smart—he knew he couldn't be seen directly investigating these people. He must have found another way to document what was happening."

As they drove through the silent city, Renee couldn't shake the feeling that they'd just stepped into something far more dangerous than a murder investigation. They were now officially at war with people powerful enough to kill a judge and corrupt enough to ensure no one asked questions.

"Taylor knew," she said softly. "When he told Boggles that the best hiding place was in plain sight... he knew they'd come looking."

Simmons's hands tightened on the steering wheel. "And he knew it might get him killed. But he kept going anyway. I guess Taylor thought it was worth taking a chance for,"

The question now was whether they could safely retrieve the evidence Taylor had died to protect—and whether Boggles could help them do it without becoming another victim.

CHAPTER 18

RENEE DUCKED INTO the alcove of a shuttered antique shop, her back to the brick wall as she dialed the number. The French Quarter was unusually quiet this morning, but she still scanned both directions before speaking.

"Boggles, this is Detective Dubois."

"Well, now, didn't spect to be hearing from you so soon, Detective."

"We found it," Renee said, speaking in a whisper despite the empty sidewalk around her. "Taylor's evidence—it's in a hidden compartment behind that huge French Quarter photograph hanging on the wall in his office."

Boggles' deep voice grew cautious. "You got it then?"

"No," Renee admitted. "We had to leave it. There were others searching his office—Domingo's men. And with the security guard…" She let the implication hang in the air.

The line went quiet for a moment. Then Boggles sighed heavily, understanding immediately what she was asking.

"Can't go in there 'til Monday," he said, "folks start Wonderin' if I show up when I ain't s'posed to. But come Monday, sho' thing, I can get it for ya."

"Will that be safe?" Renee asked, concerned about the delay.

"Safer than bustin' in there now," Boggles replied. "Ain't nobody look twice at me cleanin' the judge's office on my regular day. Been doin' that same job goin' on twenty years now."

Renee sighed. "What if the notebook's gone by Monday?"

"Or what if I show up outta nowhere and the security guard start wonderin' why?" Boggles shot back. "Listen here, sometimes you gotta sit tight. Patience. That's how you stays alive in this town."

"Monday, then," Renee agreed reluctantly. "But we need a safe way to make the exchange."

"That café on Royal Street—Fleur-de-Lis," Boggles suggested. "I get off at four, a little after gives me time to get there. Full of tourists and locals, nobody pays you no mind. You sit with a newspaper, and I'll come in after."

"Perfect," Renee said. "And Boggles... thank you."

"Just doin' right by the judge," he replied before hanging up. "He always did right by me."

The weekend passed with excruciating slowness. Renee and Kelsey reviewed the photos she'd taken of Taylor's notebook pages, but without the actual evidence, especially those SD cards, they could only speculate about the full extent of the corruption network.

By Monday afternoon, they were all on edge. So much could have gone wrong. If Domingo's men had returned to the courthouse... if the security guard had discovered Boggles in Taylor's office... if someone had spotted the hidden compartment in the frame...

* * *

At 4:20 PM, Boggles arrived at Café Fleur-de-Lis on Royal Street. The place was busy with the usual late afternoon crowd—tourists resting their feet after a day of sightseeing, locals stopping for coffee before heading home. Perfect cover for their meeting.

He spotted Renee at a corner table, a newspaper open in front of her, a half-empty coffee cup by her hand. She didn't acknowledge him as he entered. Boggles ordered a coffee at the counter, then casually made his way to an empty table near hers.

After several minutes of pretending to watch the passersby through the window, Boggles cleared his throat. "Excuse me, miss?" he called to Renee. "You finished with that part of the paper?"

Renee glanced up, catching on immediately. "Sure," she replied, folding the section she'd supposedly been reading and handing it across the small gap between their tables. "I was done with it anyway."

"I preciate it," Boggles said with a nod, accepting the newspaper and opening it in front of him.

They sat in silence, Boggles pretending to read while Renee sipped her coffee and made notes in a small notepad as if planning her day. To anyone watching, they were just two strangers sharing a café space, not even exchanging a word.

After about fifteen minutes, Boggles folded the newspaper and held it out toward Renee. "Thanks again. All done if ya want it back."

"Thanks," Renee said, taking the newspaper. As she set it on the table, she felt the weight of the notebook now hidden within its folds. Their exchange had been flawless—natural and undetectable to any observer.

They maintained this casual lack of interaction for several more minutes.

"Weather's been nice today," Renee said with a warm smile, her fingers gently closing around the newspaper.

"Can't complain," Boggles replied, sipping his coffee. "Dey say rain comin' tomorrow, though."

They maintained this casual conversation for several minutes, sharing a moment in a crowded café. Finally, Boggles checked his watch. "Well, gotta get goin' now, preciate it."

"Anytime," Renee said as she lifted her cup.

As Boggles stood to leave, Renee whispered to herself, "*Thank you, Boggles.*" She could almost hear his reply echoing in her mind: "*Just doing right by the judge.*"

Renee left the café, the notebook securely tucked inside her jacket. Outside, Kelsey was waiting in an unmarked car a block away. She walked past him once, confirming no one was following her, then circled back and slid into the passenger seat.

"Got it?" Kelsey asked, eyes constantly scanning their surroundings.

Renee patted her jacket. "Got it. Boggles came through perfectly—no problems."

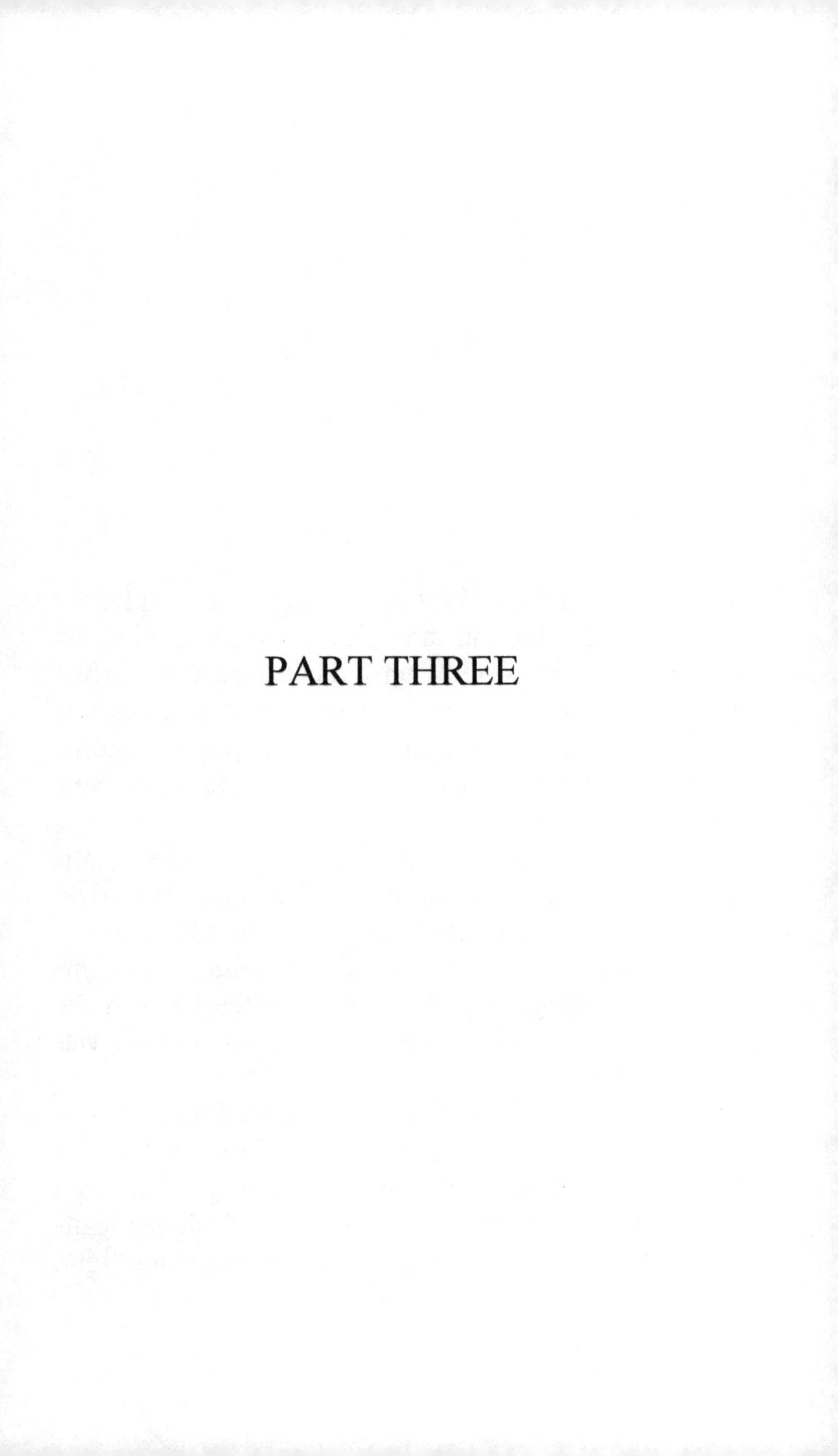

PART THREE

CHAPTER 19

JEAN-PAUL DOMINGO sat in his private study, the morning light filtering through stained glass windows that had been imported from France a century earlier. The Garden District mansion had been in the Domingo family for three generations, ever since his grandfather founded their so-called "import business" in New Orleans.

At sixty-eight, Jean-Paul maintained the appearance of a distinguished businessman. His silver hair was perfectly coiffed, his suit hand-tailored from an exclusive atelier in Milan. Nothing about his appearance suggested his position at the head of the city's most powerful drug organization—which was precisely the point.

A gentle knock at the door preceded the entrance of his son, Antoine. At thirty-six, Antoine had his father's height and build but lacked his patience and foresight. He was dressed casually in designer jeans and a silk shirt, his Rolex glinting in the morning light.

"The shipment is confirmed," Antoine said. "Kovac says everything's on schedule."

Jean-Paul nodded, not looking up from the financial report he was reviewing. "And our friends at the port authority?"

"Taken care of. The usual arrangement—they'll make sure our container gets moved to the private loading area without inspection."

"Good." Jean-Paul finally looked up, studying his son with a critical eye. "And the security arrangements? We're going to need some extra men for this delivery."

Antoine shifted uncomfortably. "Michael's handling that part. He's bringing in some additional men just like you wanted."

At the mention of Michael Reeves, Jean-Paul's expression softened slightly. He had grown to trust his head of security over the past three years. Reeves had proven himself not just competent but innovative, anticipating problems before they arose.

"Where is Michael this morning?" Jean-Paul asked.

"His usual Sunday routine," Antoine replied. "He's obsessive about maintaining patterns, says it makes him less noticeable."

Jean-Paul nodded approvingly. "He's right. Patterns create invisibility. You would do well to learn from him, Antoine."

Antoine's jaw tightened at the criticism. "I've handled everything for tomorrow's shipment, Father. It's going to go perfectly."

"It needs to," Jean-Paul said simply. "This shipment is worth more than the last three combined.

Pure product, enough to supply our network for a long time. The profit margin will be... substantial."

"And it comes at the perfect time," Antoine added, "with the Rodriguez case being dismissed tomorrow."

Jean-Paul's eyes narrowed. "You're certain about Judge Barrett?"

"Positive. He's been well compensated. The evidence will be suppressed, case dismissed."

"And the prosecutor?"

"Some junior ADA," Antoine said with a smirk. "Marshall assigned him specifically—he's never handled a major drug case before. He'll be overwhelmed, unprepared."

Jean-Paul nodded thoughtfully. "District Attorney Marshall had been a valuable asset for years," he said. "Always knowing which ADA to assign. Smart man, that DA. Have Josef attend the hearing," Jean-Paul instructed. "I want to know immediately when it's dismissed."

"I could go myself," Antoine offered.

"No. You need to focus on tomorrow's shipment. Besides, your presence would be... noticed."

The unspoken truth hung between them. Antoine's previous arrest had made him too visible in law enforcement circles. Though the charges had been dismissed—thanks to Judge Harrison and a convenient "misplacement" of evidence—his face was too well-known to risk exposing him to police scrutiny again.

* * *

An electronic chime interrupted their conversation. Jean-Paul glanced at his phone, a slight smile crossing his features. "Ah, the day begins in earnest. Show Dr. Winfield in."

Antoine opened the door to admit Dr. Gregory Winfield, Chief of Surgery at Tulane Medical Center. The doctor entered with the confidence of someone accustomed to respect, though that confidence faltered slightly in Jean-Paul's presence.

"Mr. Domingo," Winfield said, extending his hand. "Always a pleasure."

"Please, Greg, have a seat," Jean-Paul gestured to a leather armchair. "Antoine, give us a moment."

Antoine nodded and left, closing the door behind him. Jean-Paul turned his full attention to the doctor.

"How is young Miguel doing?" he asked. "I understand the procedure was successful?"

"Yes," Winfield confirmed. "The surgery went perfectly. The boy will make a full recovery, thanks to your generosity in covering the costs."

Jean-Paul waved away the gratitude. "The family has served mine loyally for years. It was the least I could do." He leaned forward slightly. "Now, about that other matter we discussed."

Winfield's expression grew serious. "I've spoken with the board members as you requested. The land acquisition for the new oncology wing... There were questions about the appraisal value."

"Questions can be answered," Jean-Paul said. "Or silenced entirely, depending on the individual asking."

Winfield nodded, understanding the implication. "Three board members remain... concerned. Peterson, Galloway, and Sinclair."

Jean-Paul made a mental note of the names. "I'll have Michael look into their personal situations. Perhaps they have needs that aren't being met. Financial difficulties. Family matters. Everyone has their price, Greg. It's simply a matter of finding the right currency."

The doctor shifted uncomfortably but nodded. They both knew the proposed hospital expansion would be built on land owned by a Domingo shell corporation—land that would be purchased at triple its market value, generating millions in clean, legitimate profits.

"Is there anything else?" Jean-Paul asked.

"No, that's all for now."

"Good. I'll have Michael contact you with our approach to the three board members. In the meantime, please send my regards to your wife. I understand her charity gala last month was quite successful."

"It was, thank you," Winfield said, rising to leave. "Your donation was most generous."

"The Domingo family has always believed in giving back to the community," Jean-Paul said, his tone just short of ironic. "We're businessmen, after all."

After Winfield departed, Jean-Paul summoned Antoine back into the study. "Have Michael look into three individuals at Tulane Medical Center—Peterson, Galloway, and Sinclair. We need leverage."

Antoine nodded. "I'll tell him when he gets back from his breakfast routine."

"Now," Jean-Paul continued, "tell me about Rodriguez. Is he still maintaining his silence?"

"Absolutely," Antoine confirmed. "He knows our reach is long. Besides, with the case being dismissed tomorrow, there's no incentive for him to flip."

"Good. And the product from his territory?"

"We've redistributed his routes among the other lieutenants. No disruption to service," Antoine added. "Normal business procedures."

Jean-Paul nodded approvingly. "You've handled that aspect well."

Antoine straightened at the rare praise. "Thank you, Father."

"Don't get complacent," Jean-Paul cautioned. "With Judge Taylor's unexpected departure, we need to be especially vigilant. The investigation into his death could create complications."

"The police have nothing," Antoine said dismissively. "A body in the swamp, no witnesses, no evidence. It's been weeks, and they're no closer to finding who did it."

"Perhaps," Jean-Paul conceded. "Nevertheless, I want you to check with our contacts in the department. Make sure the investigation remains... unfocused."

"I'll talk to Lieutenant Green," Antoine promised. "He's been reliable."

"Good," Jean-Paul rose from his desk, signaling the end of their meeting. "Now, I have matters to attend to. The shipment may be our priority, but the everyday business still requires attention."

After Antoine left, Jean-Paul moved to the window, looking out over the meticulously maintained gardens of his estate. The Domingo empire had been built on three principles: discretion, control, and leverage. They moved their product quietly, controlled those who could threaten them, and maintained leverage over anyone in a position of power.

Judge Taylor had been the first real threat to that system in decades. His death had been unfortunate but necessary—a direct response to his refusal to be controlled or leveraged. The message had been sent: no one was untouchable, not even a sitting judge.

The thought brought him no pleasure. Jean-Paul was a businessman, not a killer. Violence was inefficient, attracted attention. But Taylor had left them no choice. He had been gathering evidence, building a case that threatened everything the Domingo family had built.

Now, with Taylor gone and his evidence presumably lost, they could refocus on business. Tomorrow's shipment would cement their position as the dominant force in New Orleans' drug trade for years to come.

* * *

A soft knock interrupted his thoughts. His assistant, Elena, opened the door slightly. "Mr. Domingo, Mr. Reeves has returned. He says he has information regarding tomorrow's security arrangements."

"Send him in," Jean-Paul instructed. If anyone could ensure the shipment went smoothly, it was Michael Reeves.

Michael entered with the confidence that had impressed Jean-Paul from their first meeting. Unlike most of Jean-Paul's employees, who projected either false bravado or obvious fear, Michael carried himself with the natural authority of someone completely at ease in his own skin.

"Michael," Jean-Paul greeted him warmly. "How was your morning routine?"

"Uneventful," Michael replied with a slight smile. "Just the way I like it."

"Good. Antoine tells me you're handling security for tomorrow's shipment."

Michael nodded. "I've brought in additional men. All thoroughly vetted, none with any connection to our regular operations. They'll provide perimeter security while our usual team handles the product transfer."

"Any concerns?"

"Nothing specific," Michael said. "But a shipment this size always carries risks. I've arranged for three different exit routes and two backup locations in case we need to move the product quickly."

Jean-Paul nodded. "I like that. That's why I value you, Michael—you're thorough. What about the port authority? Are Vasquez and Miller still our main contacts?"

"Yes," Michael confirmed. "Both have been on our payroll for over three years. No signs of wavering loyalty."

"Good." Jean-Paul walked back to his desk, picking up his notebook. "Now, I need you to look into three individuals at Tulane Medical Center." He handed Michael a slip of paper with the names on it. "We need leverage to ensure their cooperation on a land deal."

Michael pocketed the paper without examining it. "Financial leverage? Or something more personal?"

"Whatever works," Jean-Paul said casually. "Everyone has their weak spots. Just find theirs."

"I'll have preliminary information by Wednesday," Michael promised.

"Excellent." Jean-Paul studied Michael for a moment. "You know, my son could learn a great deal from you. Antoine has many talents, but patience and thoroughness are not among them."

"He's young," Michael said diplomatically. "Experience is the best teacher."

"Perhaps." Jean-Paul wasn't convinced. Antoine had been "young" for a very long time. "In any case, I have one other matter to discuss. Judge Taylor's death has created a vacancy in the courthouse. We need to ensure his replacement is... amenable to our interests."

"I understand," Michael said. "I've already begun looking into the likely candidates. Judge Wilkins seems most promising, gambling debts, a history of financial mismanagement. He'd be vulnerable to the right approach."

Jean-Paul smiled. As always, Michael was a step ahead. "Excellent. Make the necessary arrangements. Now, is there anything else you need for tomorrow night?"

"Everything's in place," Michael assured him. "I'll oversee the operation personally from start to finish."

"Very good." Jean-Paul's phone chimed with another appointment reminder. "Keep me informed of any developments. I'll expect hourly updates once the shipment arrives."

After Michael departed, Jean-Paul reflected on how integral the man had become to their operations. In just three years, Michael Reeves had made himself indispensable, handling security, gathering intelligence, even managing their more delicate political relationships. Jean-Paul's only concern was that he had become perhaps too dependent on the man's capabilities.

Still, in a business built on mistrust, Michael had earned a rare commodity: Jean-Paul's confidence. And tomorrow night, that confidence would be put to the test with the largest shipment in the organization's history.

CHAPTER 20

U.S. DISTRICT COURT looked exactly as it had for decades—an imposing limestone structure that had witnessed generations of New Orleans justice, such as it was. Inside Courtroom Four, the Rodriguez hearing was about to begin.

Josef Mendoza, the Domingo family's legal advisor, sat in the gallery, his expensive suit and calm demeanor making him nearly invisible among the other lawyers waiting for their cases to be called. His presence was a formality—everything had already been arranged. Judge Barrett would find reason to suppress the key evidence, and the case would collapse.

The young prosecutor, Kevin Wright, was shuffling papers at his table, looking nervous and unprepared. Just as planned, District Attorney Marshall had assigned the most junior ADA in the office to this case, practically guaranteeing its failure. Wright had been with the DA's office for only eleven months, and this was his first major drug case.

Across the aisle, defense attorney Steven Beaumont arranged his materials. Beaumont was a fixture in New Orleans courtrooms, known for representing high-profile clients and commanding fees that would bankrupt most defendants. His services were, of course, provided to Rodriguez courtesy of the Domingo organization.

Barrett entered the courtroom, and the bailiff called for all to rise. Josef studied the judge carefully. Nothing in Barrett's demeanor suggested anything unusual—no hint that he had received fifty thousand dollars three days earlier to ensure this case never went to trial.

"Be seated," Barrett said, adjusting his robes as he settled into his chair. He glanced down at the docket, though Josef knew he was well aware of which case was before him. "Case number 47293, State versus Rodriguez."

Rodriguez sat beside Beaumont, dressed in a conservative navy suit that effectively concealed the tattoos marking him as a lieutenant in the Domingo organization. He showed no expression and betrayed none of the confidence he must have felt, knowing the outcome was predetermined.

"The State moves to admit evidence seized during the execution of a search warrant at 2010 Pelican Street," Wright said, steadying his voice. "The evidence includes roughly five kilos of fentanyl, with a street value exceeding three million dollars."

Barrett nodded; his expression appropriately serious. "Counselor Beaumont, I understand you've filed a motion to suppress this evidence?"

"Yes, Your Honor," Beaumont rose, adjusting his tie as he addressed the court. "The defense moves to suppress all evidence obtained during the search of my client's business premises on the grounds that the warrant was improperly executed."

Wright frowned. "Your Honor, the State strongly contests this motion. The warrant was properly obtained and executed according to all statutory requirements."

"Perhaps we should hear the specifics of the defense's objection," Barrett suggested, giving Beaumont his cue.

"Your Honor," Beaumont began, his voice carrying the confidence that this would be a no-contest game, "the search warrant explicitly stated that it was to be executed 'no earlier than 6:00 AM on April 17th.' However, officers from the Narcotics Division entered the premises at approximately 5:52 AM, a full eight minutes before the time specified in the warrant."

Wright looked genuinely surprised. This was clearly the first he'd heard of this particular objection. He quickly flipped through his case files, searching for the warrant documentation.

"Furthermore," Beaumont continued, "this premature entry constitutes a violation of my client's Fourth Amendment rights against unreasonable search and seizure. The timing specification in the warrant was not a mere suggestion but a legal requirement."

Barrett turned to Wright. "Counselor? Your response?"

Wright, having finally located the relevant documents, stood again. "Your Honor, while the defense is technically correct about the specified time, this minor discrepancy does not rise to the level of a Fourth Amendment violation. The officers had probable cause, a valid warrant signed by Judge Harrison, and the eight-minute difference represents a de minimis error that should not invalidate the entire search."

"The Constitution doesn't recognize 'de minimis' violations, Your Honor," Beaumont countered, "either the Fourth Amendment was respected, or it wasn't. The warrant's timing was specific, and the officers chose to ignore it."

Barrett put on a show to consider the argument, even though Josef knew it was all theater. "Do we have testimony from the officers regarding the timing of entry?"

"Yes, Your Honor," Wright said, gaining some confidence. "Detective Sergeant Phillips, who led the raid, is present and can testify to the circumstances."

Barrett nodded, maintaining the appearance of judicial impartiality. "Let's hear from the detective."

Detective Sergeant Phillips was summoned forward and sworn in. With twenty-two years of service in the Narcotics Division, Phillips presented a commanding presence in his crisp uniform.

"Detective," Wright began, "can you explain the circumstances surrounding the execution of the search warrant at 2010 Pelican Street on April 17th?"

Phillips nodded. "We arrived at the location at approximately 5:45 AM and established a perimeter. Our intention was to enter precisely at 6:00 AM, as specified in the warrant. However, at approximately 5:52 AM, we observed individuals inside the warehouse moving what appeared to be large packages toward the rear exit."

"And what did you conclude from this observation?" Wright asked.

"Based on my experience, I believed they were attempting to remove evidence, specifically, the narcotics we were there to seize. I made the tactical decision to enter immediately rather than risk losing the evidence."

Wright looked relieved. "So, your early entry was based on exigent circumstances?"

"Objection," Beaumont interrupted. "Counsel is leading the witness."

"Sustained," Barrett said promptly. "Rephrase, Counselor."

Wright nodded. "Detective Phillips, what was your reasoning for entering before the time specified in the warrant?"

"To preserve evidence that I believed was in imminent danger of being removed or destroyed," Phillips answered firmly.

Wright turned to the judge. "Your Honor, the Supreme Court has consistently held that exigent circumstances, such as the imminent destruction of evidence, create an exception to normal warrant requirements. Detective Phillips made a reasonable judgment call based on his observations and experience."

Beaumont rose again. "If I may, Your Honor?"

Barrett gestured for him to proceed.

"Detective Phillips," Beaumont began his cross-examination, "did you document these alleged 'exigent circumstances' in your official report?"

Phillips hesitated for a moment. "I noted that we observed movement inside the warehouse."

"But did you specifically document that you believed evidence was being destroyed or removed? Did you use the phrase 'exigent circumstances' anywhere in your report?"

"Not in those exact words, no."

"In fact," Beaumont continued, producing a document, "in your official report, you simply stated, and I quote, 'Entry was made at 0552 hours.' I don't see anything mentioned about suspicious movements, nor any indication that potential evidence was removed. Isn't that correct?"

Phillips shifted uncomfortably. "The report is a summary. Not every detail is included."

"A convenient omission, wouldn't you say?" Beaumont pressed. "And were these supposed 'suspicious movements' captured on any body cameras worn by officers at the scene?"

"We were not wearing body cameras during this operation."

"No body cameras," Beaumont repeated for emphasis. "So, we have no visual evidence to corroborate your claim about suspicious movements— a claim, I might add, that wasn't deemed important enough to include in your official report."

"Objection," Wright interjected. "Counsel is badgering the witness."

"I'm just setting the record straight, Your Honor," Beaumont replied calmly.

Barrett waved his hand. "I'll allow it. But watch your tone, Counselor."

Beaumont nodded respectfully. "Detective Phillips, when you entered the warehouse at 5:52 AM, did you find anyone in the act of removing or destroying evidence?"

"No," Phillips admitted. "The suspects were apprehended inside the warehouse."

"And the five kilograms of fentanyl—they were found where?"

"In a storage room at the rear of the warehouse."

"Packaged and stored, not in the process of being removed or destroyed?"

Phillips's jaw tightened. "That's correct."

"Thank you, Detective," Beaumont said, returning to his seat with the satisfied air of a cat that had cornered its prey.

Wright, sensing the case slipping away, tried to recover during redirect. "Detective Phillips, based on your extensive experience in narcotics enforcement, do suspects typically document their attempts to destroy evidence?"

"No, they don't."

"And in your professional judgment, were your actions reasonable given the circumstances you believed you were facing?"

"Absolutely," Phillips affirmed. "We had reliable intelligence that the warehouse contained a significant quantity of narcotics. When we observed movement inside, I made a split-second decision to secure the premises and the evidence."

"No further questions," Wright said.

After Phillips was dismissed, Barrett called for closing arguments on the motion to suppress.

Wright went first, his initial nervousness now replaced with the passion of someone fighting a battle he believed in. "Your Honor, the State contends that the search of the warehouse was reasonable and constitutional. While the entry occurred eight minutes before the time specified in the warrant, Detective Phillips acted on a good-faith belief that evidence was at risk. The Supreme Court has consistently recognized that the preservation of evidence constitutes exigent circumstances that may justify deviations from standard procedures."

He continued, gaining confidence. "Furthermore, the time specification in the warrant was primarily to ensure the search didn't occur during nighttime hours, which would raise additional Fourth Amendment concerns. The eight-minute discrepancy did not materially affect the defendant's rights or the fundamental fairness of the process. To suppress five kilograms of deadly fentanyl—enough to kill thousands of our citizens—based on an eight-minute technicality would be a miscarriage of justice."

Wright's argument was surprisingly compelling for such a junior prosecutor. Josef felt a momentary flicker of concern, but then reminded himself that the outcome had been decided long before anyone entered the courtroom.

Beaumont rose for his closing argument. "Your Honor, the Constitution is not a document of convenience. The Fourth Amendment protections against unreasonable search and seizure are fundamental to our legal system. The warrant explicitly stated 6:00 AM, not 'around 6:00 AM.'"

He paced slightly, his voice resonating through the courtroom. "Detective Phillips' post-hoc justification about 'suspicious movements' is conspicuously absent from his official report, suggesting it may be a convenient fabrication designed to excuse a procedural violation. Even if we accept his testimony at face value, the fact remains that no evidence was actually being destroyed or removed when officers entered."

Beaumont gestured toward Rodriguez. "My client has the right to expect that law enforcement will follow the explicit instructions of a warrant. This court should not endorse a 'close enough' approach to constitutional rights. The proper remedy for this violation is clear and well-established: suppression of all evidence obtained through the improper search."

Barrett nodded, maintaining the illusion that he was carefully weighing both arguments. He shuffled some papers, consulted a legal text on his bench, and finally looked up.

"This court takes Fourth Amendment protections very seriously," he began. "While I appreciate the State's argument regarding exigent circumstances, I find several problems with its application here. First, the lack of documentation regarding the allegedly suspicious movements raises questions about whether this justification was contemporaneous with the decision to enter early or developed after the fact."

Wright's face fell as he realized he was about to lose the motion.

"Second," Barrett continued, "even accepting Detective Phillips' testimony in its entirety, the fact that no evidence was actually being destroyed or removed when officers entered suggests that the exigency may have been perceived rather than actual."

Barrett removed his glasses, a gesture he often employed when delivering a significant ruling. "After careful consideration of the facts and relevant case law, this court finds that the execution of the search warrant failed to meet the strict requirements specified in the document itself. The time discrepancy, while seemingly minor, represents a substantive procedural error."

Josef allowed himself a small, satisfied smile as Barrett continued.

"As such, all evidence obtained through said warrant must be suppressed. Without this evidence, I understand the State has insufficient cause to proceed. Is that correct, Mr. Wright?"

Wright stood, defeated. "That's correct, Your Honor. The State has no case without the physical evidence."

"Then this court has no choice but to dismiss case number 47293, State versus Rodriguez. The defendant is to be released forthwith." Barrett brought down his gavel with an air of finality.

Rodriguez remained impressively stoic, showing no reaction to his predictable victory. Only the slightest glance toward Josef in the gallery betrayed any acknowledgment of the Domingo organization's role in securing his freedom.

As people began filing out of the courtroom, ADA Wright gathered his materials, his face a mask of frustration. He couldn't shake the thought that the whole thing had been orchestrated. The case had looked too tidy from the start.

Josef made his way out of the courthouse, pleased with how smoothly everything had gone. The system had worked exactly as intended. Even with Wright's unexpected competence, the outcome had never been in doubt.

He dialed Jean-Paul's private number. "It's done," he reported simply. "Barrett performed exactly as expected. Case dismissed."

"Any complications?" Jean-Paul asked.

"None worth mentioning. The prosecutor showed more fight than anticipated, but Barrett maintained control throughout. Rodriguez will be released within the hour."

"Excellent," Jean-Paul replied. "See that Rodriguez receives the usual compensation for his inconvenience. And Josef? Remind him that our appreciation comes with the expectation of continued loyalty."

"Of course," Josef confirmed. "I'll make that very clear."

After ending the call, Josef glanced back at the courthouse. Another day, another case dismissed, another victory for the Domingo organization. The machinery of justice in New Orleans continued to operate precisely as they had designed it, not in service of the law but in service of those with the money and power to bend it to their will.

CHAPTER 21

JEAN-PAUL DOMINGO'S study carried the weight of wealth and history. Late afternoon light came through the stained-glass windows, coloring the rugs beneath, their patterns faded by time and use. The grandfather clock in the corner ticked steadily, its brass pendulum swinging in time. It had stood in that room for generations, marking the rise of the Domingo name.

Josef Mendoza sat across from Jean-Paul, his usually composed demeanor betraying hints of concern. As the family's legal advisor for over fifteen years, Josef rarely arrived unannounced. The fact that he had done so today spoke volumes about the urgency of his news.

"You're certain about this?" Jean-Paul asked, his voice calm despite the potentially alarming information Josef had just shared.

"My source at the precinct is reliable," Josef confirmed. "Two narcotics detectives have been investigating Judge Taylor's death for weeks now. Dubois and Griffith. They were specifically pulled from narcotics to handle this case. Homicide should have taken the lead, but someone deliberately put these two on it instead."

Jean-Paul leaned back in his leather chair, steepling his fingers. The chair had been his father's and grandfather's before him. Three generations of crime lords had sat in this very spot, making decisions that shaped New Orleans' underworld.

"Narcotics detectives investigating a dead judge. That is... unusual," Jean-Paul said.

"It's more than just unusual," Josef said, pressing the point. "It's intentional."

"Who's their commanding officer?"

"Roy Simmons," replied Josef. "The same Roy Simmons who served with Taylor in the NOPD years ago, before Taylor went to law school."

Jean-Paul's eyes narrowed slightly—the only visible sign of his concern. "Old connections. Old loyalties."

"Exactly." Josef leaned forward. "My source says the detectives have been thorough. They've interviewed everyone who contacted Taylor in his final days, obtained dental records and medical histories, returned to the crime scene multiple times, and spent over an hour with his secretary."

Jean-Paul stood by the window, gazing at the manicured gardens of his mansion. The blooming roses contrasted sharply with the dark thoughts in his mind. Three gardeners worked silently among the hedges, maintaining the immaculate grounds featured in Southern Living magazine, part of the facade of legitimacy the Domingo family had preserved for generations.

"This is concerning, Josef, particularly with the upcoming shipment." He turned back to face his advisor. "What do these detectives know?"

"That's what worries me," Josef admitted. "My source couldn't say for certain. They're keeping their investigation unusually quiet. Even within the department, few people know what leads they're pursuing."

Jean-Paul returned to his desk and pressed an intercom button. "Antoine, Michael. My study. Now."

Within minutes, Antoine, his son, and Michael Reeves had joined them. Antoine slouched in a chair with the casual arrogance that often irritated his father, while Michael remained standing, alert and attentive as always.

"We may have a problem," Jean-Paul began without hesitation. "Two narcotics detectives have been investigating Taylor's death."

Michael's expression remained neutral, but his eyes sharpened with interest. "Which detectives?"

"Dubois and Griffith," Josef supplied. "Experienced officers, good records. Normally work major drug cases."

"I know who they are," Michael said carefully.

Antoine's eyes focused hard on Reeves. "How do you know them, Michael?"

"It's my job to know all who work in narcotics," Michael fired back. "They're thorough, persistent. Not the type to give up easily."

Antoine waved a dismissive hand. "So what? Let them investigate. There's nothing to find. The judge was found in the swamp, half-eaten by gators. No evidence, no witnesses."

"The fact that narcotics detectives were specifically assigned to this case suggests otherwise," Jean-Paul said sharply. "Someone suspects a connection between Taylor's death and narcotics, possibly our organization."

Michael felt a chill run through him. If Taylor had left behind evidence, if these detectives had somehow found it, they would be walking into the same danger that had gotten the judge killed. And Michael had his suspicions about who had arranged that killing—the same man slouching in the chair beside him, trying to appear unconcerned.

"Antoine," Jean-Paul said, his eyes fixed as he studied his son, "I need you to find out exactly what these detectives know. Find out if they have any concrete evidence linking our organization to Taylor or his death."

Antoine straightened, suddenly interested. "And if they do?"

"Then handle the situation," Jean-Paul replied, his voice firm. "Quietly. Discreetly. But effectively."

Michael kept his facial expressionless, though alarm bells rang in his head. He knew Jean-Paul didn't like ordering executions, but, when necessary, he would. "Handle the situation" was Domingo's euphemism for eliminating the problem permanently.

"As good as done," Antoine said, a smile playing at the corners of his mouth.

"No bodies," Jean-Paul cautioned. "Find out what they know first. If they have evidence, we need to know what it is and who else might have access to it. Then you can decide the appropriate response."

Antoine nodded, clearly pleased with the assignment. "I'll start immediately. I'll contact Vega, have him meet me at the usual place. We'll put surveillance on them, track their movements."

"Good," Jean-Paul replied. "Report back to me once you have something concrete."

"Michael," Jean-Paul continued, "in the meantime, the shipment proceeds as planned. Double-check all security arrangements. Make absolutely certain we're not exposed."

"Yes sir," Michael said, his mind racing with the implications of what was happening. "I've added additional counter-surveillance measures as a precaution."

Jean-Paul nodded, satisfied. "Good. Antoine, keep me informed of your progress. I want regular updates on what these detectives know and what actions you're taking."

"Of course, Father," Antoine said with a show of respect that Michael knew was just a pretense. Antoine only knew one way to get rid of a problem.

"That's all for now," Jean-Paul concluded. "Josef, stay behind. I have another matter to discuss."

As they left the study, Michael watched Antoine pull out his phone, presumably to contact Vega. He knew he had to move quickly. Antoine was ruthlessly efficient when motivated, and Jean-Paul had just provided plenty of motivation. Those detectives were now walking targets, and they had no idea.

CHAPTER 22

MICHAEL DROVE HIS Audi through the streets of New Orleans, keeping a careful eye on his rearview mirror. Three years of deep cover had taught him to be paranoid, to assume he was always being watched. But today, that paranoia might save two lives.

He parked in the Central Business District, entering an office building that housed several law firms. Using a keycard that identified him as a consultant for Jason & Whitney LLC—one of several cover identities he maintained separate from his Domingo persona—he took the elevator to the twelfth floor, walked through the empty reception area after hours, and entered a small office room.

Once inside, he removed a laptop from a locked cabinet and powered it up. The FBI had provided him with certain resources that even his handlers were unaware of—emergency measures specifically designed for situations like this. Among them was limited access to the NOPD's vehicle tracking system, a necessary tool for monitoring potential threats to his cover.

Within minutes, he had located three vehicles registered to the Narcotics Division, one of which was currently assigned to Detectives Renee Dubois and Kelsey Griffith. According to the GPS tracking data, their vehicle was currently at NOPD headquarters.

Michael checked his watch. If Antoine was contacting Vega, they'd likely meet first to plan their approach. That gave him perhaps a two-hour window before they began active surveillance. He needed to find the detectives before Antoine did.

He returned to his car and drove to the precinct, parking across the street so he could observe the main entrance and the staff parking lot. The wait stretched longer than expected, giving Antoine time to reach out to Vega and possibly locate the detectives first.

At 5:38 PM, Michael saw Renee leaving the building alone. He knew he had to speak with both detectives together for this to work—separate meetings would be too dangerous, too easy for Antoine to intercept.

She walked quickly to a sedan in the corner of the parking lot and drove off. Michael followed at a safe distance, being careful not to get too close. Unlike Antoine, who would probably have Vega plant tracking devices on the detectives' vehicles, Michael needed to make direct contact. Face to face was the only way to convince them their lives were in immediate danger.

He followed Detective Dubois across town, maintaining a careful distance as she navigated through early evening traffic. She was more skilled than he'd expected, taking random turns occasionally, doubling back once—the moves of someone who knew how to spot a tail. Michael kept his distance, sometimes letting several cars come between them, using his instincts and training to anticipate her route rather than following directly. She was heading away from the tourist areas and into neighborhoods where cash transactions and few questions were the norm.

After twenty minutes of careful maneuvering, she pulled into the parking lot of the Gateway Motel, a faded two-story structure on Airline Highway. The motel was a relic from the 1950s, the kind of place that had once catered to families on road trips but now served a clientele more interested in discretion than amenities. The neon sign at the entrance flickered erratically, several letters burnt out, giving the establishment an even more disreputable appearance. It was perfect for what the detectives needed—a temporary, makeshift location away from prying eyes, since no one at the station could be trusted.

Michael drove past without slowing, noting Renee entering a ground-floor room—114, according to the faded number on the door. He circled the block twice, studying the layout and checking for any vehicles that might have followed either of them.

CHAPTER 23

THE GATEWAY MOTEL had seen better days, much better days. The motel was a classic horseshoe design, two stories with exterior corridors and staircases at either end. Room 114 was on the ground floor, facing the parking lot. Not ideal from a security standpoint—too exposed, too many sight lines—but typical for cops working a case who needed quick access to their vehicle.

Its stucco exterior was cracked and discolored, painted a faded blue that might have been fashionable half a century ago. The concrete walkways showed signs of settling and decades of neglect. A small, kidney-shaped pool in the center courtyard had been drained years ago and now served as an impromptu trash receptacle for cigarette butts, empty beer cans, and debris that told stories of countless transient encounters.

For all its dilapidation, the motel offered exactly what the detectives needed—anonymity and affordability. The kind of place where the desk clerk wouldn't ask questions if you paid in cash and extended your stay day by day. The kind of place where temporary residents minded their own business, and surveillance cameras were either broken or never installed in the first place.

Michael parked two blocks away and sat for fifteen minutes, watching every vehicle that entered the area. His biggest concern now was timing—Antoine had more than enough time to get Vega and follow Renee to the motel. No suspicious vehicles appeared— no cars circling the block. Michael was good to go.

He approached on foot, keeping to the shadows cast by the motel's spotty exterior lighting. Several bulbs had burnt out and never been replaced, creating convenient pockets of darkness. He made his way to the back of the property, where a chain-link fence separated the motel from an abandoned lot overgrown with weeds and debris.

The fence presented little challenge for someone with his training. Scaling it easily, Michael dropped silently into the tall grass on the other side. From there, he worked his way around to the front of the building, staying low and avoiding the few areas where working lights created exposure zones. The front desk area glowed with the blue light of a television, where a bored attendant sat absorbed in whatever was playing on the screen. Not that it mattered—this was the kind of place where the attendant wouldn't care who came and went anyway. People appeared and disappeared at all hours, and questions weren't part of the business model.

Michael made his way down the exterior walkway, noting the few guests moving between their rooms—a woman in a bathrobe heading to the ice machine, a man in a wrinkled suit fumbling with his room key. The kind of transient population that made anonymity possible.

Seconds later, he stood outside Room 114, listening carefully for any sounds within. He could hear muffled voices—two people engaged in conversation. Both detectives were inside, exactly as he'd hoped. Taking a deep breath and knowing there was no turning back, Michael knocked softly on the door.

The voices immediately fell silent. After a moment, he heard footsteps approaching the door.

"Who is it?" a male voice called.

"Detective Griffith. You don't know me, but I need to speak with you about Judge Taylor."

The door opened a crack, chain still in place. Kelsey Griffith's wary eye appeared in the gap. "What about Judge Taylor?"

"I have information about his death," Michael said quietly. "And about why you and Detective Dubois are in danger."

"Who are you?" Kelsey's hand had moved to his side, where his weapon would be holstered.

"My name is Michael Reeves. I work for the Domingo organization," Michael said, seeing shock flash across Kelsey's face. "Actually, I'm an undercover FBI agent who's been infiltrating them for three years. And right now, you and your partner are in grave danger."

"You expect me to believe that?"

"Check my credentials," Michael said, carefully reaching into his jacket to produce an FBI badge and ID. "Call the New Orleans field office. Ask for Special Agent Carl Pinkins. Tell him 'Nighthawk' is breaking protocol. He won't be happy, but he'll confirm who I am."

The door closed. Michael could hear muffled voices inside—Kelsey and presumably Renee Dubois, discussing what to do. After what seemed like an eternity, the door opened again, but only a crack. This time, Kelsey had his weapon drawn, though held low at his side.

"Show me your credentials again. Slowly," he instructed.

Michael carefully reached into his jacket and produced his FBI badge and ID, holding them out where Kelsey could examine them closely.

"Come in," Kelsey said finally, stepping back. "But keep your hands where we can see them.

"I thought you said your name was Michael Reeves."

"I'm undercover as Michael Reeves." As he entered the room, he found himself face-to-face with Detective Renee Dubois, her revolver pointed straight at his chest. Her stance was solid and ready to fire at any moment—the kind of cop who was completely at ease with a firearm.

"Don't move," she said, her voice strong and authoritative. "We're going to verify your story."

The motel room was standard budget accommodations—two double beds, one stacked on top of the other and pushed against the wall to make space for a temporary office, with a corkboard attached to the wall and a small round table that functioned as a desk, along with a bathroom that was last updated during the Clinton administration. Kelsey kept his eyes on Michael while dialing the New Orleans FBI field office. After a brief exchange with the person who answered, he asked for Special Agent Carl Pinkins.

"This is Detective Kelsey Griffith, NOPD. I'm calling about an agent who claims to be working undercover with the Domingo organization." He paused, listening for a response. "He instructed me to tell you that 'Nighthawk' is breaking protocol." Kelsey's expression changed as he listened to the response. After a moment, he held the phone out. "He wants to speak with you."

Michael took the phone, keeping his movements slow and deliberate with Renee's weapon still trained on him. "It's me."

"What the hell are you doing?" Wells' voice was cold with anger. "You're compromising three years of work."

"They need to know. These detectives are marked."

"That's not your call to make."

"Too late now. Just confirm my identity so we can move forward."

A heavy sigh came through the line. "Fine. But this conversation isn't over."

Michael handed the phone back to Kelsey, who listened for another moment before ending the call.

"He confirmed you're FBI," Kelsey said, holstering his weapon. "He didn't sound happy about it."

"I'm breaking cover," Michael explained. "That's frowned upon, especially this close to an operation."

"Why take the risk?" Kelsey asked.

"Because Antoine Domingo has been ordered to find out what you know about Taylor and then, in his father's words, 'handle the situation.' Michael saw understanding flash in both detectives' eyes. "In Domingo's speech, that means making you disappear if necessary."

"Why warn us?" Renee pressed. "Why risk your operation?"

Michael's gaze moved to the corkboard—Taylor's notebook was visible among the documents. "Because I knew Judge Taylor. I was his source inside the Domingo organization. And I have reason to believe Antoine was behind his murder."

Kelsey and Renee exchanged glances. "You're telling us you were working with Taylor?" Kelsey asked.

"I was placed undercover to gather evidence on the Domingo drug operation. But after a year inside, I started noticing patterns—cases getting dismissed, evidence disappearing, witnesses changing their testimony." Michael paused, his expression hardening. "Jean-Paul would occasionally mention judges who were 'understanding' of his organization. I conducted my research and found that Judge Taylor never presided over a Domingo trial. I took a chance and approached him directly. And I was glad I did."

Michael glanced between the detectives. "Taylor had been investigating why cases involving Jean-Paul himself kept getting dismissed. He'd noticed the same patterns I had, but from the judicial side. We formed an alliance—me gathering evidence from inside the organization while Taylor tracked the corruption in the courts. Together, we were building a case to take down not just the Domingo operation but the entire network of corrupt officials protecting it."

Michael nodded. "The FBI was focused on the drug trafficking. Taylor was interested in the corruption that protected it—the judges, prosecutors, police officials, all on the Domingo payroll. We helped each other. He got information about the organization. I got a clearer picture of how the corruption worked."

"Why are you breaking cover now?" Kelsey asked. "If your operation is so close to completion?"

"Because Antoine is dangerous. Impulsive. And if he killed Taylor to protect the organization, he won't hesitate to kill you both." Michael gestured to the notebook. "Especially if you've found what Taylor was gathering."

"Which was?" Renee prompted.

"Evidence of systematic corruption throughout the New Orleans justice system. A network designed to protect the Domingo organization while creating the illusion of law enforcement." Michael moved closer to the table. "Taylor documented it all—which judges were paid off, which prosecutors were compromised, how cases were assigned to ensure they'd be dismissed."

Kelsey nodded slowly. "That's exactly what we've been piecing together from his notes."

"And that's why you're in danger," Michael said firmly. "Antoine and his father can't afford for that evidence to come to light. The drug operation is just business to them—if it's compromised, they take the loss and rebuild. But the corruption? That's their insurance policy. Their protection. They'll kill to keep it secret."

Renee moved to the window, carefully peering through a gap in the curtains. "So, what happens now? We've got Antoine Domingo gunning for us and an FBI agent telling us we're marked for death. Not exactly how I planned to spend the evening."

"In less than seventy-two hours, the FBI is raiding a major Domingo shipment at Pier 9. It's the culmination of my three years undercover. Once that happens, I can testify against the organization." Michael looked between them. "But that still leaves the corruption network Taylor was investigating."

"Which the FBI isn't interested in," Kelsey surmised.

"They're focused on the drug trafficking. The corruption investigation would involve taking down judges, prosecutors, police officials—messy, complicated, politically sensitive. They'd rather build their drug case, get their convictions, and move on."

"But Taylor was killed because of what he uncovered about the corruption," Renee said. "Not just the drug operation."

"Exactly." Michael's voice hardened. "And I'm not going to let his killers walk free. The drug bust will take down the Domingo organization. But the corruption? That's still out there, still protecting people who deserve to face justice."

Kelsey and Renee exchanged looks again, some unspoken communication passing between them.

"We need to get you out of here," Michael said.

"I can help you relocate. Somewhere, Antoine won't think to look. And after the operation, I can provide official testimony that corroborates Taylor's evidence."

"Why should we trust you?" Renee asked bluntly. "For all we know, this could be an elaborate setup."

"You've verified my FBI credentials," Wells said evenly. "And I'm risking my cover just by being here."

He nodded toward the open notebook on the table. "That's Taylor's, isn't it?"

Renee didn't respond. She didn't blink. Just stared at him.

"May I see it?" he asked.

She reached over and closed the notebook slowly, deliberately.

Wells didn't press. He simply said, "Then flip through it. Look for the initials—MW. I was with Taylor when he wrote that."

Renee hesitated, then reopened the notebook and began flipping through the pages. Midway through, her hand stilled. Her eyes locked on a line of handwritten notes, scribbled and half-faded. She looked up.

"You see it," Wells said quietly. "I know you do."

He stepped closer, voice low and steady. "MW—that's me. Taylor was working with the FBI. He fed us everything he could, quietly, off the record. He never used my name—only the initials-in case something like this happened. That notebook proves we were building a case."

Renee's jaw tensed.

Wells continued, "Those anonymous calls you and Griffith kept getting? That was me. I couldn't come forward—not yet. But I was trying to steer you where Taylor would've wanted you to go."

Kelsey stepped forward, arms crossed. "You knew they were going to kill him."

"No," Wells said quickly. "I didn't. But I overheard Antoine Domingo say, 'Taylor's been taken care of.'. I tried calling Taylor after that, every hour. All weekend. Nothing."

Kelsey narrowed his eyes. "So how'd you know it was him in the swamp?"

"I didn't," Wells said. "Not until I heard you two were going out there. Somebody mentioned a floater with a Loyola ring."

"Who told you that?" Renee asked.

Wells looked at her. "Taylor had a connection with Simmons. He trusted him. Asked him to put his best detectives on that case. And he followed your work, both of you. He knew you were in narcotics, saw how you flagged drug cases getting tossed on technicalities. He was planning to bring you in—as soon as he had enough to make it stick."

Renee's eyes narrowed. "How'd you know what we talked about in the car?"

Wells took a breath. "Because I bugged your Crown Vic."

Kelsey blinked. "You what?"

"I needed a way to track your progress. To help, without being seen. When you talked in the car about the floater, the Loyola ring, I put two and two together. That's when I knew. If I hadn't done it... you'd still be chasing shadows. I was trying to keep the case alive, even after Taylor went silent."

Renee's voice was quiet, but sharp. "You had no right."

"No right but every reason," Wells replied. "Because now Taylor's dead. And the people who did it? They're still out there."

"Alright," Renee said, looking up from the notebook. Her expression was still cautious, but less hostile. "If we're going to believe you, what's your plan?"

"First, we get you to a better location." Michael thought quickly. "I have a safe house the Bureau doesn't know about. I set it up as insurance in case my cover was ever compromised. You'll be secure there until the operation is complete."

"And then?" Kelsey asked.

"Then we combine forces. Taylor's evidence, my testimony, your investigation. Together, we can build a case against not just the Domingo drug operation but the entire corruption network that's protected it for decades."

They stood there in silence. Outside, a car pulled into the lot, its tires crunching over the rough asphalt. Renee glanced out the window.

"Just a guest checking in," she said. "What do we do about Domingo's men?"

Michael paused for a moment. "We set them up. They're definitely after you. I managed to find you first, but they're not far behind."

"So, what's the plan?" Kelsey asked as he started gathering the evidence they had laid out.

"This is actually an opportunity," Michael said, his eyes focused as he formulated a plan. "Here's what's going to happen: finish up here and drive back to the precinct tonight."

"And then what?"

"Tomorrow morning, get in your department vehicle and drive it to Café Du Monde. Antoine will follow you—that's a certainty. He's predictable in his methods."

Michael leaned against the dresser. "Park the car in front of the building, but somewhere Antoine can't see you. He's going to put a tracker on it. He'll want to monitor your movements before making any move against you. His objective is to find out what you know."

Kelsey's expression changed. "You want to catch them in the act."

"Exactly. I'll arrange for pictures to be taken when they place the tracker. We can use the photos to implicate them for surveilling police officers— something concrete we can use in court later.

"Then, after they leave, I'll notify you that the coast is clear, and you can slip out to the walkway behind Café Du Monde and leave the car where it is. Find alternative transportation—don't use your department vehicle again. Tell Simmons to have it towed back to the station. Don't let anyone drive it back; you don't know who you can trust.

"And don't go back to the station. It will take a while for them to figure out what happened. Antoine won't know where to look.

"After that, we go after everyone involved in Taylor's death and finish the work he started."

Renee studied Michael for a moment. "You've really thought this through," she said finally, a note of admiration in her voice. "I'm impressed."

Michael shrugged. "Three years undercover teaches you to plan ten steps ahead. Now, gather what you need."

As Kelsey packed away Taylor's notebook and the files, Renee asked, "Where will we meet you again?"

"After you ditch the car tomorrow, go to Jackson Square. There's a café on the northeast corner—Petite Amelie. I'll have someone meet you there and escort you to a safe location. Antoine will be focused on your unit at the Precinct."

Renee nodded, a firm but assuring look settling over her. "And then we finish what Taylor started."

"Exactly," Michael said, moving toward the door. "I'll leave first. Remember—act natural. As far as Antoine knows, you have no idea you're even on his radar."

"Be careful," Kelsey said. "If Antoine suspects you're working with us..."

"I've spent three years fooling the entire Domingo organization," Michael replied. "I can manage a little while longer."

As Michael slipped out the door, Renee turned to Kelsey. "What do you think? Can we trust him?"

Kelsey looked at the vacated doorway. "We verified his FBI credentials. And he knew about Taylor's notes—the 'MW reference. Plus, he's risking his entire operation to warn us."

"True," Renee acknowledged. "And that plan to catch Antoine placing a tracker... he's really several steps ahead of everyone, isn't he?"

"Seems so," Kelsey thought for a moment. "I hope his plan works."

* * *

Morning sunlight streamed through the iconic green awnings of Café Du Monde as Renee pulled the department vehicle into a parking spot. exactly as Michael had instructed, then the two detectives entered the busy café, choosing a table by the window where they could watch the unit while remaining partially obscured.

Renee and Kelsey ordered café au lait and beignets, just as they did every morning. maintaining the appearance of their routine coffee break. Twenty minutes later, her phone buzzed with a text from an unknown number: "Bait is set, see you in a few."

About thirty minutes later, another text 'fish has arrived." Renee casually glanced down the street, spotting Antoine Domingo's sleek car idling across from where she parked. Moments later, another text. 'Fish took the bait.' Glancing one more time, she saw Antoine and Vega's car now pulling away."

Leaving cash on the table, two detectives slipped out, disappearing into the Quarter's labyrinth of alleys without ever returning to their vehicle.

CHAPTER 24

MICHAEL REEVES DROVE through the rain-slicked streets of New Orleans, his windshield wipers keeping time with his racing thoughts. The city lights reflected off the wet pavement like a thousand watchful eyes.

Three years of deep cover had made paranoia his constant companion. It had kept him alive in a world where a single misstep meant death. Now, as the clock ticked down toward the operation that would take down the Domingo organization, that same paranoia might be the only thing preventing his cover from being blown.

As he approached the wrought iron gates of the Domingo estate, Michael composed himself, settling back into the identity he'd crafted so carefully. Michael Reeves, trusted lieutenant. Michael Reeves, security expert. Michael Reeves, the man who had earned Jean-Paul Domingo's confidence through calculated competence and unwavering loyalty.

Gone was Special Agent Marcus Wells of the FBI, who had just committed the cardinal sin of undercover work—breaking protocol. That could jeopardize the workings of a three-year-long investigation.

The gates opened at his approach, security cameras tracking his vehicle as he drove up the curved driveway lined with ancient oak trees. Three generations of Domingos had built their empire from this house, extending their influence through the city like poison through veins.

In the three years since infiltrating the organization, Michael had mapped every corner of the estate, including its security systems, escape routes, and blind spots. This knowledge would serve the FBI well the night they moved in, but it also made him responsible for every criminal transaction he'd witnessed and not immediately reported during that time.

He parked his Audi next to Antoine's Maserati, noticing the still-warm hood. Antoine had returned recently, likely from tying up loose ends for the incoming shipment. The countdown to the operation had everyone on edge, and Antoine's nervousness usually manifested as hyperactivity, constantly checking and rechecking details.

Inside, the mansion was quiet, as most of the staff had retired for the night. Michael moved through the grand foyer, where light spilled from beneath Jean-Paul's study door—the patriarch keeping his usual hours.

Michael headed for the kitchen instead, knowing Antoine's habits. Sure enough, he found the younger Domingo leaning against the granite island, a tumbler of bourbon in his hand, his suit jacket discarded over a chair.

"Long night?" Michael asked casually, opening the refrigerator.

Antoine glanced up, catching a brief glimpse of Michael. "Thought you'd be home by now, burning the candle at both ends..."

Michael grabbed a bottle of water, noticing the slight slur in Antoine's words. The man had been drinking heavily; drunk men often miss details, which could work to his advantage.

"Just finished reviewing security protocols. Wanted to make sure everything's airtight." He unscrewed the cap and took a drink. "You look like you've been busy, too."

Antoine glanced at Michael with a fake smile. Just handling some precautionary measures for my father. Those detectives we've been concerned about."

"Find anything interesting?" Michael kept his tone carefully neutral, professional curiosity rather than personal interest.

"Tracked them back to their precinct." Antoine rolled his glass between his palms. "Tomorrow, the tracker Vega put on their vehicle will let us know where they go."

"Smart," Michael said, leaning against the counter. "Need any help with that? I could have some of my team assist."

Antoine waved dismissively. "Vega's handling it. Don't worry about it—focus on the shipment. That's where we need your expertise." He drained his glass, reaching for the bourbon bottle to pour another. "Besides, Vega has been tracking vehicles for me for some time. All kinds of vehicles, Michael. All kinds."

Antoine's statement caught Michael off guard. Had Antoine become suspicious of him?

"Those detectives have no idea what they're dealing with, Right, Michael?"

Michael paused, still turning over Antoine's words in his mind—*'all kinds of vehicles.'*

Was Antoine just being cryptic, or was there something more to it? A deeper implication that Michael hadn't considered? He kept his expression unreadable, but the unease gnawed at him. If Vega had been tracking more than just the detectives, who else was under surveillance? And why?

Antoine poured another drink, His eyes fixed firmly on Michael. "Relax, Reeves. Just focus on what you do best."

Michael nodded slowly, but his mind was already racing. He adjusted his composure, trying to steer the conversation back on track.

"Detectives in Narcotics aren't to be underestimated," Michael cautioned. "They've seen their share of operations."

"And so have we." He swirled the bourbon in his glass, the clink of the ice breaking the silence. "But that doesn't mean we're blind to what's happening around us. Stay sharp, Michael. It's not just the shipment that's at stake here."

Antoine's eyes narrowed. "You're awfully concerned about these detectives."

"I'm concerned about anything that might compromise the shipment," Michael replied. "It's the biggest one we've ever handled. Ten million in product at risk. I don't like variables."

The tension stretched between them for a moment before Antoine relaxed. "True enough, but they're a minor issue that's being handled." He raised his glass in a mock toast. "Soon, we'll be celebrating the most successful shipment in Domingo history."

Michael forced a smile, raising his water bottle in return. "To success."

Antoine swallowed hard, then set his glass down with a sharp click against the granite. "You know what I never understood about you, Michael? Three years with us, and you're still such a mystery. No family we've ever met, no relationships, no personal life beyond your work."

"That's why I'm good at what I do," Michael replied. "No distractions."

"Or is it because you're hiding something?" Antoine's tone was light, conversational, but his eyes had sharpened.

Michael felt adrenaline spike through his system. This was danger—the real kind, the kind that had ended other deep cover operations. Antoine's paranoia, fueled by alcohol and the pressure of tomorrow's shipment, was leading him down a dangerous path.

"We all have things we don't share, Antoine," Michael said carefully. "Private matters. But nothing that affects my loyalty to your father or this organization."

"My father trusts you implicitly," Antoine said, a trace of bitterness creeping into his voice. "Sometimes I think he trusts you more than me, his own son."

And there it was—the real issue. Antoine's jealousy had been simmering for months, becoming increasingly evident as Jean-Paul relied more heavily on Michael for crucial operations.

"Your father values your judgment," Michael offered diplomatically. "He's placed you in charge of major aspects of the business."

"Yet it's you he consults first; you he listens to." Antoine pushed away from the counter, stepping closer to Michael. Close enough that Michael could smell the bourbon on his breath. "Tell me, Michael, what's your secret? How did you earn such trust so quickly?"

Before Michael could respond, the kitchen door swung open. Jean-Paul Domingo entered, still dressed in his tailored suit despite the evening hour. His silver hair caught the light, his expression unreadable as he observed the two men.

"Antoine. Michael." His voice was quiet but carried the familiar tone of authority. "I thought I heard voices."

Antoine straightened, instinctively adjusting his posture in his father's presence. "We were just discussing the arrangements, Father."

"At this hour? With that much bourbon in your system?" Jean-Paul's disapproval was evident. "The shipment requires clear heads, Antoine. I suggest you get some rest."

The dismissal was apparent. Antoine's jaw tightened, but he nodded. "Of course, Father. Good night." He shot Michael a final, unreadable look before departing.

Michael watched him go, knowing full well that despite Jean-Paul's orders, Antoine wouldn't be heading home to rest. The night was still young, and Antoine's drinking was far from over.

Silence filled the kitchen as Jean-Paul studied Michael, the older man's eyes missing nothing. Michael maintained his composure.

"My son has always struggled with jealousy," Jean-Paul finally said, moving to the espresso machine on the counter. The Italian device hummed to life. "A weakness in our line of work."

"Antoine is dedicated to the organization," Michael said carefully. "He wants to prove himself to you."

Jean-Paul nodded as he prepared two cups of espresso. "True. But his emotions cloud his judgment. Not like you." He handed Michael one of the small cups. "Your clarity of purpose is what I've always valued, Michael. Your ability to see the bigger picture."

The irony of the statement wasn't lost on Michael. His "bigger picture" included the complete dismantling of the Domingo empire within the waiting hours.

"The shipment is secure," Michael assured him, accepting the espresso. "Every detail has been addressed."

"I don't doubt it," Jean-Paul said. "Here are two envelopes for the extra security you hired. Give them one at your security meeting and the other when the delivery is secured." He moved toward the kitchen window, staring out at the garden. "Antoine mentioned the detectives investigating Taylor's death. Are they a concern?"

Michael sipped his espresso, using the moment to formulate his response. "They're thorough professionals, but I don't believe they have anything concrete. Antoine's having them tracked as a precaution."

"A prudent move." Jean-Paul turned back to face him. "Taylor's death was... unfortunate, a necessity I took no pleasure in."

Michael could feel his heart beating. This was the closest Jean-Paul had ever come to directly acknowledging his role in the judge's murder.

"The judge left us no choice," Jean-Paul continued, his voice softening with what sounded like genuine regret. "We offered him a very generous deal, gave him forty-eight hours to respond, but his silence was his answer. It seems Judge Taylor..." Jean-Paul paused. "Well, let's just say he wasn't willing to cooperate."

"Did you suspect something more about him?"

Jean-Paul smiled. "New Orleans runs on information, Michael. I've cultivated sources throughout this city for decades. One of them noticed Taylor accessing certain sealed court records, making connections about case dismissals that followed specific patterns."

"So how did it go down?"

"Robert Duran." Jean-Paul named Taylor's dinner companion without hesitation. "Antoine had connections with a former CI of Taylor's from years ago. We persuaded him to reconnect with the judge and gain his confidence. The dinner at Le Bayou Jardin was meant to determine exactly what evidence Taylor had gathered and where he kept it."

"But something went wrong, didn't it?" Michael prompted.

"Antoine decided to handle it his way. Looks like he never even tried to get information from Taylor—just went straight to eliminating the threat." Jean-Paul stared into his espresso cup. "He told me Taylor was gathering evidence and had been in contact with the FBI. But I still don't know if he was telling the truth or just feeding me a story to justify his decision."

Michael kept his expression neutral—years of practice made it second nature—but inwardly, shock rippled through him. If Taylor had been in contact with the FBI, that meant another investigation was running parallel to his own, one his handlers had never mentioned.

"And the evidence Taylor gathered?" Michael asked.

"Never found." A flash of frustration crossed Jean-Paul's features. "We searched his home, his office, and his vehicle. Nothing. Which suggests he hid it somewhere else, or passed it to someone he trusted."

"Like these detectives."

"Possibly." Jean-Paul drained his espresso cup. "Hence Antoine's surveillance. But after tomorrow night's shipment, we'll have the resources and security to handle any remaining loose ends. Including your valuable assistance, of course."

"Of course," Michael agreed, finishing his espresso.

Jean-Paul placed his empty cup in the sink. "Get some rest, Michael. We have a lot of work before the big day."

After Jean-Paul departed, Michael remained in the kitchen, processing everything he'd learned. The conversation had confirmed his worst fears—the

Domingos had directly ordered Taylor's murder, and now the detectives were next on their list. But it had also revealed something unexpected: Taylor might have been working with the FBI outside of Michael's operation.

He needed to contact his handler, but not from here. The estate was too closely monitored.

Moving carefully through the silent mansion, Michael made his way to the guest suite he occasionally used when operations ran late. Inside, he locked the door and performed his usual sweep for surveillance devices. Finding none, he still took the precaution of turning on the shower before using his burner phone to call his FBI handler. In three years, he'd never used it until now.

The number connected after two rings.

"Pinkins," came the terse greeting from the other end.

"Taylor was working with the Bureau," Michael said, keeping his voice low. "Outside my operation. Who was running him?"

A pause. "How did you find out about that?"

"Jean-Paul Domingo just confirmed it to my face. Said it's why he was killed."

Another pause, longer this time. "There are other cases that the FBI is working on besides yours," Pinkins said.

"Well, someone talked," Michael said. "And now two NOPD detectives are in the crosshairs because they're picking up where Taylor left off."

"The detectives, you broke protocol to warn," Pinkins reminded him. "Risked compromising our three-year operation."

"They have evidence, Pinkins. Taylor's notebook and surveillance recordings are concrete proof of the corruption network protecting the Domingo organization. The same network our operation completely ignored to focus on the drug trafficking."

"That wasn't your call to make."

"No, but it was Taylor's. And now it's mine." Michael leaned against the bathroom wall, the shower still running to mask his voice. "The operation is still on. Nothing changes there. But I need assurance that Dubois and Griffith will be protected."

"I can't make that promise."

"Then I can't guarantee I'll be in position tomorrow night," Michael countered.

"Three years of work, Pinkins. Do you really want to risk it all now?"

The silence stretched taut between them.

"I'll see what I can do," Pinkins finally said. "No promises. But I'll try to get a protection detail assigned."

"Not good enough. I need your word they'll be covered."

Another pause. "Fine. You'll have it. But Michael, after the operation, there will be consequences for breaking protocol. Serious ones."

"I'm counting on it," Michael replied. "One more thing—Antoine Domingo knows too much. I believe he may have had my car tracked, and if he did, he knows I was at the Gateway Motel, and that's where the detectives were."

"How the hell did that happen?" Pinkins demanded.

"Doesn't matter now. What matters is that he's suspicious; if he has information, he hasn't told his father yet. Probably trying to play the hero and trap me in front of Jean-Paul."

"We need to take him out of play."

"You want us to arrest the son of our primary target, this close to the biggest operation of the year? Are you insane?"

"Not arrest," Michael clarified. "Just detain him. Pick him up for questioning about something unrelated. Hold him until the operation is over; then, you'll be able to charge him. He has a drinking problem—his father will assume he's on another bender."

The line went silent as Pinkins considered. "Too risky."

"Riskier to let him blow my cover before the raid," Michael pushed back.

Another long pause. "I'll have to coordinate with the local field office. If—and that's a big if—we can come up with a plausible reason to bring him in without raising flags..."

"Do it tonight," Michael insisted. "He's been drinking heavily. The cover will hold."

"Fine. I'll make the call. Where can we find him?"

"He favors a club in the warehouse district called Velvet. Goes there most nights. He'll be there by midnight. He drives a Maserati. Have them pick him up in the parking lot when he comes out."

"We'll handle it," Pinkins finally agreed. "Just make sure you have this under control."

"I will." Michael ended the call.

He disassembled the burner phone, flushing the SIM card down the toilet and tucking the battery and casing into separate pockets to dispose of later. As he shut off the shower, Michael caught his reflection in the steamed mirror, the face of a man he barely recognized anymore.

Three years deep in the Domingo organization had changed him in ways his FBI training hadn't prepared him for. The constant vigilance, the moral compromises, the isolation—they took their toll. Every day required him to balance on the knife-edge between maintaining his cover and betraying his principles.

Soon, the balancing act would come to an end. One way or another, Michael Reeves would cease to exist.

The question that haunted him as he lay in bed, staring at the ceiling of his guest room in the mansion of the man he was about to destroy, was simple: When Michael Reeves disappeared, would Special Agent Marcus Wells still exist? Or had the line between his identities blurred beyond recognition?

Sleep didn't come easily. But then, it hadn't for some time.

CHAPTER 25

DAWN BROKE OVER New Orleans. Michael rose early, showered, and dressed in the same crisp suit he always wore—his armor against the day ahead.

By 7 AM, he was reviewing security protocols with his team in the estate's private office wing. Eight men, all ex-military or former contractors—men who never asked questions, just in it for the money. They were unaware that the job was part of an illegal operation, just as Jean-Paul had intended. They would be positioned strategically around Pier 9. For all they knew, they were simply creating an outer security perimeter.

"Henderson, you'll take the north approach; Garcia, the south. I want continuous radio checks every fifteen minutes," Michael instructed, pointing to the harbor schematics spread across the conference table. "The shipment arrives at 11 PM, the day after tomorrow. We secure the area by 10, no exceptions." Michael handed over the first envelope. "The other will be delivered when the delivery is secured and completed."

The men nodded, seasoned professionals who admired his attention to detail. Michael had personally selected each one, choosing men who could evaluate a situation and make the right decision when it counted. When the FBI took action, they would follow orders without question—their loyalty was to their paycheck, not to any illicit agenda.

* * *

Jean-Paul looked around. "Have you seen Antoine this morning?"

Michael shook his head. "Not since last night in the kitchen. Is everything all right?"

"He didn't come home last night," Jean-Paul said. "His bed hasn't been slept in, and he's not answering his phone."

"He was drinking heavily," Michael pointed out. "Perhaps he decided to stay somewhere else."

Jean-Paul's jaw tightened. "Yes, his... habits. Not the first time he's disappeared, probably won't be the last." He sighed, rubbing his temple. "This is exactly why I rely on you, Michael. Antoine lacks discipline."

"I'm sure he'll turn up," Michael said. "Vega could check his usual haunts."

"I've already sent him to do that," Jean-Paul replied. "In the meantime, I want you to oversee all aspects of the operation. Antoine was supposed to coordinate with our port contacts, now that falls to you."

"Of course," Michael agreed. "I'll handle it personally."

Jean-Paul studied the harbor schematics laid out on the table. "This is too important to risk any complications. Ten million in product, our largest shipment ever." He looked up at Michael. "I'm counting on you."

"I won't let you down," Michael assured him, fully aware of the double meaning in his promise.

As Jean-Paul left, Michael allowed himself a moment of satisfaction. Antoine was out of the picture, just as he'd planned. With the volatile son detained by the FBI, the operation could proceed without the risk of his suspicions reaching Jean-Paul. Now, all he had to do was maintain his cover for a little while longer.

His phone buzzed—a message from a hidden number. It was his handler, using the emergency protocol.

"OPERATION TOMORROW 9:00 PM."

Michael deleted the message immediately. His mind raced. The tactical teams would be in position by 9 PM. Jean-Paul's security detail, which he had hired, wouldn't arrive until 10.

Perfect, he thought. *If everything went according to plan, this could work.*

The double game was reaching its conclusion. Now, he just had to survive until the final move.

CHAPTER 26

THE PRIVATE DINING ROOM at Le Martinique was one of Jean-Paul Domingo's preferred meeting locations. The high-end Creole restaurant had a separate entrance, ensuring discretion. The owner—a man who'd benefited from Domingo's financing when banks wouldn't touch his business plan—ensured absolute privacy. No staff entered without knocking; no surveillance devices existed within these wood-paneled walls.

By five o'clock, the key players had gathered around the ornate mahogany table. Jean-Paul sat at the head, his silver hair immaculately styled, and his tailored charcoal suit reflecting his worth. To his right was Michael Reeves, a portfolio open before him with detailed schematics of the harbor. To his left, the empty chair where Antoine should have been spoke volumes about Jean-Paul's current irritation.

Josef Mendoza, the organization's legal counsel, occupied a seat near the far end, his wire-rimmed glasses perched on his nose as he reviewed documents. Beside him, Ricardo Vega, head of street operations, sat impatiently by the table.

Two other figures completed the assembly: Eduardo Kovac, their shipping contact with connections throughout the Gulf ports, and Dr. Lucia Vasquez, the chemist responsible for testing and processing the product upon arrival.

The table was set with fine china, crystal glasses, and silver cutlery—a pretense maintained even during such meetings. Only Jean-Paul's plate held actual food, a barely touched filet mignon that had grown cold during the preliminary discussions.

"Let's begin," Jean-Paul said, closing the menu he'd been idly examining. "As you all know, this shipment represents a significant milestone for our organization: millions in pure product, enough to supply our network for months." His eyes moved around the table, studying each face. "I expect nothing less than perfection from each of you."

He nodded toward Kovac. "Eduardo, walk us through the arrival process."

Kovac, a lean Croatian with black hair and the weathered face of a lifelong sailor, leaned forward. " Tomorrow night, the ship—*Estrella del Mar*—will dock at Pier 9 at approximately 11 PM. Container 47-C-118 is registered as machine parts from a nonexistent Venezuelan manufacturing company." His accent gave his precise words a melodic quality. "Our contacts at the port authority have ensured it will be offloaded last and diverted to the private loading area at the south end of the terminal."

"Timeline?" Jean-Paul prompted.

"From docking to our possession—forty minutes maximum. The container will be accessible by 11:40 PM."

Jean-Paul turned to Vega. "Transport?"

Vega straightened, his muscular frame straining against his suit that looked better on a hanger. "Three vehicles. A lead car to scout for trouble, the transport truck itself, and a follow car for security. All vehicles are clean and purchased through shell companies, accompanied by appropriate documentation. Drivers have been selected for reliability, not connection to our usual operations."

"The route?" Michael inquired, his pen poised above a detailed street map.

"Primary route through the Warehouse District to the processing facility in Algiers. Two alternate routes were prepared in case of complications. Police scanner monitoring throughout the operation." Vega tapped his finger on the map. "Checkpoints here, here, and here, where our spotters will confirm the route remains clear."

Jean-Paul nodded approvingly, then shifted his attention. "Dr. Vasquez, your facility is prepared?"

The woman adjusted her designer glasses, her expression clinically detached. "Fully equipped and staffed. We can begin processing immediately upon arrival. Initial testing will confirm purity, followed by cutting and packaging according to distribution requirements. The entire batch can be ready for street distribution within 36 hours."

"And security for the facility?" Jean-Paul asked, turning back to Michael.

Michael opened a second folder. "Three concentric layers. Outer perimeter—four men stationed at strategic positions with sight lines to all approach routes. Inner perimeter—motion sensors, cameras, and two roving guards. Final layer—biometric access to the processing area itself, limited to essential personnel only." He laid out a series of photographs showing the warehouse from multiple angles. "The building's commercial zoning classification means law enforcement would require specific probable cause for any action. We've maintained the cover of a medical supply distribution center, complete with legitimate business paperwork."

Jean-Paul examined the photos. "And our personnel?"

"All vetted," Michael assured him. "No one with outstanding warrants, no one with known connections to law enforcement, no one with substance abuse issues." He closed the folder, eyeing each one in the room. "Every individual involved has something to lose if this goes wrong—family connections, financial dependencies, or dirt that could ruin them if it leaks."

"Distribution timeline?" Jean-Paul turned to Vega again.

"Phased rollout beginning forty-eight hours after processing completion. We'll use our established network, but with additional cutouts between supply and street-level dealers. Priority goes to our highest-margin territories first: Uptown, Garden District, and Warehouse District. Secondary distribution to Mid-City and Gentilly by end of week."

Josef Mendoza cleared his throat. "I've prepared the financial infrastructure to handle the increased revenue flow. Multiple channels, properly insulated from each other." His scholarly tone made drug money sound like an academic subject. "Primary laundering mechanisms are in place through the restaurant chain, the real estate holdings, and the art gallery. Secondary laundering through the offshore accounts in Cayman and Singapore."

Jean-Paul nodded, satisfied. "Contingencies?"

Michael took the lead. "Three safe houses prepared if we need to go dark. Emergency transportation standing by at all times. Cash reserves at each location. If necessary, we can suspend all operations and disappear within thirty minutes of your order."

A silence fell over the table as Jean-Paul considered everything he'd heard. He took a slow sip of his Bordeaux, savoring it as if it were a casual dinner rather than the orchestration of a multi-million-dollar drug shipment.

"And Antoine?" he finally asked, his voice carrying a dangerous edge as he gestured to the empty chair. "Has anyone heard from my son?"

No reply.

Jean-Paul's jaw tightened. "Find him," he said to Vega. "Discreetly. Ensure he's presentable and not drunk."

"Yes, sir."

"Would you like me to oversee the port authority arrangements in Antoine's absence?" Michael asked.

"Yes," Jean-Paul replied. "Handle it personally. Antoine's unreliability has become a concern."

A subtle shift in the room's atmosphere followed this statement—something between tension and relief.

Antoine's volatility was well-known among the inner circle.

"One final matter," Jean-Paul continued. "Those detectives investigating Judge Taylor's death. Where do we stand on that situation?"

Vega straightened. "Surveillance in place as of this morning. Trackers on their vehicle. We know they've been gathering evidence on Taylor's death, but that's all we know for sure."

"Evidence of what, precisely? Has anyone figured out how far they've gotten in their investigation?"

Josef adjusted his glasses nervously. "Based on our sources at the courthouse, Taylor was documenting the pattern of case dismissals."

"And this evidence is now in the hands of two narcotics detectives," Jean-Paul stated. It wasn't a question.

"Maybe—we don't know that," Michael said. "Even if they do, without Taylor's context, they may not understand the full implications."

Jean-Paul studied Michael's face for a long moment. "After tomorrow night's shipment is secure, these detectives become our priority. I want them handled. Permanently."

Murmurs of agreement circled the table.

"Michael, you'll coordinate that operation as well." Jean-Paul's tone made it clear this wasn't a request.

"Of course," Michael replied, his expression betraying nothing of the cold dread settling in his stomach. Jean-Paul didn't usually give orders like this—clean, final, and personal. The very detectives

Michael had tried to protect were now marked for execution, with him cast as their executioner.

Jean-Paul stood, signaling the meeting's conclusion. "Tomorrow night, gentlemen—and Dr. Vasquez—our organization takes a significant step forward. The Domingo name has been synonymous with New Orleans for three generations. After tomorrow, our influence extends throughout the Gulf Coast."

As the others gathered their materials, Jean-Paul gestured for Michael to remain. When they were alone, the older man placed a hand on Michael's shoulder—a rare gesture of physical connection.

"My son's absence concerns me," Jean-Paul admitted quietly. "Not just for this operation but for the future of our family business."

"Antoine is passionate," Michael offered diplomatically. "Sometimes that passion leads him to... impulsive decisions."

Jean-Paul's laugh held no humor. "A generous assessment. The truth, Michael, is that Antoine lacks the temperament this business requires—the discipline, the patience." His grip on Michael's shoulder tightened slightly. "Qualities you possess in abundance."

"Sir?"

"After tomorrow's success, I believe it's time to formalize your position within our organization. Not just security, but operations. Perhaps more."

The implication hung in the air between them— Michael was being offered what should have been Antoine's birthright.

"I'm honored by your confidence," Michael said.

Jean-Paul patted his shoulder. "We'll discuss details after the shipment is secure. For now, ensure everything is ready. I'd prefer Antoine be involved, but I've learned to prepare for his... absences."

"I understand."

* * *

After the meeting at Le Martinique concluded, Michael followed Jean-Paul to his waiting car. The Domingo patriarch's driver stood at attention by the black Mercedes sedan, but Jean-Paul waved him back, indicating he wanted a private word with Michael.

Jean-Paul turned to face his trusted lieutenant. "You'll take care of the port authority arrangements," then, he confirmed, "Antoine should have wrapped up the preliminary work, but..." He let the sentence trail off, his disappointment in his son clear.

Michael nodded, projecting the calm demeanor that had earned him Jean-Paul's trust. "I'll take care of it immediately. In fact, I'd like to visit the port this afternoon to inspect the area personally."

Jean-Paul's eyes lit up with approval. "Excellent initiative, Michael. This is exactly why I rely on you."

"If I'm handling security, I need to see the terrain firsthand," Michael explained. "There's a significant difference between reviewing schematics and actually walking the perimeter."

He pulled out his phone, opening a map of the port area. "I want to verify sight lines, identify potential vulnerabilities, and establish optimal positions for our security. Especially since you had me bring in extra personnel."

"Always thorough," Jean-Paul said, a hint of appreciation in his voice. "Antoine would've just made a phone call and called it done."

"I need to know every entrance, exit, blind spot, and vantage point," Michael continued. "I need to see how the light falls at night, where shadows could conceal threats, how sound carries across the water."

"This is why you've become indispensable," Jean-Paul said. "You understand that success is built on meticulous preparation."

Michael felt a little smile creeping onto his face. "From what I've seen, successful operations rely more on preparation than execution. The strongest security is the kind that anticipates problems before they begin."

"Go today," Jean-Paul encouraged. "Take whatever time you need. Make it perfect."

"I'll meet with the port supervisor, verify that our contacts are in place, and establish the security perimeter for the delivery," Michael assured him. "By the time the shipment arrives, I'll have mapped every square inch of that pier."

This is what distinguishes you, Michael. This attention to detail. Antoine..." His expression darkened momentarily.

"Different approaches, sir," Michael replied diplomatically.

"Indeed." Jean-Paul straightened his suit jacket. "Very well. Visit the port, make your preparations."

"Of course."

Jean-Paul moved toward his car but paused before getting in. "This shipment represents more than just profit, Michael. It establishes our position for years to come. Nothing can go wrong."

"It won't," Michael assured him. "By the time the shipment arrives, Everything will be set."

As Jean-Paul's car pulled away, Michael allowed his expression to shift just slightly. The weight of deception—a burden he'd carried for three years—pressed down on him. He would indeed ensure everything was in place, though not for the outcome Jean-Paul expected.

He checked his watch, calculating how much time he needed at the port to gather the necessary information. It would be a delicate balance—appearing to strengthen security while actually ensuring its failure.

The day would be busy but essential. The operation depended on his thoughtful preparations today. Those preparations required him to play his role perfectly, right up until the moment it didn't.

And Jean-Paul, the man who had just offered him a place in the family business—a man who, in another reality, Michael might have genuinely respected—would spend the rest of his life in prison.

The burden of betrayal, even of a criminal enterprise, sat heavily on Michael's shoulders as he left Le Martinique and stepped into the humid New Orleans air where cicadas chirped their endless chorus from nearby oak trees.

The final pieces were moving into position. The endgame had begun.

CHAPTER 27

THE AFTERNOON SUN BEAT down on Pier 9 as Michael Reeves walked the perimeter, a clipboard in hand and sunglasses shielding his eyes. To any observer, he appeared to be conducting routine security preparations—a diligent lieutenant of the Domingo organization ensuring tomorrow's shipment would proceed without complications.

In reality, each notation he made, each photograph he took with his phone served a dual purpose.

"The container will be offloaded here," he said to the port supervisor accompanying him, pointing to the southern loading area. "I need to verify sight lines from all approaches."

The supervisor—a heavyset man named Garvey, who had been on the Domingo payroll for years—nodded. "We'll have the area cleared by ten tomorrow night. No other ships scheduled for unloading, no dock workers except the ones on your approved list."

Michael made a show of noting this information. "And the access road here?" He indicated the narrow service road running behind the loading area.

"Restricted access. Gate locked after eight PM," Garvey assured him.

Michael nodded, mentally calculating how long it would take FBI tactical teams to breach that gate. The narrow road would funnel Domingo's escape vehicles, creating an ideal chokepoint for the operation.

"I'll need the maintenance access codes for these doors," Michael said, gesturing to the large warehouse at the edge of the pier. "In case we need an alternate extraction route."

Garvey looked uncomfortable. "Those aren't supposed to be shared with—"

"Jean-Paul Domingo is personally invested in this shipment," Michael interrupted, his voice carrying just enough edge. "He wants all contingencies covered. All of them."

The supervisor relented, writing the codes on Michael's clipboard. Another piece of intelligence that would find its way to the FBI before nightfall.

As they continued the tour, Michael paused at strategic locations, taking photos that captured the pier's layout, security camera positions, guard rotations, and potential blind spots.

Michael stopped abruptly at a particular section of the pier, studying the sight lines. "This area concerns me," he said, pointing to where the dock intersected the main access road.

Garvey frowned. "We've never had issues before—"

"I'd like you to place two shipping containers here," Michael said, gesturing to the spots he had in mind. "One here and one directly on the other side. It will block the view from the street." He made a show of scanning the perimeter. "This seems to be the only area that has open access to viewing from the street. I need that blocked."

"Two containers?" Garvey scratched his head. "I suppose we could move a couple of empty ones from the south lot."

"Make it happen," Michael said firmly. "I want them in place by tomorrow afternoon at the latest."

"I've brought in eight specialists for perimeter security," Michael explained, pointing to different positions on his map of the pier. "My men. Hand-picked. They'll create an outer security ring while Domingo's regular crew handles the product."

"Your own guys?" Garvey raised an eyebrow.

"Mr. Domingo wanted added security for this job. He authorized it directly," Michael replied, his tone leaving no room for debate. "That's all you need to know."

"I'll position them here, here, and here," Michael continued, marking the locations in front of Garvey. Each position was strategically chosen to appear as if it secured the pier, while actually having something else in mind. "They'll establish a secure perimeter by 9 PM, well before the shipment arrives."

Garvey nodded, seemingly impressed. "Sounds like you've thought of everything."

"What about police patrols?" Michael asked casually. "Any changes to their routines lately?"

"Same as always. Harbor patrol passes by around 9 PM, then not again until the morning," Garvey replied.

At the northern edge of the pier, he stopped, gazing out over the water. From this vantage point, he could see the entire approach the Estrella del Mar would take tomorrow night.

"I want to place two of my men here," he told Garvey, pointing to the observation platform. "Best view of any approach by water."

"Whatever you need, Mr. Reeves. Mr. Domingo's instructions were clear—you have full authority."

Michael spent another hour inspecting every inch of Pier 9, mentally choreographing the FBI raid that would unfold there tomorrow night. Each recommendation he made to enhance the Domingo security plan cleverly created openings that could be exploited. Each "secure" location he established for his handpicked men would become a carefully designed weak point in the defensive perimeter.

"My team will run communications on a separate channel," Michael added as they finished the inspection. "More secure that way. I'll be the liaison between them and Domingo's regular crew."

This arrangement would allow him to control the flow of information during the raid, delaying any warning to the Domingo organization until it was too late.

As the sun began to set across the pier, Michael completed his final notes. The weighted feeling in his chest wasn't entirely professional. After three years undercover, the line between deception and betrayal had blurred in ways his FBI training hadn't prepared him for.

These men—Garvey, the dock workers, even some of Domingo's soldiers—were not all hardened criminals. Many were simply people caught in a system of corruption that predated their involvement. Tomorrow, some would go to prison. Others might resist and face worse consequences.

"I think we're covered," Michael said finally, shaking Garvey's hand. "My men will be here at 8 PM, I'll be here at 7:00 PM. I need you and your dock workers gone by the time I get here."

"Understood, Mr. Reeves. It's always a pleasure working with a professional."

As Michael walked back to his car, he paused to take one final photograph—an innocent shot of the harbor at sunset that would appear on his phone. However, embedded in the image's metadata were the final coordinates for the FBI extraction point, where he would shed the identity of Michael Reeves forever.

He started his car and drove away from Pier 9, leaving behind the elaborate stage he had just set for tomorrow night's performance—the final act in a three-year charade that had consumed his life and altered his sense of self in ways he was only beginning to understand.

In a little over twenty-four hours, it would all be over. The Domingo organization would fall. The corruption network would be exposed.

And Michael Reeves would cease to exist.

CHAPTER 28

THE SAFE HOUSE Michael had arranged was a modest bungalow in Gentilly, far from the Domingo organization's usual territory. Its peeling paint and overgrown lawn suggested abandonment, but inside, it had been quietly maintained—a forgotten property on the FBI's confidential assets list.

Michael arrived at precisely noon, parking his car two blocks away and approaching on foot, checking repeatedly to ensure he wasn't followed. Three years of deep cover had made such precautions second nature.

Renee opened the door before he could knock. "Clear?" she asked, her hand resting near her holstered weapon.

"Clear," Michael confirmed, stepping inside.

The living room had been transformed into an operational center. Maps of New Orleans covered one wall, with red pins marking key locations in the corruption network Taylor had uncovered. Kelsey sat at a folding table, covered with files, with his laptop open in front of him.

"You're taking a big risk coming here today," Kelsey said, not looking up from his screen. "If the Domingos suspect anything..."

"Jean-Paul trusts me completely," Michael replied, removing his jacket. "He thinks I'm coordinating with our port contacts all morning. I have until three before anyone expects to hear from me."

Renee closed the blinds, though they'd already been mostly drawn. "So, it's happening tonight?"

Michael nodded, but the tension betrayed his calm exterior. "Everything's in place for the takedown. I've created blind spots in the security perimeter, stationed my own men at key locations, and made sure the FBI has all the intel they need."

He spread a detailed map of the harbor across the table. "The raid will come from three directions simultaneously. Maritime units from the water, tactical teams through these access points," he indicated several locations, "and a containment team to block any escape routes."

"And Jean-Paul has no idea?" Kelsey asked.

"None. He thinks it's going to be the crowning achievement of the Domingo organization." A hint of something like regret crossed Michael's face. "Three years I've spent earning his trust, and tonight I destroy everything he's built."

"He's a drug dealer responsible for countless deaths," Renee reminded him.

"I know." Michael straightened. "The Domingo operation ends tonight. But that's just one piece of what Taylor was investigating." He looked between the two detectives. "What about your end? Do you have all your ducks in a row for the city corruption case? The judges, the DA, all of it?"

Renee exchanged a glance with Kelsey before answering. "Taylor's notebook gave us the framework. We've spent the past week connecting the dots, tracking money, and matching case dismissals with specific judges."

"We have enough to start," Kelsey added, turning his laptop to show Michael a complex spreadsheet—documented patterns of case assignments, evidence suppression, and suspicious financial activities. Judge Harrison, Judge LeBlanc, Judge Barrett—they're all implicated, and possibly the District Attorney himself.

"And Captain Simmons has been crucial," Renee said. "He's kept this entire investigation off the books, away from anyone who might be compromised."

Michael studied their evidence board, nodding slowly. "It's impressive work. But exposing corruption this entrenched won't be easy. These people have powerful friends."

"That's why we need you," Kelsey said directly. "You were inside, part of the Domingo organization. You saw firsthand how they manipulated the system, who they paid off, how the protection network functioned."

"We need your testimony," Renee added. "Taylor's evidence gets us started, but your firsthand account bridges the gaps. You can connect the

Domingo family directly to the judges and prosecutors."

Michael moved to the window, carefully peeking through the blinds at the quiet street outside. Years of living as Michael Reeves had taken a toll. Sometimes, in unguarded moments, he couldn't remember which parts of himself were real and which were constructed for his cover.

"After the operation, Michael Reeves ceases to exist," he said quietly. "Once the FBI raid happens, my identity is burned. I'll be extracted and debriefed, then likely relocated with a new identity."

"But you'll testify first," Kelsey insisted. "You have to. Without you, the corruption case falls apart."

Michael turned back to face them. "The FBI's priority is the drug operation. The corruption network is secondary to them, politically complicated, and potentially embarrassing for law enforcement. They may not want me to get involved."

"So what?" Renee challenged. "Judge Taylor died because he was trying to expose this corruption. Are you going to let that be for nothing?"

The question hung in the room, heavy with accusation and truth. Michael's jaw tightened.

"I worked with Taylor for almost a year," he said finally. "He trusted me when he didn't have to. He risked everything for what he believed was right." He met Renee's gaze directly. "I'll testify. Whatever it takes."

Relief washed across both detectives' faces.

"But there's a condition," Michael continued. "The corruption case moves forward immediately— not next week, not after the drug case is processed—

immediately. These people have connections; they'll start covering their tracks the moment word of the Domingo raid gets out."

"We're ready," Kelsey assured him. "Simmons has a team standing by. The moment the raid happens, they move to secure records and evidence before it can disappear."

"Good. After tonight, things will move quickly. The FBI will want to control the narrative and limit exposure. You'll need to be aggressive."

"We will be," Renee promised. She hesitated, then asked, "What happens to you after all this?"

Michael's expression became unreadable. "That's up to the Bureau. New assignment, probably. New identity, definitely." He checked his watch. "I need to get back. Jean-Paul expects a final briefing at three."

"Be careful," Kelsey said. "If they suspect anything..."

"They won't," Michael assured him, though they all knew the stakes. "I've been playing this role for too long to let it mess up now."

As he prepared to leave, Michael paused at the door. "One more thing—Antoine is missing. The FBI has him in custody, but Jean-Paul doesn't know that."

"Is Antoine totally secure?" Renee asked.

"Yes, he is being held in a private location," Michael replied. "Probably will never be able to see the light of day again if we can convict him in Judge Taylor's death. A special team is guarding him."

"But you're still concerned," Kelsey observed, noting the tension in Michael's shoulders.

Michael nodded. "Antoine is resourceful when motivated. And he had suspicions about me before they picked him up. If he somehow gets word to Jean-Paul before the raid..."

The implication was clear. Michael's cover—and possibly his life—would be in immediate danger.

"What time is your final briefing with Jean-Paul?" Kelsey asked.

"Three to four, at the estate. Then I head to the pier by seven to oversee final preparations."

Renee said. "If anything looks wrong, will there be a way to warn you?"

Michael nodded. "The FBI has a trigger. If I mention certain code words that only they know during any conversation, they'll move in right away. But let's hope it doesn't come to that."

He opened the door slightly, checking the street one final time before slipping out. All his undercover work had culminated in this day. In less than twelve hours, the Domingo empire would fall, and the corruption that had protected it would be exposed.

CHAPTER 29

MICHAEL REEVES SAT in his parked car three blocks from the Domingo estate, rain drumming steadily on the roof. The weather forecast called for showers throughout the evening—less than ideal for a tactical operation, but it would provide additional cover for the FBI teams.

He checked his watch: 4:45 PM. With his briefing to Jean-Paul complete, he had a narrow window to set everything in motion before heading to the pier.

Michael pulled out his burner and dialed his FBI handler.

"Pinkins," the familiar voice answered on the second ring.

"It's me," keeping his voice low despite being alone in the car. "I need eight men at Pier 9 by 7:00 PM. Have them dressed as dock workers, tactical gear in duffel bags."

"Eight men as dock workers?" Pinkins sounded skeptical. "Did something change?"

"Just send them," Michael replied firmly. "Once I secure the scene, I'll signal for you to bring in eight more SWAT officers."

The line went silent for a moment as Pinkins considered. "And after that?"

"Once I secure the scene, they'll all be positioned inside the shipping containers."

"And when the eight security men Jean-Paul had me hire arrive, I'll position them at their security posts."

"Wait, Domingo wanted you to hire eight additional security men? Why didn't you just use eight of our men?"

"Because Antoine was becoming suspicious of me, and I worried he was going to vet those men. I was running out of time. So, I did what I had to do. Just shut up and listen, will you? When I can make sure Garvey and his men are gone, and we get closer to the ship's arrival, I'll gather them between the containers on the pretense of a final briefing."

"And then?"

Michael, becoming frustrated, continued. "And then I'll tell them plans have changed, hand them their final payment from Jean-Paul, and send them away."

"They might not want to leave without an explanation."

"I'll handle that," Michael said firmly. "They'll get their explanation."

Another pause, longer this time. "This is unorthodox, Reeves."

"This whole operation has been unorthodox from the beginning. Things are constantly changing and I'm flying by the seat of my pants. Give me some credit,"

Michael countered. "I need those men off-site before the shipment arrives. They're not hardened criminals—I specifically chose them because they'd be unlikely to fight when the situation changes."

"Alright," Pinkins finally agreed. "Eight at seven, disguised as dock workers. And then an additional eight upon your request."

Michael checked his watch again. "I assume you have all the rest of the teams waiting out of sight."

"Yes, we're all ready. I just hope you are."

"One more thing—Antoine?"

"Still secured," Pinkins said. "No communications in or out."

"Good. I'll see you on the other side of this."

* * *

The rain began to slacken as Michael arrived at Pier 9 at precisely 6:30 PM. Tonight was the night. The two shipping containers he'd requested stood exactly where he'd specified, creating a narrow corridor that blocked the view from the street—and would soon serve a very different purpose than Garvey imagined.

Michael performed a methodical sweep of the area, checking every corner, every potential hiding place. The pier was deserted except for Garvey, who waited in his small office near the main entrance.

"Evening, Mr. Reeves," Garvey greeted him, rising from behind his cluttered desk. "Everything's set up just like you wanted."

"Any stragglers?" Michael asked, scanning the security monitors that showed different angles of the pier.

"Just me," Garvey assured him. "Everyone else is gone for the day. The place is empty."

Michael nodded, hiding his relief. "Good. I'll take it from here, Garvey. My security team will be arriving shortly."

"You want me to leave too?" Garvey asked, glancing at his monitors.

"Yes," Michael said decisively. "I need complete control of the perimeter."

Garvey didn't argue; he simply reached for his jacket. "You'll handle the documentation for the container?"

"All taken care of," Michael assured him. "Enjoy your evening."

As Garvey walked to his car, he saw eight men carrying duffel bags heading down the dock. As soon as his car disappeared from view, Michael moved quickly. He pulled out his secure phone and sent a single text: "Site clear. Proceed with phase two."

At precisely 7:30 PM, eight more men in tactical gear arrived on the dock.

Michael directed the first eight men, the ones carrying duffel bags, into the southern container. "Stay inside until I signal," he instructed. "Do not change into your tactical gear yet."

The other eight men, already in full tactical gear, he sent to the northern container. "You'll hold position here. No one moves until Domingo's distribution team arrives and the ship docks. Understood?"

"Understood," acknowledged the SWAT team leader. "We stay hidden until you give the signal."

The men moved efficiently, disappearing into their respective containers. The doors closed behind them, concealing sixteen heavily armed FBI agents waiting like a coiled spring to be released.

Now came the most delicate part of the operation. At precisely 8:00 PM, right on schedule, the eight contractors Michael had hired as Domingo's security team began arriving in pairs. Former military and private security professionals, they were competent, reliable, and—most importantly—unconnected to the Domingo organization.

Michael greeted each team as they arrived, directing them to predetermined positions around the pier. By 8:30 PM, all eight men were present, creating a security perimeter that looked impressive.

Michael spent the next hour supervising preparations around the dock. As the clock approached 9:30 PM, he signaled to the eight contractors he had hired as Domingo's security team.

"Gather up," Michael called to them, gesturing to the space between the two shipping containers. "Final briefing before positions."

The contractors assembled promptly, forming a tight semicircle around Michael. These were professionals—alert, observant, their eyes constantly scanning their surroundings even as they listened to instructions.

"There's been a change of plans," Michael announced, keeping his tone steady.

The contractors exchanged glances, instantly wary.

"What kind of change?" asked Davis, a former Army Ranger who seemed to have assumed leadership of the group.

Michael reached into his jacket and removed a thick envelope. "Mr. Domingo has decided to use his regular security team for tonight's operation. Your services won't be needed after all."

He held out the envelope. "This contains the full payment agreed upon. Mr. Domingo appreciates your time and hopes to work with you again in the future."

Davis made no move to take the envelope. "That's not how these arrangements work, Mr. Reeves. We were contracted for the full operation."

The other contractors shifted slightly, hands moving subtly closer to concealed weapons.

Michael had anticipated this reaction. Without breaking eye contact with Davis, he rapped twice on the shipping container.

The container door slid open. Three FBI agents in full tactical gear emerged, weapons at the ready—not pointed at the contractors, but visible enough to make the situation clear.

The message was unmistakable. This wasn't a negotiation.

Davis stared at the FBI agents, then back at Michael, understanding dawning in his eyes. "You're not who they think you are."

"No," Michael agreed quietly. "I'm not. And this operation isn't what you signed up for." He extended the envelope again. "Take the money and leave. Now. What happens here tonight isn't something you want to be part of."

The contractors exchanged glances, a silent communication passing between them.

Davis reached out and took the envelope. "We were never here."

"That's right," Michael confirmed.

Without another word, the contractors turned and walked away, disappearing into the rainy night as quietly as they had arrived.

After the contractors left, the three FBI agents returned to their container.

Michael approached the first container and tapped on the metal door. It opened just enough for him to slip inside, where eight FBI agents in civilian dock worker attire waited.

"Listen up," he said. "I'm going to position you around the perimeter—same spots where the contractors would have been. Maintain normal security posture, stay visible, but blend in."

The agents nodded, understanding the crucial role they would play in the deception.

"When the ship is close to docking and the offloading preparations begin, I'll signal you to return here. You'll have just a few minutes to change into tactical gear and get into position inside the container."

Michael checked his watch, then continued. "Once inside, you'll remain silent and ready. The second container already holds the other tactical team. When I give the final signal, both container doors will open simultaneously. You'll join forces with the other team and execute the takedown."

The agents filed out of the container, spreading across the dock to their assigned positions. To the untrained eye, they were simply the security team Michael had hired—just part of the normal preparations for a major shipping operation. No one would suspect they were the first wave of what would soon become the largest drug bust in the city's history.

At 10 PM, the first vehicles containing Domingo's distribution team began arriving at the pier. Vega, the organization's head of street operations, led the convoy—three black SUVs and a large box truck for transporting the product once it was offloaded. Ten heavily armed men from the Domingo organization deployed around the pier—guards, loaders, drivers.

Michael greeted them with the steady confidence that had earned him Jean-Paul's trust. "Everything's secure," he reported to Vega. "Perimeter is established, all access points controlled."

Vega nodded, clearly pleased with Michael's efficiency. "Jean-Paul sends his regards. He's monitoring from home."

As 11:00 approached, the running lights of the Estrella del Mar appeared, cutting through the night. The container ship's massive silhouette grew larger against the horizon, its deck stacked with shipping containers of various colors and sizes. Only one mattered—Container 47-C-118, containing ten million dollars in product.

As the ship's horn announced its arrival, Michael's hand moved to his radio. Two quick taps—the signal his FBI agents had been waiting for. They disengaged from their positions and melted back toward the shipping containers.

The dock erupted into activity as Domingo's crew prepared for the offloading. Vega barked orders, directing men into position as the ship's crew secured the vessel to the pier. In the commotion, no one noticed the absence of Michael's security team, now sealed inside their container, rapidly changing into full tactical gear.

Inside the first container, the agents worked with military precision, strapping on body armor, checking weapons, and activating communications equipment. The other tactical team was already prepared in the second container, having been in position for hours.

"Listen up," Michael said, slipping briefly into the first container to address the now-equipped agents. "You all need to understand something crucial about tonight's operation."

The agents paused their preparations, giving Michael their full attention.

"My cover must be maintained throughout this entire raid," Michael stated firmly. "When you move on Domingo's crew, you treat me exactly like them. No special treatment, no acknowledgment of who I really am."

Jenkins, the team leader, frowned. "You want us to arrest you with them?"

"Exactly," Michael confirmed.

"As far as anyone outside this container knows, I'm Domingo's security chief, Michael Reeves. I'll appear to resist just like the rest of them. When the raid goes down, you take me down. Hard enough to be convincing, but try not to break anything I'll need later."

A few of the agents smiled and exchanged glances.

"What about the other teams?" one asked. "They need to know, too."

"Pinkins is briefing them separately. If Jean-Paul Domingo ever discovers I was FBI, anyone he thinks I might have spoken to becomes a target. That includes detectives working the corruption case, witnesses, informants—everyone."

"Got it," Jenkins said, nodding. "You'll be heading out with Domingo's crew, then?"

"Yes. Pinkins will handle the extraction later, away from prying eyes," Michael confirmed. "But until then, I'm just another perp you took down. Are we clear?"

"Crystal," Jenkins assured him. "We'll make it look good."

"Good. Now get back in position and stay hidden until I give the signal. No matter what happens, no matter what you see or hear, you don't move until Domingo's people are all here and the shipment is being unloaded."

Michael exited the container, and the door closed behind him. The pier fell quiet again, the calm before the storm.

Vega directed operations from the pier, positioning his men strategically as they prepared to offload Container 47-C-118, containing the shipment.

At precisely 11:20 PM, as Domingo's men began transferring the opened container's contents to their waiting truck, Michael pressed his radio transmit button and spoke the words that would trigger the operation:

"Execute. All teams go."

The doors of both shipping containers exploded outward simultaneously. Sixteen FBI agents in full tactical gear emerged, weapons raised, their shouts of "FBI!" cutting through the night.

At the same instant, FBI agents who had been concealed aboard the ship emerged from hiding, weapons drawn. They had infiltrated during the vessel's last port call, hiding in maintenance areas throughout the journey.

And from the water itself came the third prong of the attack—three unmarked boats, each carrying ten FBI tactical agents, approached swiftly from different directions. They swarmed up the pier's ladders, cutting off any escape by water.

The Domingo organization's men reacted with stunned confusion, immediately followed by resistance. Gunfire erupted across the pier as several of Domingo's more hardened criminals opened fire.

Michael had prepared for this moment for three years, but now came the most dangerous part of his mission—one Pinkins had strongly opposed. Instead of revealing himself as the architect of the Domingo organization's downfall, Michael had to maintain his cover.

Near the ship, a fierce firefight had broken out between Domingo's men and the FBI agents who had been onboard. Bullets ricocheted off metal surfaces, sending sparks flying. Two of Domingo's men used the container being offloaded as cover, firing from behind it at the advancing agents.

One FBI agent took a round to the shoulder, spinning him backward. His teammates immediately dragged him to safety while returning fire.

As they moved, the FBI team from the southern container cut off their escape route. Caught in the crossfire, two more of Domingo's men went down.

The gunfire intensified for nearly two minutes before beginning to taper off. The Domingo organization, though well-armed, was completely outmatched by the coordinated FBI assault.

Vega, bleeding from a graze to his arm, continued firing until his magazine emptied. As he attempted to reload, an FBI agent tackled him from behind, driving him face-first into the pier with enough force to split his lip. The man fought viciously, managing to elbow the agent in the face before another two agents piled on, finally subduing him.

Drawing his weapon, Michael fired several carefully aimed shots well above the heads of the FBI agents, looking to all observers like he was defending the operation alongside Domingo's men. The firefight was intense but brief. The FBI teams had overwhelming force and the element of surprise. Within minutes, most of Domingo's men were face down on the pier, hands zip-tied behind their backs.

Michael, fighting alongside them as expected, found himself tackled by an FBI agent. He was thrown roughly to the ground, his face pressed against the wet concrete as his hands were secured behind his back.

Michael struggled convincingly as he was hauled to his feet. Across the pier, he saw Vega watching, blood running from a cut on his forehead, his eyes filled with rage but not suspicion. To Vega and everyone else in the Domingo organization, Michael appeared to be just another casualty of the raid—captured rather than killed only because he had surrendered when overwhelmed.

As he was led toward the FBI vehicles, Michael caught Pinkins's eye briefly. The smallest nod passed between them—acknowledgment of a plan executed perfectly. Michael's cover remained intact. If any of Domingo's people escaped the net, they would report that Michael had been captured fighting alongside them, not that he had betrayed them.

* * *

Fifteen miles away in the Garden District, another FBI team, accompanied by Detectives Renee Dubois and Kelsey Griffith, pulled up to the elegant gates of Jean-Paul Domingo's mansion. The operation had been precisely timed—the raid at the pier and the arrest at the mansion happening at exactly the same moment, giving no opportunity for warning calls.

As agents swarmed the grounds, Renee and Kelsey approached the front door with the FBI team leader. The mansion's security personnel, seeing the overwhelming force, offered no resistance.

Inside, they found Jean-Paul Domingo in his study, calmly drinking bourbon as he monitored communications from the pier—communications that had suddenly gone silent. He looked up without surprise as the agents and detectives entered.

"Jean-Paul Domingo," Renee announced, "you're under arrest for drug trafficking, conspiracy to commit murder, and racketeering."

To her surprise, a smug smile spread across Domingo's face. He set down his glass and leaned back in his chair with the ease of a man completely unconcerned.

"This is hardly the first time I've been arrested, Detective," he said, his tone almost bored. "I was innocent then, and I'm innocent now."

Kelsey stepped forward with handcuffs. "Stand up, please."

"I don't think I will," Jean-Paul replied, remaining seated. "I'm innocent of everything you're trying to accuse me of. My businesses are all legitimate enterprises. You're making a serious mistake."

"Save it for court," Renee said. "You have the right to remain silent—"

"I want my lawyer," Jean-Paul interrupted, his voice hardening. "Josef Mendoza. Call him immediately. I won't be saying another word until he arrives."

The FBI team leader nodded to two agents, who moved to either side of Domingo's chair.

"Mr. Domingo, you can stand up on your own, or we can assist you," he said firmly. "But you are leaving this house in custody."

With a theatrical sigh, Jean-Paul stood, straightening his custom suit jacket. "My lawyer will have me out by morning," he said, extending his wrists for the cuffs. "This is harassment, nothing more."

As they led him from the mansion, he asked casually, "I assume my security chief, Michael Reeves, has been similarly inconvenienced by your overzealous actions tonight?"

"Reeves is in custody," Renee confirmed, careful to maintain the fiction.

Jean-Paul nodded, his smug expression never wavering. "Good. When this is all sorted out, I'll be sure to compensate him well for this indignity."

As Jean-Paul Domingo was escorted to a waiting vehicle, his expression of absolute confidence never faltered. He truly believed his network of corruption would protect him, just as it always had.

* * *

Back at the pier, Michael was placed in the same transport vehicle as several of Domingo's top lieutenants, maintaining his role until the very end. The door slammed shut, and as the vehicle pulled away from Pier 9, Michael allowed himself the smallest smile in the darkness.

Phase two—the exposure of the corruption network that Judge Taylor had died investigating—was just beginning.

In a secure FBI facility miles away, the real work would soon begin.

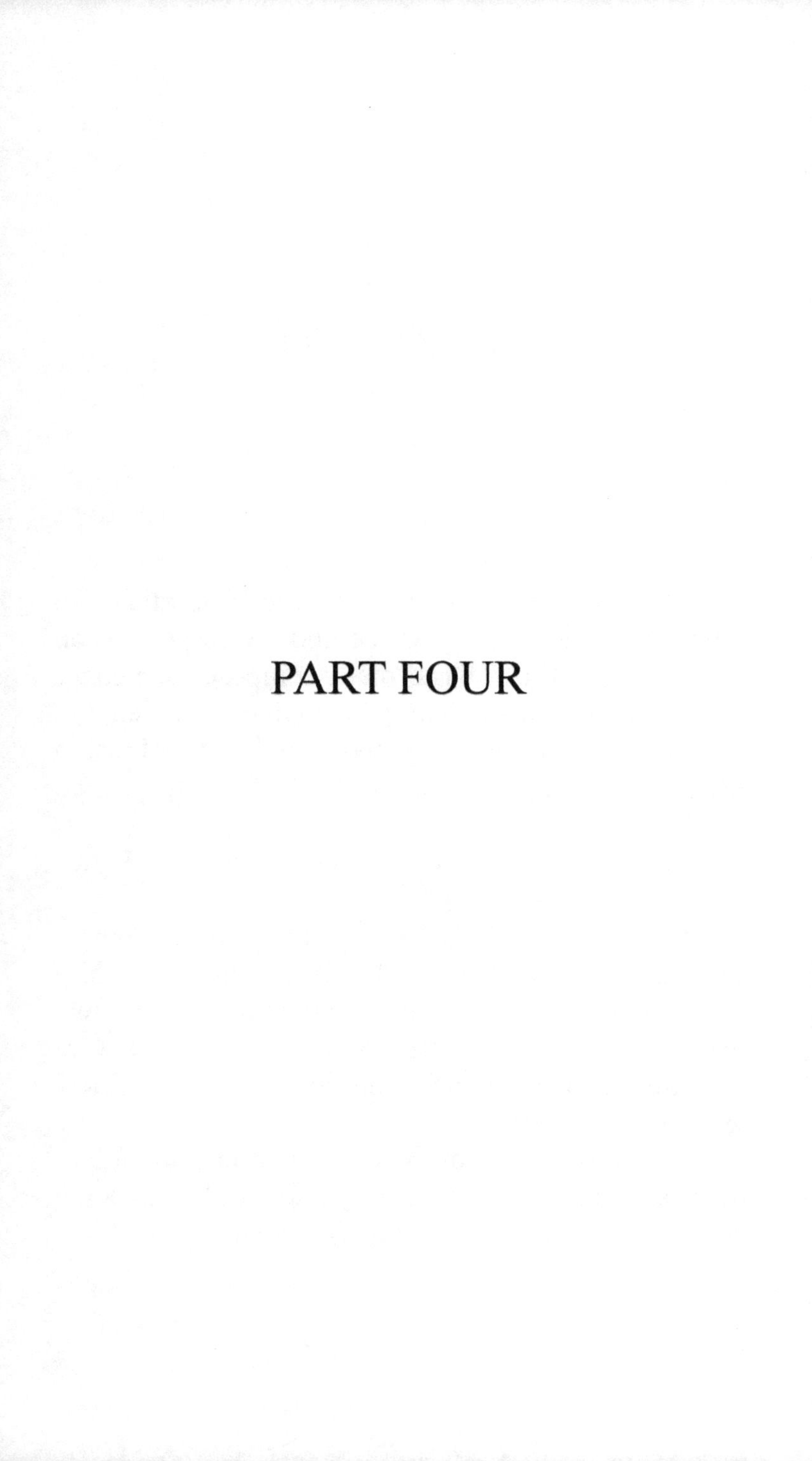

PART FOUR

CHAPTER 30

"THEY GOT HIM!" Callahan announced, striding into Simmons' office where Renee and Kelsey had been reviewing case files. His normally composed demeanor was animated with barely contained excitement. "Robert Duran was apprehended at Houston International Airport trying to board a flight to Mexico City."

"Duran? Taylor's dinner date?" Renee straightened up immediately.

"The very same," Callahan confirmed, dropping a folder on Simmons' desk. "FBI agents intercepted him at the gate. They were conducting their own investigation into the corruption cases that we were unaware of. He's being transported back to New Orleans as we speak."

Simmons leaned forward, flipping open the folder to reveal a grainy airport security photo of Duran being led away in handcuffs. "Good. That's very good."

"This could be the breakthrough we've been waiting for," Kelsey said. "Duran was the last person seen with Taylor before he disappeared."

"Not just that," Callahan added. "According to Agent Wells, Duran was specifically recruited by Antoine Domingo because of his past connection to Taylor."

"As Taylor's former CI," Renee nodded, the pieces clicking into place. "The perfect Trojan horse."

Simmons checked his watch. "When will he arrive?"

"Within the hour," Callahan replied. "They're bringing him directly to the federal building downtown. His attorneys are already negotiating a plea deal in exchange for testimony."

"Let's go," Simmons said, rising from his chair. "I want to be there when this piece of garbage starts talking."

* * *

The federal holding facility downtown was a stark contrast to the aged grandeur of the Orleans Parish Courthouse. Its modern glass-and-steel structure housed temporary detention cells and interview rooms where federal prisoners awaited processing or transfer.

In the observation room, Renee watched through one-way glass as Robert Duran was led in, his wrists shackled to a chain around his waist. Gone was the confident man from the restaurant security footage. This Duran was haggard, unshaven, with dark circles under bloodshot eyes.

His attorney, Ellen Martindale, was already seated at the metal table. As Duran took his place beside her,

Callahan and Simmons entered from the opposite door, carrying files and a digital recorder.

"Interview with Robert Duran, case number 473-291. Present are Special Agent Nelson Carter, Special Agent Donna Fitzgerald, ADA James Callahan, and NOPD Captain Roy Simmons. The subject, Robert Duran, and his attorney, Ellen Martindale."

"Before we begin," Martindale interjected, "I want to confirm that the US Attorney's Office has agreed to consider my client's substantial cooperation in charging and sentencing recommendations."

"That depends entirely on how substantial that cooperation proves to be," Callahan replied. "Full disclosure, complete truthfulness, and willingness to testify against all co-conspirators."

Martindale nodded. "My client understands."

Callahan leaned in as he locked eyes with Duran. "Let's start from the beginning. How did you get involved with Antoine Domingo?"

Duran shifted uncomfortably, glancing at his attorney before responding. "About four months ago, I was deep in gambling debts. Owed money to some dangerous people." He swallowed hard. "Antoine approached me at a bar in the Quarter. He said he knew who I was and about my history with Judge Taylor."

"And what history was that?" Callahan asked, though they all knew the answer.

"Years back, I was Taylor's CI," Duran explained, his voice shaky. "He arrested me for dealing near a school, but instead of throwing the book at me, he offered me a deal. I'd provide information on my suppliers, and he'd help me get into a program, maybe reduce my charges."

"And did he?" Simmons prompted.

"Yeah," Duran nodded, a flicker of something like shame crossing his face. "Taylor kept his word. Got me into rehab, helped me find legitimate work after. For a while, I was straight—five years clean, steady job."

"Until?" Callahan pressed.

"Until I got into gambling. Started small, but... you know how it goes." He stared at his shackled hands. "Anyway, Antoine knew all about this. Said he'd clear my debts if I helped him with something."

"Which was?" Simmons asked.

"Getting close to Taylor again. Finding out what he knew, what evidence he'd gathered about the Domingo organization." Duran's voice dropped even lower. "Antoine was obsessed with Taylor, convinced he was going to expose everything."

Behind the glass, Renee exchanged glances with Kelsey. Taylor had been right all along—the evidence he'd been gathering had been significant enough to frighten the Domingos.

"So, you agreed to spy on the judge who once helped you," Callahan stated, not bothering to hide his disgust.

"I told myself it was just information," Duran said defensively. "Just finding out what Taylor knew. I didn't know it would end up... the way it did."

"When did that change?" Callahan asked. "When did it go from intelligence gathering to murder?"

Duran was silent for a long moment. "The day before our dinner at Le Bayou Jardin. Antoine called me in, said the plan had changed. Said Taylor had become too dangerous, had evidence that could destroy everything they'd built."

"And you went along with it," Callahan said, his tone making it clear it wasn't a question.

"I didn't have a choice!" Duran's composure cracked. "Antoine showed me pictures of my sister's house, her kids playing in the yard. Said accidents happen every day in New Orleans." He looked down. "Besides, by then, I was in too deep. If Taylor ever found out I was working with Antoine..."

"Tell us about the night at Le Bayou Jardin," Simmons redirected. "Step by step."

Through the glass, Renee watched Duran's body language as he began recounting the events of that night. Despite his nervous energy, there was something rehearsed about his delivery, as if he'd prepared this version of events carefully.

"Antoine had it all planned out," Duran explained. "Three other men were involved—Victor Suarez, Manny Ortiz, and Luis Vega. I knew Suarez from before, when I was using. The other two, Antoine, brought, were already on the payroll."

"The plan was precise," he continued. "I'd have dinner with Taylor. About an hour in, Suarez would arrange for a fake phone call to draw Taylor away from the table. I'd excuse myself to the restroom at the same time Ortiz and Vega would position themselves to block the view from the host stand, and Suarez would slip something into Taylor's wine."

"Fentanyl," Callahan stated.

Duran nodded. "Dissolved in a liquid. Almost tasteless in red wine."

"Then what happened?" Callahan asked.

"It went exactly as planned. Taylor went to take the call; I went to the restroom. Ortiz and Vega blocked the view while Suarez doctored the wine." Duran's voice had taken on a mechanical quality as if distancing himself from the events. "When Taylor returned, he didn't suspect anything. We continued talking. He drank more wine."

"What did you talk about?" Callahan asked. "Was Taylor sharing information with you?"

"That's the thing," Duran said, looking up. "He wasn't. He kept the conversation casual, asked about my family, my job. Looking back, I think... I think he suspected something wasn't right."

In the observation room, Kelsey nodded slightly. "That sounds like Taylor," he murmured. "Cautious to the end."

"By about nine-thirty, Taylor was showing signs," Duran continued. "Slurring words, having trouble focusing. I called for the check, told the maître d' that Taylor wasn't feeling well. We helped him outside, and I called for a taxi."

"Where was the taxi supposed to take him?" Callahan asked.

"An empty house on Prytania Street that was for sale. Suarez and Lucia Vasquez were waiting there."

"Lucia Vasquez?" Simmons interjected. "Antoine's medical specialist?"

"Yes," Duran confirmed. "She had the fentanyl patches. Said oral ingestion wasn't reliable enough. The patches would ensure a lethal dose."

"The taxi driver believed it was Taylor's house?" Callahan asked.

"We told him Taylor's daughter would be waiting. Suarez and Vasquez posed as concerned family members." Duran's voice had grown softer. "The driver never suspected anything."

"And then?" Simmons prompted.

"They transferred Taylor to an SUV. Vasquez applied the patches. They... they were going to take him to Barataria." Duran looked away. "That's all I know. I wasn't part of that."

"Who was?" Callahan demanded.

"I don't know who they are. And Antoine never told me."

"And after?" Callahan pressed.

"Antoine paid me. Told me to lay low, maybe leave town for a while." Duran's shoulders slumped. "I took the money. What else could I do? But I couldn't sleep. Kept seeing Taylor's face as he started feeling the effects. The confusion in his eyes..."

Martindale placed a hand on her client's arm. "My client has provided substantial assistance," she reminded Callahan. "We expect this cooperation to be noted in any charging decisions and sentencing recommendations."

Callahan nodded slightly but continued his questioning. "Was Jean-Paul Domingo aware of this plan?"

Duran hesitated, glancing at his attorney. "Not at first, not according to Antoine. This was Antoine's operation. He said his father was too soft, too cautious. Antoine wanted to prove he could handle threats to the organization."

"But Jean-Paul knew afterward?" Simmons asked.

"Yes. Antoine told me later that his father was angry about how it was handled—said it was sloppy, drew too much attention. But he didn't disagree with the outcome." Duran looked directly at Callahan. "Antoine said his father told him, 'Next time, consult me first.'"

"And where can we find Suarez, Ortiz, and Vasquez now?" Callahan asked.

"Suarez has a place near Audubon Park. Ortiz, I'm not sure. After the operation, Antoine mostly kept us separated." Duran paused. "Vasquez, I heard she fled to Mexico after the FBI raids began."

As Callahan and Simmons continued questioning Duran about specific details, Simmons slipped out to the observation room, already on his phone, arranging for teams to locate the men Duran had named.

"Captain," Renee said, "you think he's telling the truth?"

"Most of it," Simmons replied. "The core details match what we already know from the security footage and forensic evidence. He's probably minimizing his own role, but the rest rings true."

"So, Antoine ordered the hit, not Jean-Paul," Kelsey noted.

"But Jean-Paul condoned it after the fact," Renee pointed out. "Makes him an accessory after the fact at minimum."

"We've got them both," Simmons said, pocketing his phone. "Teams are moving on Suarez and Ortiz now. We'll have the full circle of Taylor's killers by morning, except for Vasquez.

"Now we can add murder charges to the drug trafficking and corruption counts."

"What about Taylor's wife?" Renee asked.

Simmons shook his head, a somber look crossing his face. After a pause, he replied, "The poor woman had a breakdown since they found her husband's body. She's in the hospital. No one's been able to talk to her."

"Sorry to hear that, the poor woman's been through enough," Renee said. "We'll just have to wait and hope that she can pull through. At least we'll be able to provide the family with some answers."

* * *

Three hours later, Renee stood in the break room of the federal building, staring into a cup of coffee that had long since gone cold. The events of the day had left her drained yet restless, caught between the satisfaction of finally knowing who had killed Taylor and the nagging awareness that their work was far from complete.

The door opened, and Wells entered. Though they'd known each other only briefly while he operated as Michael Reeves, seeing him now, fully in his FBI identity, was still a mental adjustment. He looked as tired as she felt, the strain of his years undercover etched into the lines around his eyes."

"Just got word," he said, pouring himself coffee without bothering to check if it was fresh. "They've got two of them. Suarez surrendered at his apartment. Ortiz was picked up at a bar in Metairie."

"And Vasquez?"

Wells shook his head. "Still in the wind. Last seen crossing into Mexico. We've notified the Mexican authorities, but..."

"But she's probably gone," Renee finished for him.

"For now." Wells took a sip of coffee, grimaced, but drank it anyway. "Each arrest yielded additional evidence. Vega is already talking, hoping for leniency.

He led agents to a storage unit with the burner phones they used to coordinate the operation."

"And Suarez?" Kelsey asked, joining them.

Wells set his cup down. "Had a notebook detailing payments from the Domingo organization—including a special bonus for what he called the 'judicial retirement.'" He paused, locking eyes with Kelsey. "But the real prize came from Ortiz. He had a recording on his phone—a conversation with Antoine discussing how to handle the 'Taylor situation' days before the murder."

"Insurance policy," Renee surmised.

"Exactly. Didn't trust Antoine to protect him if things went wrong."

CHAPTER 31

MONTHS FOLLOWING the dramatic pier raids had been a careful chess game. While Jean-Paul and Antoine Domingo sat in federal custody, the corruption network they had described remained largely intact, and unaware of how much the FBI actually knew.

Federal prosecutors had made a strategic decision: let the corrupt judges and officials continue their normal routines while building an airtight case. Judge LeBlanc still presided over his docket. Judge Barrett continued dismissing cases on technicalities. DA Marshall maintained his office, unaware that every move was being monitored.

The FBI had been patient, allowing the network to operate while gathering additional evidence. They needed more than what they had to take down the entire system—they needed documentation, recordings, and financial records that would make convictions certain.

Pre-trial motions for the Domingo case had consumed months, with defense attorneys challenging evidence and seeking dismissals. But prosecutors had carefully avoided revealing the full scope of what they knew. The corruption network believed they were still safe, still protected.

Of the major players, only the Domingos and those who had been arrested in the initial raid. Antoine faced murder charges in Judge Taylor's death, while Jean-Paul maintained his innocence on racketeering and drug charges.

CHAPTER 32

RENEE CHECKED HER weapon one final time before securing it in her holster. Today wouldn't require gunfire—at least she hoped not—but the weight at her hip was reassuring nonetheless. In the kitchen of her small apartment, coffee brewed, strong and black, the way she'd learned to drink it during long stakeouts.

Her phone buzzed with a text from Kelsey: "Ready?"

She replied with a simple "Yes" before picking up Taylor's notebook from the table. She ran her fingers over the worn leather cover, thinking of the judge who'd documented everything and paid dearly for it. "Today's for you," she murmured.

Across town, Callahan straightened his tie in the mirror. The weight of what they were about to attempt settled on his shoulders like a physical burden. He'd prosecuted hundreds of cases in his career, but none carried the stakes of today's hearing. His phone rang.

Wells's handler at the FBI was confirming the final arrangements.

"Everything's in place," the agent assured him. "Just proceed as planned."

Captain Simmons stared at the evidence board in his office at the precinct one last time. Three years of Michael Reeves's undercover work and Taylor's meticulous documentation had created an ironclad case. If—when—it worked, it would reshape the city's justice system for a generation. He checked his watch. It was time.

As morning broke over New Orleans, the principals in the day's drama converged on the courthouse from different directions, each carrying a piece of the puzzle that could finally bring down the Domingo organization and the corrupt officials who had protected it for decades.

None of them knew exactly how the morning would unfold. They had planned, prepared, and anticipated every contingency. But in a city where power and money had dictated justice for generations, nothing was certain until the final gavel fell.

* * *

The court buzzed with unusual energy for a Monday morning. Reporters crowded the hallways, jostling for position outside Courtroom Three, where the most significant case of the year-perhaps the decade—was about to begin.

Inside the courtroom, security was tight. U.S. Marshals stood at every entrance, their watchful eyes scanning the assembled crowd. Court officers conducted thorough searches of everyone entering, and the gallery was strictly limited to authorized personnel, family members, and select media representatives.

At the prosecution table, James Callahan organized his notes. Though he projected calm confidence, inside, he felt the weight of what they were attempting. Across the aisle, the defense table remained empty, awaiting the arrival of Jean-Paul Domingo and his attorney.

In the gallery's front row sat Renee Dubois, Kelsey Griffith, and Captain Roy Simmons, their expressions carefully neutral despite the significance of the moment. They had worked around the clock since the raid, preparing for this day, knowing that the real battle was just beginning.

The side door opened, and Antoine Domingo was led in, hands cuffed before him. Despite three weeks in federal custody, he maintained the arrogant bearing of a man born to privilege. He was directed to a seat in the gallery, separate from the general public but with a clear view of the proceedings. Two U.S. Marshals flanked him, their presence a reminder that he, too, faced serious charges.

Antoine's eyes swept the courtroom, fixing briefly on Renee and Kelsey with undisguised contempt before settling on the empty defense table. The door opened again, and Jean-Paul Domingo entered with his attorney, Josef Mendoza. Despite the orange jumpsuit, Jean-Paul carried himself with the dignity of a businessman rather than a prisoner. He showed no reaction upon seeing his son, though Antoine straightened perceptibly at his father's entrance.

"All rise," the bailiff called. "The Honorable Judge William Harrison presiding."

Renee felt the excitement run through her. She turned to Kelsey, "This is going to be good." The judge most deeply implicated in Taylor's notes, the one who had dismissed more Domingo cases than any other, was presiding over this case.

Harrison took the bench, his silver hair and distinguished features projecting the gravitas of his position. "Be seated," he said, his voice carrying the cultured tones of old New Orleans. "We are here for the preliminary hearing in the matter of United States versus Jean-Paul Domingo."

He surveyed the courtroom over his reading glasses. "Given the high-profile nature of this case, I'll remind everyone that I expect complete decorum. Any disruptions will result in immediate removal." He turned to the prosecution table. "Mr. Callahan, is the State ready to proceed?"

"The government is ready, Your Honor," Callahan replied, standing.

"Mr. Mendoza?"

Josef Mendoza rose with the confidence of a man who had never lost a high-profile case. His every movement calculated to project authority as he addressed the court. "The defense is prepared, Your Honor."

"Very well. Mr. Callahan, you may begin."

Callahan approached the bench, "Your Honor, the government brings before you a case of extraordinary scope and significance. Jean-Paul Domingo stands accused of operating a continuing criminal enterprise involved in drug trafficking, money laundering, racketeering, and conspiracy to commit murder."

Harrison's expression remained impassive as Callahan continued.

"The evidence seized during the raid at Pier 9 includes ten million dollars' worth of pure fentanyl, financial records linking Mr. Domingo to numerous shell corporations used to launder drug proceeds, and documentation of his direct involvement in the organization's operations."

Mendoza was on his feet immediately. "Objection, Your Honor. The prosecution is making sweeping assertions without establishing the admissibility of this supposed evidence."

"Mr. Callahan," Harrison said, "I remind you that this is a preliminary hearing, not a trial. Please stick to establishing probable cause."

"Of course, Your Honor," Callahan replied. "The government will demonstrate that there is more than sufficient evidence to bind the defendant over for trial on all charges."

For the next hour, Callahan methodically outlined the government's case. With each new piece of evidence he introduced, Mendoza objected, and with suspicious regularity, Harrison sustained those objections or limited the scope of what the prosecution could present.

In the gallery, Renee leaned slightly toward Kelsey. "Right on script," she whispered. "Harrison's shutting down every significant avenue."

Kelsey nodded, acknowledging Renee's concern. "Callahan's got this, I'm sure."

After Callahan introduced physical evidence from the raid, carefully navigating Harrison's increasingly restrictive rulings, Mendoza rose for cross-examination of the FBI agent who had testified about the chain of custody.

"Agent Thornton," Mendoza began, "is it not true that the container allegedly containing fentanyl was seized before any connection to Mr. Domingo could be established?"

"The container was registered to one of Mr. Domingo's companies," the agent replied.

"One of his legitimate import companies, correct? With proper documentation?"

"On paper, yes."

"So, you have no direct evidence linking Mr. Domingo personally to any illegal contents that may have been in that container?"

The agent hesitated. "The documentation and—"

"Just answer the question, Agent," Harrison interrupted. "Do you have direct evidence linking Mr. Domingo personally to the contents?"

"Not direct physical evidence of him handling the container, no."

Mendoza smiled slightly. "Thank you, Agent. No further questions."

As the morning progressed, a pattern emerged. Each piece of evidence presented by the prosecution was systematically undermined, each witness's testimony limited in scope. To the casual observer, it might have appeared that the government's case was falling apart. But Renee, Kelsey, and Simmons were hoping for a different outcome. Harrison would be incriminating himself if Callahan played his cards right.

Just before the lunch recess, Mendoza called his first witness—Reverend Thomas Blackwell, a prominent community leader known for his charity work in the city's poorest neighborhoods.

"Reverend Blackwell," Mendoza began after establishing the witness's credentials, "how long have you known Jean-Paul Domingo?"

"Nearly twenty years," the Reverend replied, his deep voice resonating through the courtroom.

"And in what capacity have you known him?"

"Mr. Domingo has been the single largest donor to our youth center since 2005. Without his generous contributions, we could not have rebuilt after Hurricane Katrina."

"Would you characterize Mr. Domingo as a pillar of the community?"

Callahan rose. "Objection, Your Honor. Character testimony is not relevant at this stage."

"Overruled," Harrison said immediately. "The witness may answer."

"Mr. Domingo has always demonstrated the highest character in my dealings with him," Reverend Blackwell stated. "He's provided scholarships for dozens of underprivileged children, funded our after-school programs, and personally mentored several young men who might otherwise have fallen into trouble."

Mendoza nodded appreciatively. "And have you ever seen any indication that Mr. Domingo was involved in illegal activities?"

"Never. He's a businessman and philanthropist, nothing more."

After Reverend Blackwell's testimony, Mendoza called his second witness—Dr. Eleanor Prescott, Chief of Pediatric Oncology at Tulane Medical Center. Her elegant appearance and crisp white coat lent an air of authority that commanded attention as she took the stand.

"Dr. Prescott," Mendoza began after establishing her credentials, "how long have you known Jean-Paul Domingo?"

"Nearly twelve years," she replied, her voice carrying the measured tones of someone accustomed to delivering both hope and devastating news. "We met when he approached our hospital about establishing a children's cancer treatment fund."

"Could you tell the court about that fund and Mr. Domingo's involvement?"

Dr. Prescott sat straighter, her expression softening slightly. "The Domingo Children's Cancer Initiative has provided treatment for over three hundred children whose families couldn't afford care. Many of these children would not be alive today without it."

"And what was Mr. Domingo's role beyond the initial funding?"

"He didn't simply write a check and disappear," Dr. Prescott explained. "Jean-Paul personally visited the children's ward monthly. He knew the names of every patient, their favorite toys, their birthdays. When we needed specialized equipment that insurance wouldn't cover, he purchased it without hesitation."

Mendoza nodded. "Could you share a specific example of Mr. Domingo's personal involvement?"

"There was a boy—Miguel Canjura, eight years old, terminal diagnosis. His last wish was to see a Saints game from the owner's box." Dr. Prescott's professional demeanor momentarily yielded to genuine emotion. "Jean-Paul not only arranged it but spent the entire game with Miguel, introduced him to the players afterward. When Miguel passed away three weeks later, Jean-Paul attended the funeral and established a scholarship in the boy's name."

"In your professional opinion, Dr. Prescott, what kind of man does such things?"

"In my thirty years of medicine," she answered without hesitation, "I've found that people reveal their true character in how they treat those who can offer them nothing in return. Children with cancer—especially those from disadvantaged backgrounds—have no political connections, no wealth, no influence. Jean-Paul's dedication to them shows a compassion that can't be faked."

From his seat at the defense table, Jean-Paul maintained a dignified humility, eyes downcast as if uncomfortable with the praise. It was a masterful performance, Renee thought—the philanthropist embarrassed by public recognition of his good deeds.

"Has Mr. Domingo ever used his charitable work for publicity or personal gain?" Mendoza asked.

"Quite the opposite," Dr. Prescott said. "He specifically prohibited the hospital from naming the wing after him, despite it being standard practice for donors of his magnitude. He insisted that any recognition would detract from the focus on the children."

Callahan rose for cross-examination, his expression carefully neutral. "Dr. Prescott, are you aware that charitable donations can provide significant tax benefits?"

"Of course," she replied coolly. "But the tax deduction on a million-dollar donation doesn't compare to simply keeping the million dollars. Philanthropy, even with tax benefits, means giving away more than you get back."

"And you've never observed anything that suggested Mr. Domingo's charitable work was motivated by anything other than selfless concern?"

"Never," she stated firmly. "In twelve years, I've watched him sit with dying children, console grieving parents, and celebrate miraculous recoveries—all away from cameras, away from publicity. That's not the behavior of someone seeking a tax write-off."

As Dr. Prescott stepped down, Mendoza looked satisfied. The picture he was painting for the court was clear—Jean-Paul Domingo as the misunderstood benefactor, the businessman whose legitimate philanthropy was being overshadowed by unfounded accusations.

In the gallery, Renee couldn't help but admire the strategy. Mendoza was creating reasonable doubt not by attacking the evidence but by making it emotionally difficult to reconcile the philanthropist with the criminal. It was the same duality that had allowed Jean-Paul to operate for decades—the respectable face hiding the ruthless crime lord beneath.

After one more character witness—a prominent businessman who had partnered with Domingo on various civic projects—Harrison called for the lunch recess.

In the hallway outside, Callahan joined Renee, Kelsey, and Simmons in a quiet corner away from prying ears.

"Harrison's worse than we expected," Simmons murmured. "He's not even trying to hide his bias."

"Which is exactly what I expected," Callahan replied. "He's showing complete judicial misconduct."

"How can you let this charade continue?" Renee asked.

"One more hour," Callahan replied. "Let Mendoza put on a few more of his character witnesses."

The atmosphere had shifted subtly as they returned to the courtroom after lunch. Reporters sensed something brewing, though none could have predicted what was coming.

Mendoza called two more witnesses who testified to Jean-Paul Domingo's sterling reputation and community involvement. With each glowing character assessment, Jean-Paul's expression grew more confident, almost smug. In the gallery, Antoine appeared increasingly relaxed, occasionally exchanging knowing glances with his father.

When Mendoza concluded his presentation, Harrison appeared satisfied, turning to Callahan with an almost dismissive air. "Does the government wish to present any rebuttal witnesses?"

Callahan stood, his face revealing nothing. As he began to speak, he briefly made eye contact with Renee and Kelsey, giving them a slight wink.

"Yes, Your Honor. At this time, the government wishes to call a protected witness."

Harrison frowned. "A protected witness? This is the first I've heard of this."

"Your Honor," Callahan said, approaching the bench with a sealed folder, "pursuant to Federal Rule of Evidence 509 regarding state secrets and informant privileges, I have here an order signed by the Director of the FBI and countersigned by the Attorney General authorizing the disclosure of this witness's identity specifically for these proceedings." He handed the folder to Harrison. "The witness has been operating in a special capacity until the recent arrests."

Harrison examined the documents, his brow furrowing deeper with each page he read. "Mr. Mendoza, approach the bench."

As the attorneys conferred quietly with the judge, Renee and Kelsey remained expressionless, though tension radiated through the courtroom.

After several minutes, Harrison addressed the courtroom, a new edge of wariness in his voice. "The court will allow the prosecution to call its protected witness. However, I am ordering additional security measures. The courtroom will be temporarily cleared of all spectators except for essential personnel."

A murmur of protest rose from the reporters present.

"Bailiff, please clear the courtroom," Harrison ordered. "The marshals will remain, as will counsel for both sides."

"Please allow the detectives working on the case to remain," Callahan added.

Harrison reluctantly agreed.

Once the courtroom had been cleared of reporters and other observers, Harrison nodded to Callahan. "You may proceed, Mr. Callahan."

"The government calls Special Agent Marcus Wells."

The name meant nothing to anyone in the courtroom except those few who had been briefed on the operation. Jean-Paul and Antoine Domingo showed no reaction, merely looking toward the door with mild curiosity about this unknown witness.

A side door opened, and two FBI agents in suits entered, scanning the courtroom before nodding to someone in the hallway.

Jean-Paul's eyes widened in confusion. "What is this?"

Antoine, from his seat in the gallery, leaned forward, staring at his father.

As the man approached the witness stand, Mendoza rose. "Your Honor, what is the meaning of this?"

The bailiff approached with a Bible. "Do you swear to tell the truth, the whole truth, and nothing but the truth, so help you God?"

"I do," the man replied calmly.

Callahan approached the witness, his expression revealing nothing of the bombshell about to be dropped. "For the record, please state your name and occupation."

The man straightened in the witness chair, his eyes moving from Jean-Paul to Antoine Domingo before focusing straight ahead.

"My name is Marcus Wells. I am a Special Agent with the Federal Bureau of Investigation."

The effect was immediate and electric. The courtroom seemed to freeze for a heartbeat before erupting in shock. Jean-Paul Domingo's composed facade shattered entirely. The color drained from his face as if someone had opened a valve; his eyes widened in disbelief, which quickly transformed into horrified understanding. His mouth opened and closed wordlessly, blood visibly draining from his face as decades of criminal confidence collapsed. For the first time in his life, Jean-Paul Domingo looked genuinely afraid.

The man he had trusted most—the man he had invited into his home, shared meals with, confided in about both business and personal matters—had been systematically dismantling his empire from within for three years. Every secret, every connection, every protection he believed secure had been exposed. The realization seemed to age him physically, his shoulders sagging as if under an impossible weight.

Wells himself seemed to transform before their eyes. The deferential posture and watchful demeanor of Michael Reeves melted away, replaced by the assured bearing of a federal agent. He sat straighter, his voice carried differently, and even his facial expressions changed subtly—no longer the careful, measured responses of a man playing a role but the direct gaze of someone who could finally show his true self. The skilled mimicry that had protected him for three years was discarded like a snake shedding its skin.

Antoine's reaction was even more visceral. He lurched to his feet, face contorted with rage, a vein pulsing visibly at his temple. His eyes bulged, and for a moment, it seemed he might vault over the gallery railing.

"You lying no good—" His words choked off as he fought to control himself, his hands clenched so tightly that his knuckles turned pale. The look he directed at Wells contained such pure hatred that even the U.S. Marshals flanking him tensed in preparation for violence.

"Order!" Harrison slammed his gavel as the marshals moved quickly to restrain Antoine. "One more outburst, and you'll be removed from these proceedings!"

Jean-Paul stood up. The implications were catastrophic—his operations, his contacts, his protection network—Wells had been privy to it all.

Even Harrison appeared shaken, a subtle tremor visible in his hands as he gripped his gavel, no doubt wondering what this FBI agent might have witnessed regarding his own corrupt dealings with the Domingo organization.

"Mr. Domingo, please sit," Mendoza urged his client, but Jean-Paul appeared not to hear, his eyes fixed on Wells with a mixture of shock, betrayal, and dawning horror.

"Special Agent Wells," Callahan continued once order had been restored, "could you please explain your role in the investigation of Jean-Paul Domingo and his organization?"

What followed was the most devastating testimony the Orleans Parish Courthouse had ever witnessed. Wells began to dismantle the Domingo empire piece by piece, his calm, measured voice describing in precise detail the criminal activities he had observed over three years. He linked Jean-Paul Domingo directly to drug shipments, money laundering operations, and violent enforcement actions against rivals.

Most damning of all was his testimony about the corruption network that protected the organization— the judges, prosecutors, and police officials who had been bought and paid for by Domingo money.

"Special Agent Wells," Callahan asked, "could you detail the structure of the Domingo organization's corruption network? Who were the key players, and how did they operate?"

Wells nodded, his testimony shifting to a breakdown that left no room for ambiguity.

"Jean-Paul Domingo operated what he called 'the insurance policy'—a comprehensive system of protection that cost the organization approximately three million dollars annually." Wells's voice remained steady, professional. "The network was hierarchical and compartmentalized."

From the bench, Harrison leaned forward slightly, appearing to listen with judicial interest, though Renee noticed his hand seemed to be tightening around his pen.

"At the top were several key judges," Wells continued, "operating as the final safeguard for the organization's interests."

A ripple of murmurs passed through the courtroom from the select group of federal officials and law enforcement personnel permitted to remain after the general public and media had been cleared. Harrison tapped his gavel once, restoring order, though noticeably showing his agitation.

"Judges LeBlanc and Barrett each received monthly payments of twenty-five thousand dollars in offshore accounts," Wells testified, his eyes carefully avoiding the bench. "In exchange, they provided what Jean-Paul termed 'judicial insurance'—ensuring that cases against Domingo associates would be dismissed on technical grounds."

The courtroom fell silent. Harrison trying to remain impassive.

"Below the judges were Assistant District Attorneys who received fifteen thousand monthly. They ensured case assignments went to junior prosecutors when Domingo associates were charged. These inexperienced attorneys would then face defense counsel like Steven Beaumont, who was on retainer with the Domingo organization for one-point-two million dollars annually."

Jean-Paul's expression remained frozen, but his attorney's frantic note-taking betrayed the devastating impact of Wells's precise testimony.

"The organization maintained extensive documentation," Wells continued. "In Jean-Paul's private safe at the Garden District estate, he kept ledgers recording every payment—dates, amounts, recipients, and specific cases influenced. I personally observed him updating these records on the first of each month."

Callahan approached with a document. "Agent Wells, does this appear to be one of those ledgers?"

Wells examined it. "Yes. This is a photocopy of the ledger from March through August of last year. The third column lists case numbers with notations about expected outcomes."

Harrison shifted in his seat, reaching for the water glass beside him. His hand trembled slightly as he brought it to his lips.

"You'll notice that cases 47293, 52177, and 48901 all have the notation 'TD'—total dismissal—next to them," Wells pointed out. "All three were indeed dismissed on technicalities."

"And who presided over those cases?" Callahan asked.

"Judge Barrett handled two of them. Judge LeBlanc the third."

Callahan produced another document. "And this bank record showing deposits to an account in the Cayman Islands?"

"That corresponds to payments to Judge Barrett. Each deposit coincides with a major case dismissal. For example, the deposit on April 17 for fifty thousand dollars—double the usual amount—was made the day after Barrett suppressed crucial evidence in the Rodriguez heroin trafficking case."

In the gallery, Renee and Kelsey exchanged glances. The specificity of the testimony was undeniable—dates, amounts, account numbers, all meticulously documented by a witness who had been at the heart of the organization.

Harrison dabbed at his forehead with a handkerchief. The movement was casual, but the slight shake in his hand signaled his growing tension.

"The system extended beyond the courthouse," Wells continued. "Five officers in the evidence management division received regular payments to 'misplace' critical evidence. Lieutenant Gregory Wilson in Narcotics ensured certain investigations were derailed before they gained momentum. Three port authority officials facilitated the smooth entry of shipments. Even the zoning commission had two members on the payroll to ensure Domingo properties received favorable treatment."

With each new detail, the comprehensive nature of the corruption became clear. This wasn't random or opportunistic—it was systematic, calculated, and entrenched throughout New Orleans' justice system.

"In total, thirty-seven officials across multiple agencies received regular payments," Wells concluded. "Jean-Paul often referred to it as 'the cost of doing business in New Orleans.' He estimated that each dollar spent on corruption saved the organization ten dollars in potential losses from prosecutions and seizures."

Harrison's breathing had become shallow, though he maintained his composure. The courtroom had grown uncomfortably warm, and he loosened his collar slightly.

Callahan walked to the evidence table and picked up a worn leather notebook. "Agent Wells, are you familiar with this item?"

Wells nodded solemnly. "The two detectives provided this to the FBI as evidence in their investigation."

A visible shock ran through the courtroom at the mention of the murdered judge. Harrison froze, his eyes fixed on the notebook.

"By the way, Your Honor," Callahan said, turning to lock eyes with Antoine Domingo, "FBI agents picked up Robert Duran in Houston. Word is, he's singing like a bird."

He shifted his attention to Agent Wells, wagging the notebook in his hand. "My apologies, Agent Wells. And what exactly does this notebook contain?"

"Judge Taylor meticulously documented the pattern of case dismissals over several years. He tracked which judges handled which cases, the unexpected rulings, the procedural 'errors' that always seemed to benefit one organization." Wells's voice took on a note of respect. "He identified the same corruption network that I witnessed from inside the Domingo organization. Working independently, from the judicial side, he came to the same conclusions."

"Special Agent Wells," Callahan said, his voice cutting through the tension, "you've named Judges LeBlanc and Barrett in this corruption network. Were there other judges involved?"

The courtroom fell completely silent. Even Jean-Paul Domingo seemed to hold his breath.

Agent Wells didn't answer right away, as if waiting for tension to build.

"I need to—" Harrison began, his voice cracking. He cleared his throat, attempting to reclaim his authority. "The court will take a brief recess."

Harrison's eyes widened, darting between Callahan and the federal prosecutor who had quietly entered the courtroom midway through Wells's testimony. The realization that this had been orchestrated—that he had been deliberately set up to preside over his own exposure—hit him with visible force.

"I—this court—" Harrison floundered, decades of judicial confidence evaporating under the weight of Wells's testimony and the growing murmurs in the courtroom. For a man who had controlled his courtroom with an iron fist for twenty years, this loss of command was perhaps more devastating than the allegations themselves.

He made a final attempt to assert control, raising the gavel with a hand that shook so badly the movement was almost spastic. He tried to take control, but his voice failed him as he saw FBI agents taking positions near the exits. He lowered the gavel without striking it, the gesture of capitulation unmistakable.

When the federal prosecutor approached the bench with papers in hand, Harrison seemed to physically shrink in his chair. His face, once flushed with indignation, drained to an ashen gray. The man who had entered the courtroom as one of New Orleans' most powerful judges now sat hunched and diminished, head down as he waited for Agent Wells' final statement.

"Agent Wells," Callahan said, "I'll ask again, were there any other judges involved?

With no pause or hesitation this time, "Mr. Domingo referred to Judge William Harrison as, in his words, 'our most reliable asset on the bench,'" Wells stated, his voice carrying clearly through the now-silent courtroom."

Mendoza was on his feet, objections spilling from his lips, but it was too late. The damage was done.

"William Harrison," the prosecutor announced, "you are under arrest for conspiracy, accepting bribes, and obstruction of justice."

Harrison's last pretense of control shattered as federal agents approached the bench. The gavel slipped from his fingers, clattering against the wooden bench with a sound that echoed through the suddenly silent courtroom like the final note of a requiem for corrupt justice.

Callahan looked hard at Harrison's eyes. "Given the serious nature of these allegations, particularly those involving Your Honor, I move that this case be immediately transferred to another judge to avoid even the appearance of impropriety."

Harrison appeared frozen, unable to respond.

At that moment, the courtroom doors opened, and a group of FBI agents, led by the federal prosecutor, entered.

Two agents approached the bench as the courtroom erupted in chaos. Reporters who had been silently let back in rushed for the doors, scrambling to break the story. Antoine struggled against his restraints until the marshals subdued him. Jean-Paul sat perfectly still, his empire visibly crumbling around him.

As Harrison was led from the courtroom in handcuffs, the federal prosecutor turned to address the remaining officials. "This courtroom is now under federal jurisdiction. Judge Martha Williams from the Eastern District will be taking over these proceedings."

Outside the courthouse, the operation was already expanding like a carefully orchestrated symphony. Black SUVs with federal markings converged on locations throughout the city, each carrying teams with specific targets identified in Wells's testimony and corroborated by Taylor's evidence.

At the District Attorney's office, a team of FBI agents strode through the main entrance just as DA Marshall was preparing for a press conference about an unrelated case. The look of stunned disbelief on his face as agents approached with a warrant matched the expressions of his staff, who watched in frozen silence as the city's top prosecutor was led out in handcuffs.

Across town, Judge LeBlanc was in the middle of a golf game at the country club when federal agents approached his cart on the seventh hole. His playing partners—two prominent developers and a city councilman—backed away as if corruption might be contagious.

In Courtroom Six, Judge Barrett was just calling his docket to order when agents entered through both doors. The bailiff, recognizing the inevitable, stepped aside without resistance as Barrett was informed of the charges against him. The spectators in his courtroom erupted in shocked whispers as he was escorted out, his judicial robe billowing behind him like a dark flag of surrender.

Lt. Gregory Wilson was at his desk in the Narcotics Division when agents arrived. Unlike the judges and the DA, Wilson made no attempt to maintain dignity—he bolted for the back exit only to find more agents waiting there. His attempted escape became immediate evidence of consciousness of guilt.

By noon, the coordinated sweep had netted twenty-seven arrests—judges, prosecutors, police officials, and court administrators, all of whom were identified in Wells's testimony and Taylor's evidence. Each piece of the corruption network that had protected the Domingo organization for decades was being systematically dismantled.

News helicopters circled overhead as the courthouse became the epicenter of the largest corruption bust in New Orleans' history. Reporters crowded the steps, broadcasting live updates as one official after another emerged in handcuffs.

"Sources confirm that this operation, codenamed 'Clean Slate,' is the culmination of a multi-year FBI infiltration of the Domingo criminal organization," one reporter announced breathlessly. "The scale of corruption being alleged is unprecedented, potentially affecting hundreds of criminal cases over the past decade."

Inside the federal command center established in a nearby building, Simmons watched the operation unfold on multiple screens. Maps of the city displayed real-time updates as each target was taken into custody. Red icons turned green with each successful arrest.

"Twenty years," he murmured, almost to himself. "It took twenty years, but we finally got them."

Beside him, Callahan nodded. "Taylor would be proud. His evidence was the key that unlocked everything."

As federal agents continued to execute warrants across New Orleans, the city's judicial system was being reborn—painful and chaotic but cleansed of the corruption that had infected it for generations.

"Phase one complete," Callahan said quietly. "The bait was taken exactly as we hoped. His obvious bias created the opening we needed."

"And now?" Renee asked.

"Now we move on to see if there's anything we missed," Simmons replied. With Harrison's arrest as the triggering event, federal warrants were executed across the city.

As they watched the unfolding operation, a court officer approached them. "The judge assigned to take over the case is ready to proceed with arraignments," he informed them. "Judge Martha Williams from the Eastern District. She's waiting in Courtroom One."

Callahan nodded. "Tell her we'll be right there."

As they prepared to enter, Renee paused, looking back at the doors of Courtroom Three, where just moments ago, one of the city's most respected judges had been revealed as a corrupt ally of the Domingo organization.

"It's like Taylor used to say," she remarked quietly. "The people closest to the light cast the longest shadows."

"Not anymore," Simmons replied. "Today, we're turning on all the lights."

They walked together toward Courtroom One, where the true cleansing of New Orleans' justice system was about to begin—a process started by a judge who had given his life to expose the truth, and completed by those who had taken up his cause.

CHAPTER 33

THE STRIPED CAT was exactly the kind of jazz club tourists never found—tucked away on a side street off Frenchmen, with no flashy sign, just a simple painted cat silhouette on a weathered door. Inside, the lighting was low, the air thick with decades of music and cigarette smoke. Old album covers and black-and-white photographs of jazz legends lined the walls, watching over the small tables and worn wooden bar.

They found a table near the stage just as Boggles and his quartet were setting up. The courthouse janitor looked transformed behind his piano, his large frame somehow more graceful, his movements precise and confident in a way they'd never seen before.

"The Courthouse Kings," Simmons read from the small sign by the stage. "Fitting."

When Boggles spotted them, a wide smile spread across his face, he leaned into the microphone. "Listen up, y'all—we got us some real special folks wit' us tonight. The ones who done finally brought some justice for our friend, New Awlins. Give it up, now!" A murmur went through the small crowd, followed by appreciative applause. Renee, Kelsey, Simmons, and Callahan nodded in acknowledgment, slightly embarrassed by the attention.

"Judge always said he'd come hear us play sometime," Boggles continued, his deep voice resonating through the club. "Never got da chance. So we're playing this here first one for him." His fingers moved across the keys, starting a slow, soulful rendition of "Sweet Lorraine." The saxophone joined in, followed by bass and drums, the music filling the small club with a bittersweet melody that somehow conveyed both loss and hope.

A waitress brought them drinks—bourbon for Simmons and Kelsey, wine for Renee, and scotch for Callahan. They raised their glasses in a silent toast to Judge Taylor, then sat back to let the music wash over them.

"You know," Callahan said during a break between songs, "Taylor used to say that jazz and justice had a lot in common. Both rely on rules and structure, but also require improvisation and heart."

"He also said they both work best when everyone plays their part," Simmons added. "No one instrument dominates; everyone contributes to something larger than themselves."

As Boggles and his quartet launched into their next number—a more upbeat tune that had people tapping their feet—Renee watched the musicians working together, each finding their moment to shine while supporting the others.

"We did good work," she said finally. "All of us. Taylor would be proud."

"It's not over," Kelsey reminded her. "The remaining. trials will take months, maybe years."

"But the system is working again," Callahan said. "That's what matters. For the first time in a long time, justice in New Orleans isn't for sale."

The music swelled around them, vibrant and alive, filling the club with its energy. Outside, New Orleans continued its eternal dance of light and shadow, sin and salvation, corruption and redemption. But tonight, in this small corner of the city, those who had fought for justice could finally take a moment to celebrate what they'd accomplished.

As Boggles' fingers danced across the piano keys, Renee raised her glass once more.

"To Charles Taylor," she said quietly. "Who showed us that one person with courage can still make a difference."

"To Taylor," the others echoed.

In the swirling notes of jazz filling the Striped Cat, they could almost imagine the judge was there with them, finally getting to hear the music he'd always meant to enjoy. Justice, like jazz, would play on—sometimes struggling against corruption and greed, sometimes soaring with truth and integrity, but always, always worth fighting for.

The case that had begun with a body in the swamp had exposed a cancer in the city's justice system. But it had also revealed something else—that light could still break through even in the darkest corners of New Orleans.

"How about our FBI friend Marcus Wells?" Renee asked the others.

Callahan replied with a smile. "He's one hell of an agent. I'm sure we'll be hearing from him again."

As Boggles and his quartet played on into the night, the music drifted out into the streets of the Crescent City—a city of contradictions where beauty and decay, honesty and corruption, darkness and light had always existed side by side. Tonight, at least, in this small corner of New Orleans, the light seemed a little stronger, the music a little sweeter, and the future a little more hopeful.

Disclaimer

This is a work of fiction. Names, characters, businesses, places, events, locales, and incidents are either the products of the author's imagination or used in a fictitious manner. Any resemblance to actual persons, living or dead, or actual events is purely coincidental.

The city of New Orleans and its institutions are depicted in a fictional context. The portrayal of law enforcement, court procedures, and legal systems is dramatized for narrative purposes and may not accurately reflect actual processes, protocols, or jurisdictions.

This novel contains mature themes, including references to drug trafficking, violence, corruption, and criminal activity. It is intended for adult readers.

No portion of this work may be reproduced, distributed, or transmitted in any form or by any means without the author's prior written permission, except for brief quotations embodied in critical reviews and certain other noncommercial uses permitted by copyright law.

Also available
by
MICHAEL TENNANT

CAN YOU
SLEEP
ON A
STORMY NIGHT

In a world teetering on the precipice of oblivion, three unlikely allies are thrust into a quest that will challenge the very fabric of their reality.

They are brought together by an enigmatic figure known only as "The Old Man." As they embark on a journey to unravel the secrets of ancient prophecies, they find themselves in a battle that will determine the fate of humanity.

Navigating a world plagued by a growing sense of darkness, the trio must confront the startling realities that lie hidden within the pages of ancient texts. With each step, they uncover a web of connections that spans across time, pointing to a truth that could shatter the very foundation of everything they once believed in.

Michael Tennant weaves a masterful narrative that will keep you on the edge of your seat until the final, breathtaking revelation.

"Can You Sleep On A Stormy Night" is a thought-provoking novel that challenges readers to question the world around them and to contemplate the profound implications of the choices they make.

As the story races towards its climax, readers will find themselves on the edge of their seats, confronted with startling revelations that will leave them questioning everything they thought they knew.

"Can You Sleep On A Stormy Night" is a story that will linger long after the final page is turned, inviting you to ponder the great mysteries that shape our world and discover the transformative power of truth in the face of darkness.

So buckle up and prepare for the ride of a lifetime. "Can You Sleep On A Stormy Night" is more than just a novel — it is an invitation to embark on a journey of the soul, to confront the darkness that threatens to engulf us.

A heartfelt thank you to my wonderful daughter Erin for her incredible help with this book. I truly appreciate her support and kindness throughout this journey.